THE MEGALIGHT CONNECTION

THE MEGALIGHT CONNECTION

A NOVEL BY WILLIAM M. GRIGGS

E & L PRESS

P. O. BOX 1967

CHICAGO, IL 60690

© 1990 by William M. Griggs

All Rights Reserved.
No part of this publication may be reproduced
or transmitted in any form or by any means,
electronic or mechanical, including photocopy, recording,
or any information storage and retrieval system,
without permission in writing
from the publisher.

Libarary of Congress Cataloging-in-Publication Data
Griggs, William M., 1952-
The megalight connection : a novel / by William M. Griggs.
p. cm.
ISBN 0-9622869-5-8
I. Title.
PS3557.R48955M4   1989   89-11954
813'.54--dc20

Cover design by William M. Griggs.

For Stephanie and Louisa

INTRODUCTION

*B*efore there was Eden, there was Zarkon. Located in a distant galaxy, the planet Zarkon supported a thriving civilization.

Zarkonians placed a powerful emphasis on family. But their understanding of "family" extended beyond immediate blood lines to include all of the people of Zarkon. The entire planet was one large tightly knit family.

Zarkonians knew nothing about crime, war, pollution, hatred or loneliness. There were no thefts because if someone needed or wanted something, another would gladly give it, usually without being asked. There was little room for violence or hatred on a planet where everyone felt kinship toward everyone else. They lived close to the soil and were taught at an early age how to care for their environment, always making sure that everything they did was in harmony with the other creatures with whom they shared the planet.

Zarkonian society owed its unique character to the fact that Zarkonians were connected to the Megalight. The Megalight served as both father and mother to the entire universe and all its teeming galaxies and solar systems. It stood then as it does now, beyond space and time, and yet permeating the core of all that exists.

This Megalight connection acted as a sort of invisible umbilical cord, providing the Zarkonians with spiritual nourishment and a sense of wellbeing. It made them strong enough to love and secure enough to trust. It produced a faith that reduced the severest of problems- from droughts to floods- to temporary challenges. The Megalight connection was the source of their linkage with each other and of their harmony with the environment.

In some ways the Megalight connection resembled human intelligence. Everyone had it, but to varying degrees. This connection, like intelligence was a gift that could be squandered through neglect, or enhanced through diligent application. For Zarkonians, the greatest sin- -the *only* sin, was slothfulness in the development of one's Megalight connection. Only a small percentage of the population regularly committed this sin. They were known as *fools*. *Fool* represented more of a reputation than a title, since it was not something that one sought to earn.

It was a reputation that was granted grudgingly, only after insufferable transgressions-unnecessary arguments, unbelievable disputes over almost anything.

Because they were self-centered and motivated by fear (fear of failure, fear of success, fear of commitment, fear of isolation, the list goes on) they were easily spotted and quickly shunned.

All of Zarkonian society was based upon one guiding principle: becoming one with the Megalight. The Zarkonian creed emphasized strengthening self to overcome obstacles rather than constantly trying to remove those obstacles. It was a sentiment not unlike the one that would be expressed eons later on Earth through the Negro Gospel Song, *Lord Don't Move My Mountain*.

There was but one path toward self strengthening, and that path led inward. This inward path also led to a keen sensitivity to self and awareness of self. The most amazing by-product of the Zarkonian individual's self awareness was an awareness and sensitivity to his neighbor. When this sensitivity was fully developed they could send and receive feelings and thoughts from one another.

The Zarkonian's telepathic powers were directly related to their Megalight connections. Their powers increased or diminished as their Megalight connections grew or shriveled. They recognized themselves as distinct, individual drops in the same sea of life; a sea that began and ended with the Megalight.

Linkage to the Megalight also meant knowledge. The connection fed advice and instructions which the Zarkonians were free to accept or reject. Whenever someone snapped his fingers or slapped his head in the wake of a bad decision and proclaimed, "something told me not to do that!" others would simply smile in the shared knowledge of what it meant to ignore the consul of the Megalight.

1

"This is a perfect day," the beautiful young bride Chuka said aloud to the life within her swollen belly, "to go limpin hunting." Limpins were small mushroom-like vegetables that were said to affect the Megalight connection the same way oysters are said to affect the libido. The rainy season had ended and the dry season had not yet hit its full stride, which meant the limpins would be plentiful. So it was not surprising that young Basalt and his also pregnant wife, Nizinga, also decided to search for limpins.

"I think I know just the spot to look for limpins," Basalt told Nizinga as they prepared to leave their hut. "It is secluded, so we will not have to worry about others having already picked over all of the best limpins. But if we find as many as I think we will, then I guess we will have to tell the others about this spot."

"Are you sure you want this location because there will be limpins there, or do you just want to go some place secluded?"

"Well, there is always one way for you to be certain," Basalt's eyes twinkled as he hinted at that other most intimate activity two people could share: a probe.

"I do not think I really want to know," Nizinga laughed with a naughty sort of roll of the eyes that indicated she already knew the answer only too well.

Although the spot they were to pick the limpins in was secluded, the most direct route to it was not. So Nizinga and Basalt meandered through the countryside just outside their native village of Saroppo (pop. 5,000, located in the southeastern section of the eastern continent). They made an additional detour when Nizinga complained of being thirsty. When they found a stream, they mostly kicked the water on each other, and Nizinga never got around to drinking any. When Basalt said he was so hungry he did not think he could take another step, they found a grove of fruit trees. But they became so engrossed in playing hide-and-seek among the trees that Basalt somehow forgot to eat any fruit.

"If you get any bigger, we will have to hide among the mountains," he kidded her.

"Well, if it were not for you, I would not be big at all!" she retorted.

"And another thing, oooohh,"

"What is the matter?" he asked, his face awash with concern.

"Here, feel." she placed his hand on her huge belly.

He felt her belly pelting outwardly with such force that it startled him.

"I think our baby wants out!"

"Any day now. Any day now."

When they finally arrived at the limpin patch, Nizinga decided that she wanted to take the probe that Basalt had offered earlier. They sat upon the ground, holding hands and facing one another. They bantered briefly over who would probe whom first, and Nizinga emerged as the victor.

Slowly Basalt yielded his mind to the psychic energy that she directed at him. He felt her energy pierce his mind, and he opened it even further. "Know me," he transmitted to her, and she responded by going deeper into his thoughts, all of which were about her. This was not a fact-finding probe, based on the need for information, but rather a pleasure probe, done simply for the ecstasy of doing it. She rolled her energy around his thoughts and delighted in the sheer joy of love without doubt. The tension was exquisite! She experienced so much of him-his feelings for her, some of his anxieties-she was careful to avoid certain areas, for that truly would have been an invasion of privacy-that it felt almost like he was inside of her, instead of the other way around. Yet, through all the delicious feelings that enveloped her, she had to maintain her energy level at a steady stream, or else the probe would fade. She tasted a rainbow and smelled a symphony. She heard flowers and saw softness. She probed until she had almost reached the periphery of his soul. Then it was time to gradually withdraw.

Slowly she backed her energy out of him, slowing a bit here, lingering a bit there, as especially tender lumps of feeling snagged her progress. When she had completely withdrawn, she could only sit in silence for a few moments, savoring the probe, before she could speak again.

"Now it is your turn," she purred.

Gingerly, he pushed his energy out of his own mind and into hers. He would go beyond her thoughts to the tip of her emotions and then retreat. "Come all the way in and know me," she conveyed to him, but he continued to retreat once he had gone so far. "If that is the way you are going to probe, then I am going to block you," she mentally pouted at him.

Basalt apologized by sending his probe deeply into Nizinga's psyche. Warm, exhilarating impulses cascaded over him as Nizinga's feelings materialized within his mind. When he completed his probe, there was no need to communicate that the time had indeed come to look for limpins.

"How does this one look?" she asked, holding a freshly plucked limpin.

"Woman, are you trying to kill us?"

Although limpins were popular for their healing and cleansing properties, as well as their exquisite taste, some were poisonous. While Nizinga was new to limpin hunting, Basalt was an expert.

"See these tiny veins running along the stem? Well, they indicate that there is a chance that this limpin might not be safe. Now this," he proclaimed while flashing another limpin, "is as safe a limpin as you will ever find. After all, I want no harm to come to my son that you are carrying."

"You mean our daughter," she rejoined, laughing as she nibbled the limpin.

"That is not how you eat limpins!" Playfully he snatched the vegetable from her hand and attacked it. Not to be outdone, she grabbed the limpin from his hand and gulped the remainder. Basalt's eyes widened as he flew into a mock anger. He lunged at her, but then pulled her gently to the ground beside him. The laughter subsided as they gazed into one anothers' eyes.

Suddenly a look of disbelief, then horror swept across Basalt's face. In an instant, Nizinga's expression mirrored her husband's. The impossible had happened. The limpin had been poisonous. Basalt reach across the grass and grasped his wife's hand. There was no time for panicking. Telepathically, he communicated what had to be done.

Their minds merged to form a single telepathic voice that went out in search of Menes, Basalt's guardian. Their message resembled a sort of X-ray photograph; it included their exact location and situation. Although transmitting the message drained their life forces, they had to continue until they could feel the message lock into Menes' spiritual aura. Finally, they found him. He would know what to do.

Without speaking a word (they had not communicated verbally since discovering that the limpin was poisonous) they redirected their energy toward Nizinga's belly. There was a slim chance that if they tried to conserve their energy, they might be saved. But having located Menes, they knew that the baby's odds for survival would increase with each bit of energy they fed into it. Being only a few weeks away from the baby's due date, they concentrated on the infant.

An hour later, Menes arrived. He carried a small bag full of medical supplies-roots, herbs, concoctions, and instruments. He found Basalt and Nizinga both spiritually dead, their souls having returned to the Megalight. They had been able to keep Nizinga's body physically alive, turning it into a sort of living incubator. The lungs breathed and the heart beat, but spiritually, there was no one home.

The sight of the lifeless Basalt and Nizinga stunned Menes. The moisture in his mouth evaporated only to reappear in his eyes. He had just been with them the night before. When they had mentioned that they would probably look for limpins; he had, ironically, chided Nizinga to listen to Basalt in that one particular area because they could be dangerous for someone who did not know how to spot the poisonous ones. He allowed himself one heavy sigh before digging into his medical bag. His grief would have to be postponed.

Menes pulled a small knife from his sack and quickly sterilized it with the juice from the healing kukasia plant. He could not know how much time he would have before Nizinga's body would stop functioning, but he knew that every second counted. He would have to work quickly and with precision. One false move could kill the baby. His arms ached and his tired mind almost succumbed to a powerful feeling of aloneness. He would have to utilize the discipline for which he was widely known and admired, to suspend his emotions. Through the sheer force of his will he forced the tears from his eyes.

Urgently he asked the Megalight to guide his hands as he cut Nizinga's still heaving belly. The tension in his weary arms and hands began to subside. He could feel his prayer being answered and yielded his mind and members to the Megalight spirit that began to operate through him. He became almost a spectator as his hands moved quickly and methodically in retrieving the unborn fetus. Shortly he was spanking the behind of a healthy baby boy. When the infant screamed, Nizinga's body stopped breathing.

2

"**D**o you want to be part of supper for my special family tonight? Are you tender enough? Mature enough?" Chuka interrogated a limpin not more than five miles from the spot where Basalt and Nizinga fatally encountered a limpin. "Only the best limpins will be good enough for my special husband and the special baby I am carrying, so you will have to be a special limpin to make it into tonight's stew." she giggled out loud.

Even before she became married and pregnant, Chuka had acquired the habit of talking to birds and trees and streams and stones. She had already been known for her playful nature, and having been blessed with a marriage to the man she truly loved, and now carrying *his* baby; she seemed to smile and laugh almost all the time. Although her playfulness was widely acknowledged, it was her intelligence upon which her reputation had been built. Once one of her peers mistakenly asked her why she talked to rocks. She answered that since the spirit of the Megalight was present in all things, talking to rocks gave her another avenue through which to converse with the Megalight. No one asked her that question again.

She possessed a natural inquisitiveness about most things, but she was particularly intrigued by the way two substances could be united to form something completely different. She loved to concoct potions by trying new combinations of herbs and medicinal roots. No mixologist or herbalist was safe from her never ending onslaught of questions whenever she was in their vicinity; and she seemed to always be in their vicinity.

She had excelled in practically every area of education, especially Motherhood training. Zarkonians felt that parenthood was too important not to have established guidelines. While the men received instructions in fatherhood during their manhood training, the women were trained specifically in motherhood. Much of the Zarkonian training centered around controlling one's thoughts. They knew that if they were not constantly vigilant, negative fears and doubts could crop into their consciousness at any time and disrupt the flow of positive energy. They were taught to block out the negatives; to fight doubt with faith, fear with courage. Sometimes children were instructed to draw the most hideous figure they could imagine. Then each child would take a turn finding and explaining something beautiful in the sketch. Eventually, they would turn the entire drawing into a thing of beauty to everyone, including the artist.

Because Zarkonians knew that the thoughts a mother fed her baby were every bit as important as the food she ate, this training -- "thought management" -- they called it, was accelerated whenever a young woman became pregnant for the first time.

Mothers who maintained positive tranquil thoughts generally produced sweet-tempered babies who slept throughout the night. Such babies often laughed and seldom cried. Expectant mothers who allowed themselves to worry produced frightened babies. These babies were nervous and irritable and they craved inordinate amounts of attention. Fortunately, worried mothers and fretful babies were the exception because the additional training was usually enough to offset that possibility.

Chuka, however, had required no such additional training. She instinctively internalized so many of the principles involved in the classes that she was called upon to instruct others, including some older women (a rarity on Zarkon where knowledge was mostly passed down from the elders, not up).

If there was a single fault for which Chuka was sometimes reprimanded, it was that she loved to daydream so much that she would occasionally allow her mind to wander when it might have been dangerous to do so. She had almost become supper for one of the larger predator animals once because she had not taken care to mentally scan the area for danger. Luckily, Lima, the man who was to become her husband, happened onto the scene and was able to direct the animal away from her before it could harm her.

Even this slight adventure in limpin picking was interrupted by memories of the breakfast she shared a few hours earlier with Lima. While she was still sleeping, he had gathered fresh fruits to mix with the grains she would prepare. She heated the cereal mixture despite Lima's protestations that it was not necessary. She needn't have bothered. They were so absorbed with laughing, kissing and teasing one another that the food got cold anyway.

An exotic fragrance intruded upon her reminiscence and gently pulled her back into the present. The scent was delicious, unlike anything she had ever smelled before. It was more than just inviting, it was *intriguing*. Where did it come from? What was it? The limpins would have to wait.

Changes in the wind direction led her astray a few times, but the fragrance had a magnetic quality about it that persisted beyond the whims of the air currents. It was almost as if she was smelling it with her eyes, ears and skin. The bouquet grew in intensity as she followed its trail until she found herself standing on a small hill. The trail of the scent stopped.

Something was strange. Very strange. She couldn't quite put her finger on it, but something was wrong. She was thoroughly familiar with the area, and now she was standing on a mound that *wasn't there before*.

The instant the truth hit her, the ground vanished from beneath her feet. Darkness enveloped her as she tumbled down a short narrow tunnel. She strained to adjust to the darkness. "Remain calm and rely on your training," she thought to herself. *When darkness is all around you*, she had been taught, *that is the time that your inner light will shine at its brightest.*

She thought about assuming the lotus position but realized how ridiculous the idea was in her condition. "Pull yourself together and send. You should be able to lock onto Lima in no time," she tried to encourage herself.

She eased herself down against the cold dank floor. The moisture caused her thin wrap to cling to her. The hard rocks jutted against her soft skin, but she hardly had time to notice the discomfort. Did it matter whether she closed her eyes when trying to send in complete darkness? She decided to close them. She wanted to do things the same way she had always done them.

First, she knew she had to remove the tension from her body. Beginning with her toes, she focused on each part of her body: the ankles, calves, knees, and up, ordering each part to relax. She concentrated on each segment of her body until she could feel the tension leave it, or at least until she felt that she had done the best she could under the circumstances. Although her rhythm eluded her, she was still able to achieve a modicum of control. She was ready to begin sending.

From deep within, she pulled on energy as she had never done before. Her message sort of gurgled up within her and pushed out. It streamed from her consciousness, billowing and collecting. Billowing and collecting. Becoming ever stronger, more concentrated. And yet ...

Something was terribly wrong. The message kept billowing and collecting because it wasn't getting out from wherever it was that she was trapped. It was as if there was some kind of force field around her. *"Stay Calm!"* she almost screamed at herself. "Stay calm," she repeated to herself. Over and Over. "Stay calm." But she could not feel the life presence of anyone. It was as if she was the only living being on the entire planet. She could feel the panic coming over her, lapping her in waves of ever increasing intensity.

"I will not give in!" she cried bravely, all the while realizing that she fought a losing battle. She prayed that she was having a nightmare and would soon awaken to find herself safe in the warmth of her husband and friends. But it was a prayer that she knew could not be answered. *Try to think. It is dark. I am cut off. I cannot send any messages and I cannot feel any life presence.* There was only one place she could be. She tried to get a hold of herself as the realization of where she was burst upon her. She screamed and the echo resounded back upon her, pulling her even further from the thin grip she had managed to keep on herself. By the Megalight's eyes! NOOOOOOO!

She was in a forbidden cave. The caves were forbidden for two reasons; the first being that they were comprised of negative energy radiating metals and minerals. These metals and minerals were so powerful that they negated the Zarkonians' powers of telepathy and empathy. For a Zarkonian to be cut off from all life forces was tantamount to being buried alive.

Because they were so dangerous, all of the forbidden caves were mapped out and clearly marked. There were not supposed to be any for several more miles.

Chuka barely noticed that the hard jagged rock bruised her back as she made her way to her feet. She had to get out of there. She ran as fast as she could, stumbling in the darkness until she fell. Tears streamed down her face as she cried aloud, pleading with the Megalight and whomever else might listen, that no harm had befallen her baby.

As she laid on the cold damp floor, she noticed that fragrance again; the one that got her into this mess in the first place. She raised her torso and tried to get a fix on the scent. Having no other options that she could think of, she followed the aroma through the darkness, until she glimpsed a dim orange glow. She crawled toward the light. The closer she came to it, the stronger the fragrance became. She picked up the orange, cantaloupe-sized sphere. She knew that it was forbidden fruit: the other reason the caves were forbidden.

In all of Zarkon, nothing was more strange, not to mention **dangerous**, than the forbidden fruit. It required neither sunlight nor soil. It grew out of the rocks in the caves, deriving its sustenance from the negative energy in the rocks. Chuka had heard stories about the fruit. She had been told that its aroma was hypnotic; that the fruit had a magnetic quality about it, a magnetism that could sap the will of the strongest man or woman. She had also been told about the devastating effects the fruit had on people; how it attacked one's Megalight connection until it was almost completely severed. (Because it was a divine gift from the Megalight, only the

Megalight could completely break the connection).

Now she found herself in the bowels of a forbidden cave, clutching a piece of forbidden fruit. Never in her wildest imaginings had she ever dreamed that something like this could happen to anyone she knew, let alone to *her*.

Even though the glow from the fruit illuminated only a few cubic feet of space, it was infinitely reassuring in the otherwise pitch black cavern. The fruit also radiated a comforting warmth that seemed to soften the edges of her terror. She caressed her cheek with the sphere. A warning issued forth from the core of her being, telling her to get rid of it. But it was too late. The emanations from the fruit were louder than her own internal warning system. Her will power was squeezed between the mesmerizing fruit and her isolation. She began to yield to the fruit, assigning to it all responsibility for whatever might happen.

She continued to caress her face with the fruit, allowing it to brush against her lips, then licking them ever so lightly. Nectar. Like she had never tasted before. She sat transfixed, torn between devouring and discarding the fruit. She pricked it with her teeth. It had the consistency of an overripe peach, and a sweetness that defied description. She bit the fruit again, this time more boldly. She bit again and again, until her jaws stretched to contain it. The sticky juice dripped from her chin and dribbled through her fingers. She sucked the musty air hungrily through her nostrils as she attacked the fruit. She had just begun to feel revitalized when the juice reached her stomach. It felt as if it had turned to acid. An unbelievable searing pain shot through her abdomen as the fruit dropped from her hand. Nothingness engulfed her.

When she awoke, her lungs and nostrils were bulging with fresh air. She stared at the bright orange of her eyelids for a moment, then covered them with her forearm; even through her eyelids, the sun was blinding. The chirping of birds and the smell of grass confirmed it. She was outdoors. She was back at the limpin patch where she had first encountered the strange aroma.

Had she been dreaming, or had she really been inside one of the dreaded forbidden caves? Everyone knew there were no forbidden caves in the vicinity. She decided to ignore the nagging little voice that came from within her: the one that insisted that the experience had been real. It was a voice that the Chuka who left to go limpin hunting that morning would have heeded. But that was the old Chuka. The old Chuka knew fear, but was not intimately related to it. That Chuka loved truth as passionately as she loved her husband. But the new Chuka-the Chuka with a stomach filled with forbidden fruit-knew only the truth that her fear allowed her to know.

If the experience had been real, then it would have negative consequences for her baby. Therefore, it was a dream. It was as simple as that.

For several minutes she had been vaguely aware of the weight which rested lightly upon her belly. In her hazy world, it had taken that long to register that the object was not a part of her body. She had to force herself to focus her eyes-she was not up for another surprise. As she adapted to the bright sunshine, she was able to make out that the object was a pamphlet of some sort. How could it have come to rest on her stomach? Even if the cave experience had been real- which she had since decided it definitely was not- there was no memory of any document of any kind. Jerkily her hand reached for the paper. What a strange title! She sensed there was something evil about the pamphlet, that she should get rid of it. But the terrible secret of her cave experience longed for company. Like a child with one dirty hand who would rather dirty his clean hand than wash the dirty one, she clung to the pamphlet. She knew it would be powerful. She would read it later.

She stood, caressing her belly, and lecturing herself on the need to get home right away. That worthless husband of hers would probably want to know where she had been. The later she came in, the more he would want to know, and she really did not feel like being bothered with his infernal questions. She would have to think of something to tell him as it was, but that could wait until it had to be dealt with.

She walked heavily along the path back home. Suspiciously she eyed a few squirrel-like animals, the same type of animals she had greeted that morning. "Stay away from my baby!" she hissed at a little furry creature who had been too busy gathering food to even notice her.

The crippling of her Megalight connection had transpired so traumatically that it had created a schism in her mind, and a war within her soul. It was a war between her feelings and her thoughts, between the old Chuka and the new. It married her to the pain of isolation, a pain so horrible that it could only be endured by infusing it with tremendous ego. She was no longer special because of what she shared with others, but because of what she could *not* share. Her pain became her scarlet letter, her badge of courage. A perverse pride began to form around her emerging sense of self-sufficiency. She could no longer distinguish between self-sufficiency and self-dependence. She had secrets now that could help define her otherness. The afterpain of her experience was exquisite because it could not be shared. No one could be trusted, except her baby.

Just as she was beginning to realize how truly special she was, it was also becoming apparent to her that her baby would be even more special than she. The baby became the only noncontroversial part of her being.

The new Chuka could slide back and forth between several realities, choosing truths as they fit whatever her purposes might be at the moment. But one reality remained constant. She would kill anyone or anything that tried to come between her and her baby.

3

"Chuka, are you all right? I have been worried sick about you. I could not feel your vibrations for more than four hours today! Where have you been? What happened?" the concern spewed from Lima machine gun-style as his wife approached.

Chuka swallowed hard. She knew she would have to deal with his questions, but she had procrastinated in creating a story for him. She had already decided that she wasn't going to spend a lot of energy making up something just so he would believe it. She would tell him whatever she could think of, and then it would be up to him as to whether he wanted to accept it. If he did not, well, she would make sure that the consequences would be worse for him than for her.

"I am sorry you were worried about me. There really was no need. I went to fetch some limpins and I just fell asleep for a bit. I was probably on a wavelength that you could not pick up while I was asleep. You know, being pregnant can alter a woman's wavelength."

"I have never heard of such a thing."

"You," Chuka's eyes flashed a brilliant anger from which she recovered almost instantly, "have never been pregnant. Or have you?"

"I cannot understand why you are reacting this way. I am only showing the same concern for you that I have always shown. It is the same concern that you have always shown for me. But, perhaps you are right. Maybe I did overreact a bit. I am just thankful that, by the Megalight's grace, you are safe. But where are the limpins? I will wash them for you."

"When I woke up, I did not bother to pick any because I knew that you would be worried. There is other food that I can prepare." She avoided his embrace and proceeded to her cooking station.

An awkward silence pervaded the rest of the evening. No matter what Lima said, Chuka would only respond in monosyllables. Lima loved to make jokes. The problem was that he was never very good at it. His jokes were always considered *klival*, or "corny." Only Chuka enjoyed his jokes. She would always laugh, sometimes at jokes that even Lima did not like. She could always find something of value in anything Lima did.

This night, Lima made several stabs at humor. Chuka met each with a look that said, "You did not mean to say that."

Dinner, which was usually the most talkative time around their hut, was eaten in almost total silence.

He tried sending gentle probes at her, but she blocked him viciously. She had blocked his probes before, but always in a playful manner. In the past, it had felt like someone had put a trampoline in the way of his probe. But tonight, it felt like a steel wall had been put in the way. After a half-dozen futile attempts at probing, an exasperated Lima tried a verbal approach.

"Chuka, something is wrong. I do not know what happened to you today, but I do know that something happened. You will not talk to me. You have been blocking my probes all evening. You have never done that before. You must know that I would never do anything to hurt you. I *love* you. *Please.* Tell me what the problem is and I will help. With the Megalight as my witness, I will help you. But I cannot help you if you will not share the problem with me."

For an all too brief moment, Lima's plea touched and awakened the old Chuka. She turned her back to him to hide the tears that welled in her eyes. She itched to tell him of her ordeal; to have him hold her in his arms and tell her that everything would be all right. The old Chuka was about to tell him when the new Chuka took over. *No one must ever know that you were in the forbidden cave.* She opened her mouth, not knowing which Chuka would speak, or what would come out. Just then there was an urgent ringing of the bell at the entry of their hut.

Lima ignored the ringing, feeling that Chuka was about to disclose something. But the interruption gave the new Chuka a chance to regain firm control. When Lima sensed that no response was forthcoming, he answered the door.

"Do you not care to know what that was about?" Lima returned to find his wife utterly indifferent to the brief doorway visit.

"I assumed you would tell me soon enough."

"Basalt and Nizinga are dead. Poisoned limpins. But Menes was able to save the baby."

"I am glad the baby is all right."

4

"Thank you again, Otumba," Menes said to the matronly woman as she prepared to leave his home. "This child had his parents snatched from him before he even breathed his first breath. But he has been truly blessed to receive mother's milk and mother's *love* from the finest women in all of Zarkon, and that especially means *you*."

"Hush now. You know I love little Jawala as if he were my own. He *is* mine. When the Megalight gives a life, he does not give it only to the people that he used to bring it here. He gives it to everyone. Anyway, the baby will be fine with me tonight. You get some rest. Your aura is so jagged these days, I hate to think of what I might find if I were to probe you."

Otumba's words jolted Menes. He had always been very proud of keeping his thoughts on such a high plane that anyone could probe him at almost anytime, and there would be no thoughts there for which he might feel ashamed. (Of course, probing was such a personal activity that it was seldom done between persons other than spouses, and then, almost always with permission.) But had Otumba probed him, she would have found that for the first time in the many years of their friendship, Menes was looking at her with more than brotherly eyes. For just a few seconds, he had allowed himself to wonder about the comfort her ample body could afford him at a time like this. Nothing carnal, just a moment in which he felt the need to be held. Cuddled. He thought to himself how some needs could never be completely erased.

"Stop sleeping with your eyes open! Menes, I have been standing here trying to finish my goodbys, and you have not heard a single word that I have said."

Something in Menes' vibrations touched Otumba. She put the baby down and walked to where he sat. She cradled his balding head between her large breasts and kissed him gently on the crown of his head. "Rest now, dear friend. We all love you."

Once Otumba had gone, Menes tried to gather his mental energies, but he was too tired. The events of the last few days kept replaying themselves in his mind. He kept hoping that somehow the ending would come out differently, somehow make *sense*, but it never did. Basalt and Nizinga were dead. A limpin expert had died of limpin poisoning. As much as he had loved his late wife, Lakwanda, he had found it easier to accept her death, or *transition*, as they called it.

Lakwanda had always been there. Before puberty had complicated his life, and before he had been able to recognize his feelings for her, she had been there. Even as a youngster, Menes had always preferred thinking of large intellectual concepts and ideas, than of love. He was more comfortable with the *idea* of love than the reality. It had been said that love would not only have to trip him, but also to throttle him before he would recognize it. Yet, he had always been conscious of Lakwanda. Petite. Intelligent. Graceful. Skilled at almost everything she tried. Although she was but a wisp of a woman, the joy of knowing her came from uncovering the layers of strength she possessed. She had developed the most extraordinary Megalight connection Menes had ever witnessed. She had achieved that rare state of relaxed determination that melted any and all obstacles that stood in her path to perfection. During the last few years of her life her mistakes gradually diminished to the point of virtual nonexistence. She always *said* the right thing. Always *did* the right thing. She developed the knack for saying exactly what a person needed to hear when that person was experiencing pain. Her ability to anticipate became positively uncanny.

In the months before her transition, an almost eery serenity replaced her usual liveliness. She smiled more with her eyes than with her mouth. It was a piercing smile that could make a person stop and reflect on whether or not he had done a good deed that day.

Having been blessed with an exceptional Megalight connection himself, Menes knew where her mercurial growth was leading. *Why did she have to be so precocious?* She was still a young woman. Much too young for this to be happening, Menes had rationalized.

Hoping that if she lost her temper, her progress might be impeded just enough to prolong their time together, Menes tried to start a fight one evening over Lakwanda's failure to repair a garment that he had already told her he was going to discard anyway.

"I work hard in the fields, and I cannot get you to sew one little *tshamos* for me. Is that too much to ask?" he had ranted.

Lakwanda smiled at him.

"You are so busy gossiping with the village women that you do not even have the time to prepare a decent meal for me. Look at this slop that you have thrown before me. Do you expect me to eat this garbage? I cannot recall the last time you spent any effort preparing a reasonable meal for me."

Lakwanda's eyes moistened as she smiled even more intently. Menes was always the most poised man she had ever known. He always tried to be correct, even if it meant doing something painful; like the time just before they were married when he suspected that she might have been better off with another suitor and offered to withdraw. For the first time in all the years she had known him, Menes was stepping out of character and allowing his heart to rule his head. His outburst-his love for her-touched her in a spot that she thought surely only the Megalight could reach.

Menes turned his back to her, but her smile continued to rain on the fires of his mock anger. He picked another argument.

"Tell me, how far do you have to go to fetch cool water? No. Do not tell me, I know. I know because it was I who dug the irrigation channel and installed the pump so that you would not have to go to the stream for water."

Her eyes brimmed, but the tears clung stubbornly inside her lashes, as if falling might somehow condone Menes' tirade. She used every ounce of her formidable strength in resisting the urge to hold him. Through her clouded eyes, through her nose, her ears, her very pores, she sent to him what he already knew only too well: that all his efforts were useless.

"What is a man supposed to ..." his voice and his resolve faltered together. "I am going out for some air."

That night, through a poignant probe, Menes apologized for what he had done, and she thanked him for loving her enough to do it.

They knew that their next probe would be their last. It came three nights later. They shared their sorrow and focused two lifetimes of loving into a few fleeting moments. Menes perceived the tiniest glimpse of the journey that awaited Lakwanda, and that glimpse made him feel ashamed for trying to stop her. They went to sleep knowing that only one of them would awaken the next morning. Lakwanda had simply grown to the point where her transition was the only thing left. She had honorably completed all of the work involved in life on the planet, and was now ready to graduate to a higher level of existence. Menes recognized how honored he had been.

In keeping with Zarkonian custom, Lakwanda's body was quickly and quietly buried. Instead of funerals, Zarkonians held memorial services where they came together and joined psychic forces to give the departed a boost on the journey to the Megalight. Memorial services were supposed to be festive occasions, characterized by feasting and dancing. A joyful memorial service was considered an expression of ultimate love: love that can let go. It was also a statement of faith that the departed had lived his life in such a way that something better awaited him following his transition. Only fools, those who demonstrated little linkage to the Megalight, were mourned. It was felt that the death of a fool signalled the end of the Megalight's patience with him. For fools, death was considered a failing mark in the test of life.

Menes danced and laughed throughout Lakwanda's memorial service. She had enriched his life so deeply that he could not bare to have her memorial be remembered as anything less than splendid. Even the lone regret that had blemished their marriage had been corrected. They had never been able to have children. But late one night as Menes was about to step out for a walk, he almost tripped over a baby boy that had been left at his doorway. That baby was Basalt.

Neither Menes nor Lakwanda ever learned how the baby came to be put there. There had been unconfirmed rumors that a strange, caped man had been seen around their home carrying a baby on the night in question. Menes and Lakwanda correctly interpreted the baby to be a gift from the Megalight.

The boy was so quick that the entire village came to wonder how the people who produced him could possibly have abandoned him. (For it had been said that a cornstalk would never produce a tomato.) He was everything any parent could ever ask for in a son: bright, helpful and funny. While his mathematical skills were just a bit above average, his grasp of language was such that he challenged even Menes by the time he was in his fourteenth year. It seemed that not a single day went by that he did not find a way of making Menes and Lakwanda thank the

Megalight anew for sending him into their lives.
His smile endeared him to just about everyone. Actually it was more like a grin. Even after he had disobeyed, he could flash that grin and melt whatever anger might have been directed at him. Some people said that Lakwanda developed her own unique style of smiling just to deal with Basalt's.
Basalt got along well with just about everyone, but his closest friends were Chuka and Lima. He and Chuka had been so close that Menes and Lakwanda were mildly surprised when he announced that he was going to marry Nizinga. They may have been surprised, but they were hardly disappointed. Nizinga was bright and, like Menes, slightly reserved. She did not wrap herself tightly in her reserve; she let it fall from one shoulder, allowing for the possibility of wide-stroked rainbows and other sweet or spicy facts beneath the surface. Had there been such a thing as royalty, she surely would have been a queen. There was a gentle relaxing quality about her that bore testimony to a well-developed and ever expanding Megalight connection.
Menes had been preparing himself for the role of grandfather. He was going to take his grandchild fishing, and teach it even more than he had taught Basalt, since he was older and wiser now. As grandfather, he would assume many of the joys of parenting without the responsibilities. He had visualized the evenings of dinner at Basalt and Nizinga's, holding his grandchild in his lap, watching the generations grow. Now Basalt and Nizinga were dead. Mysteriously. He could have accepted almost any other fate--mauled by a hungry wild animal after being caught with their guards down--struck by lightning even--but poisoned limpins? Basalt simply knew limpins too well to have made that kind of mistake. It was as if there was some cruel, ironic joke taking place. A joke that was not funny.
The village drums pounded the news to the sister villages of the cluster. Saroppo was one of five villages situated around a thirty-mile radius. Many of the villages were arranged in clusters to promote exchanges among the people. These exchanges kept the villages from becoming isolated. They knew isolation choked kinship. Kinship provided their collective Megalight connection with expression. Like unemployed muscles, unexpressed linkage to the Megalight would dwindle to the point that any claim of being made in the image of the Megalight would be rendered hollow.
The responding *thunkathunka thu thunka thunka thunka*

from the drums of the sister villages-Zambutu, Milanhi, Olimpar, and Shinozi-crowded the air with condolensces extolling the virtues of Basalt and Nizinga and praising the will of the Megalight. They hammered out the news of Basalt and Nizinga to the wind, which carried it to villages beyond the cluster.

Many travelers came to pay homage to the houses of Basalt and Nizinga. Because of Menes' reputation, many had come expecting a huge feast and party. The locals tried not to disappoint the travelers. Although they rarely ate meat, other than fish and a few fowl, on this occasion practically every kind of small game had been prepared. Some were roasted in open pits, while others were baked in small metal ovens that collected and condensed the sun's rays. Still others were blended into the countless savory stews that were prepared. Many of the visitors brought exotic spices that added a dash of excitement to already mouth-watering dishes. Sweetbreads and fruit-filled confections abounded. It would have been easier to find a drowning fish than a small child whose hand had not been spanked as payment for attempted pilfering of sweets. Musicians came from around the area to perform and share techniques. Dancers and jugglers entertained. But ...

The music, while technically flawless, sounded flat. The dancing and singing were forced and jokes elicited laughter before the punchlines were delivered. As skillfully as the food had been prepared, the next day no one would be able to say what the menu had been. Menes knew he bore the brunt of the blame for the mood of the memorial.

Menes had built a lifelong reputation as an interpreter of dreams and spiritual powerhouse, through his love of simplicity and truth. "Eliminate purpose, and confusion will take its place. Eliminate confusion and vision will replace it." This had been his motto.

He had wanted desperately for this memorial to go as smoothly as Lakwanda's had gone. But poisoned limpins? His confusion had tainted the ceremonies. Something was wrong and someday he hoped to know the truth. There were so many questions and so few answers. And what about the feelings he *thought* he experienced toward Otumba? No matter how diligently one kept one's thoughts orderly and neatly processed, love, or the mere possibility of love, could blow through with the force of a two year old, leaving a path of chaos and devastation in its path. In the six years since Lakwanda's transition, not to mention the twenty they were married, he had never seriously looked at another woman. Had his eyes finally been opened to a new possibility with Otumba, or was it just a fleeting reaction to the immediate stress? More confusion.

He had known Otumba for close to a decade. She had moved to Saroppo after her children had become grown and wed. She and her late husband had reared five sons and two daughters together. After her daughters married, they insisted on coming home to her to complain about their marital problems. None of their problems were very serious; but Otumba knew that as long as she was around, they would come to cry on her shoulder instead of working things out with their mates. One day she told them she was leaving and migrated to Saroppo.

It had often been said that those things which appear to be opposites may often be identical. If it were true, then, perhaps, it might explain Menes' attraction to Otumba. Where Lakwanda was petite, Otumba was large and buxom. Lakwanda was quiet, Otumba, gregarious; differences of style, not substance. Both women were warm and generous, although Otumba expressed herself more gruffly. Both women made people feel good about being around them.

Menes found that trying to sort his feelings toward Otumba was even more draining than trying to understand what happened to Basalt and Nizinga. For a diversion, he went out to check the clear night sky. He wondered about the mysteries each of the thousands of stars could unfold. He lay down to close his eyes for what he thought was only a few minutes when he awakened to the ringing of his entryway bell. It was Lima.

"I am sorry to bother you, but I thought you might be up by now. I can come back this evening."

"Lima, it is always a pleasure to see you, but what is all this mumbling about being up and this evening when it is already well past evening."

Lima walked to the sunhole along the wall and lifted the shade leaves. Sunlight burst into the room like water from a dam.

"I did not realize I had slept so late. Obviously, I was in need of a reprieve from consciousness. No matter. Fix us some tea. I can see that you are deeply troubled."

"Reprieve from consciousness," Lima thought to himself. Despite his troubles, Lima could never ignore the way Menes talked. Anyone else simply would have said "sleep." But the way he talked was just one of the many things that Lima loved about Menes, or "Mashari," the title of exalted teacher which had been bestowed upon Menes, and by which he was commonly called. But enough of that. Lima had come on an important mission.

Menes stared into his tea as Lima told him about Chuka's disappearance and subsequent strange behavior. *It had happened on the same day that Basalt and Nizinga died.* That sounded about as coincidental as crops following rain.

"She just is not the same anymore," Lima repeated as he concluded his story.

"Have you talked to anyone else?" Menes asked.

"Oh, I started to talk to my father, but I knew that could be construed as asking for family intervention in marital affairs. I have been around to some of the women in town trying to determine what changes are considered normal when a woman is pregnant for the first time. But I have not given anyone the kind of detailed information that I just shared with you."

"What did the women have to tell you?"

"Not much. Although I really did not give them very much to go on. One said something about the Megalight working strange and mysterious ways. Another mumbled something about how the changes that can occur during pregnancy can be unpredictable. But I know that what is happening with Chuka is far too drastic and far too sudden to be a mere side effect of being pregnant. It had something to do with her disappearance. I cannot say if it is related to what happened to Basalt and Nizinga. About the only thing that I can say with the utmost certainty is that it is really frightening.

"Repeat what you have told me to no one," Menes counseled. "You must not even think about it until after the baby is born."

Lima looked as if he had just been told to walk across the planet on his hands.

"I realize that I have not asked you to do an easy thing. But you must remember that the time the baby spends in the womb is its most crucial period of development. There has already been more than enough negativity surrounding this child. We cannot afford anymore. It will be difficult, but it will also allow you an opportunity to utilize the training you have been receiving all of your life. You must maintain positive thoughts until after the baby has safely arrived. Return to me three days after the baby has been born and we should know how to proceed by then. When is the baby due?"

"Any day now."

"Excellent."

"What are you going to do in the meantime?"

"I am not quite sure yet. Obviously there will be some fasting and meditation. But the full process will not be revealed to me until after it has begun."

"Mashari, you know that Basalt and Nizinga were like a brother and sister to me. I know that ... Well, what I am trying to say is ..."

"I know what is in your heart. I have always regarded you as my other son. But right now we must not allow events that have already transpired to interfere with those things which we have yet an opportunity to influence. Time, like water, is precious because it is fluid. You may thank me by following my instructions and keeping an eye turned inward for the grace of the Megalight."

Lima inhaled the sunshine as he strolled away from Menes' hut. Talking to Menes had always seemed to make things better when he was a little boy, and it still did. Even when Menes did not have the answer, he could always boil a question down so that it no longer seemed impossible. He had a way of transforming a catastrophe into a project. Nothing seemed to faze him. And he had that poetic way of talking. It was as if the language Menes used made everything so neat. So solvable.

Lima struggled valiantly to keep his spirits high for the next three weeks. Whenever Chuka said something insulting or disrespectful, he pretended she had said something else, and tried to turn the conversation around to make a joke. But the advent of the fourth week brought with it an erosion of his will. Why was the baby so late? How much longer could he keep trying to make peace with a woman who wanted none? What happened to the woman he loved and married? There were a few rare moments when he caught a glimpse of the old sweet Chuka. But the old Chuka was a wisp of smoke that evaporated whenever he tried to touch it. The new Chuka was more concrete. Unfortunately.

Finally, the time came. Lima and Chuka had gone to bed. Lima was just about to doze off when he felt a strange psychic energy emanating from Chuka. From the time that Chuka's pregnancy had been first diagnosed, the men of Saroppo had instructed Lima regarding what to expect and what to do when the baby came. He knew, actually he *sort* of knew (he wasn't sure of anything since Chuka had changed so much) that the energy he felt was the signal of Chuka's labor.

Chuka let out a silent, siren-like scream. It could be picked up for about a half-mile radius. But it was on a special frequency that could only be picked up by other mothers. Mothers who had not yet gone to bed, dropped what they were doing and raced toward Chuka and Lima's home. If they were in bed, they awakened and threw on whatever was handy. Those with teenaged daughters brought them along. More than one amorous husband was left clinging to a pillow as the women responded to Chuka's cry.

Once assembled, the women sprinkled kukasia leaves on the floor in the main room. Lima was ushered back into the sleeping room and given firm instructions to stay there until summoned. As many as possible of the women lay their hands on Chuka's bulging abdomen. Two of them held her hands. The others made contact with whatever parts of her body were available. The teenaged girls were instructed to form a circle behind their mothers. Each girl extended her right arm to touch the girl next to her, and placed her left hand on her mother's back. In this way the girls not only learned about child birth, but they also contributed by keeping the energy flowing in an unbroken circle.

Normally, once everyone was in place and the energy had begun to flow, it would only take a few painless minutes for the birth to take place. The circle usually began with the woman who had given birth to the most children. The energy was increased with each woman that it traveled through until it took on a swirling nature, like a slingshot, increasing with each revolution until it hit a crescendo. When it peaked it was flung directly into the laboring mother who used it to effortlessly slide the baby out into the world. But something unusual happened with Chuka.

Every time the women flung the energy into Chuka, she consumed it, rather than of converting it. The energy flowed into her and stopped. The women started another circle of energy only to have it end in Chuka's belly. Six times they completed the energy cycle, and six times it was consumed inside of Chuka. She writhed, she kicked and screamed so violently that Lima had to be restrained from bursting into the room. Finally, on the seventh cycle, after more than three hours-two hours and seventeen minutes longer than anyone could remember ever being required- a healthy baby boy, with considerable help from the women, made his way into the world.

5

"Mashari, it is so good to see you again," Lima exclaimed. "I understand you were in Zambutu?"

"Yes I was," Menes answered. "I had experienced a strong urge to get away for a few days. Otumba kept Jawala for me. But I must admit that I was almost embarrassed by my need to get away. There was the possibility that I had wanted to get away to escape from the terrible goings on that have transpired around here lately. But as I thought it through, I realized that if my motive had been escapism, I would have been aware of it and dealt with it differently.

"While I was in Zambutu I interpreted a very strange and powerful dream, easily the most powerful dream that I have ever encountered. I have never felt so intimately connected to the dream of someone that I had never met before. I realize now that my desire to get away was actually a call from the Megalight to interpret that dream."

"Intriguing. Tell me, how many dreams have you interpreted?"

"Too many to count."

"I figured that. The dream you interpreted must truly have been a wondrous one. I suspect that this dream may have some bearing on the recent mysteries that we have encountered around here. Can you tell me about it?"

"I would love nothing more than to share this dream with you. But I cannot. I too, sense that this dream is connected to these recent events, but it is only a feeling that I cannot substantiate. The dream contained layers of meaning, and I have only been able to grasp the most rudimentary of those levels. It may be years before I ever unravel all of its meaning, if ever.

"I wanted you to know about the dream because I wanted you to know that knowledge is still unfolding. But you need not be concerned with the particularities of the dream. Your cup is already full. If you have been following my teachings, you have been more than busy enough trying to empty that cup."

"Mashari, as always, you speak with the wisdom that only the Megalight can grant. And it is a wisdom that the Megalight grants sparingly. Although my cup has been somewhat full, it has not been so filled that I could not do something for the child of the man and woman who were as a brother and sister to me." Lima reached into one of the many folds of his robe and brought forth a hand-carved wooden figurine. "I tried to capture the spirit of what you mean to me. I wanted to give him something that, when he is older and confused or afraid, will provide comfort."

Menes grasped both the sculpture and Lima's extended hand without taking his eyes away from Lima's face. He had told Lima about the dream primarily because he had wanted to involve Lima in something beyond his immediate problems. Yet Lima had spent his time working on a gift for little Jawala. Menes fingered the small sculpture. It was of a man in meditation. Although the eyes were closed, there was no mistaking the look of serenity on the doll's face.

"Thank you, my son. Now tell me, how is your family?" the gleam in Menes' eyes vanished as he asked the question.

"I wish I could say," Lima answered with a sigh. "The baby is in excellent physical condition. Chuka seems none the worse for wear. But ..."

"Please continue."

"Every time I have tried to hold that baby, Chuka has come up with some excuse to take him from me. The only time I have been able to hold him for any period at all has been while she was asleep. And she seems to awaken almost the instant I pick him up. She has no right to act the way that she does, but I'm convinced that she is not herself. And besides, what can I do? Punch her? I am sure that you have already heard about the strange circumstances surrounding the baby's birth."

"Yes, I had heard. Fathers and husbands were called upon in the middle of the night to retrieve their daughters and wives. The women were too tired to return home without assistance. As a matter of fact, not one of the women who was in attendance has been out of bed in the three days that have elapsed since the baby was born."

"Speaking of three days ..."

"A magnificent segue, my son. Very well. I have not been able to determine the exact nature of the problem. I have, however, determined that you are indeed in the midst of a situation that could have far reaching and volatile repercussions." The words danced casually from Menes' lips as if he had been discussing the weather. But Lima knew, given Menes' serious nature and his penchant for understatement, that when he used words like "far reaching," and "volatile," he was speaking of something very very big.

"There is something in the air," Menes continued, "a foreboding. Whatever it is, it is not unrelated to these mysterious deaths, your problems with Chuka, or the fact that so many women are bedridden due to energy depletion suffered while attempting to help bring your child into the world. These things cannot be coincidental. Yet I do not know if there is a guiding force or principle or, for that matter, an individual or groups of individuals that is responsible for these matters. But I can tell you that the will of the Megalight is being grossly violated. I cannot say whether evil is the cause of conflict with the Megalight or the result, any more than I can say whether the *chumu* came first or the egg. But I can state, uncategorically, that where there is conflict with the Megalight there is evil. Now, as to the particulars regarding Chuka, that is information that I may not discern. You must be the agent through which the mystery is solved."

"Me? I have only the tiniest fraction of your insight. Why me?"

"Because you are her husband. Your union is primary. I sense that she is in trouble, which means that you both are in trouble. Whatever is affecting Chuka may be near the very core of her being. Because of your spiritual union, you may be the only one who can reach her at her point of despair. Do you understand?"

"What must I do?"

"You must go to the Kolowon River. Go to the area where the great tree is located, where I first taught you how to swim. Make sure you scan the area for danger. If there are forces behind these problems, they may intervene at this point. There is a plant there that you must find. Unfortunately, I do not know what it looks like. You must lose yourself in meditation until the plant is revealed to you. Once you have found the plant, remove the leaves and shake them onto the ground. Meditate over the leaves. You should receive some images, although the information you receive at this point will be incomplete. Next, you must....What are you doing?"

Lima peered through the shade leaves covering Menes' sun hole. "I thought I saw Chuka. But I must have been mistaken. There was no one there."

"That can happen when one is overly preoccupied with someone, even if that someone is one's spouse. As I was saying, after you have learned all that you can from the leaves, you must brew them into a tea. Meditate again while the tea is brewing. Remember, the most important aspect of all of this will be your ability to meditate. The plant will only enhance the process that essentially begins and ends within you. Once you have drunk the tea, if you have followed these steps correctly, you should know what the problem is. If knowledge of the problem does not provide a solution, then return to me and I will help you plan your course of action."

"Mashari, I ..."

"The return of joy to your home will be thanks enough for me. Now do what you must!"

Lima tried to walk away from Menes, but his feet kept running. He was almost at the river when he remembered he would have to stop at home to get utensils with which to make the tea. After checking to make sure that Chuka was not there, he picked up a small pot and gourd and then dashed to the river.

Once he reached the great tree, he began to settle himself down for meditation. He almost remembered to scan for danger, but he had been here hundreds of times. He could not stand another second of being at war with the woman he loved. Otherwise, he followed Menes' instructions through the finding of the plant, the reading of the leaves and the making of the tea. Involuntarily he shuddered as he read the plant leaves. The images he received, though blurred, were of Chuka. The emotions, the horror, were unmistakable.

The scant images he had been able to receive began to get fuzzier and fuzzier. He knew they were fading because his emotionalism was blocking his reception. He knew what he would have to do. He would have to dig beneath his thoughts and feelings. Move beyond his memories -- keepsakes of his own evolution -- to remember all that he had forgotten just so he could forget it again, this time with a purpose. He knew that on the other side of his thoughts and feelings, past the "what ifs" and the "maybes" lay the point where he simply would "be."

His journey was a difficult one. He had to pass through thoughts without thinking them, and emotions without feeling them. He had to act without action, for the slightest ripple would bring him back to himself. This, for Lima, was the ultimate test of relaxed determination.

Briefly he felt an intrusion upon his space. A familiar presence. But he could not come directly from this state of meditation without ruining the whole process and possibly killing himself. Gradually he returned to the world.

The tea was ready.

As he sipped the tea, he could not help noticing that it had a strangely familiar taste. His spirits plummeted as Chuka's entrapment in the cave played itself out in his mind's eye. Her terror slashed his heart. She had suffered so much and *he had not been there for her!* Tears rolled down his face when he opened his eyes. Somehow, someway he would make it up to her. Somehow, if the Megalight would only give him the strength, he would make things right for her and his baby, little Nagap. He sensed someone coming up behind him.

"Chuka!"

She said nothing. She just stared through him as if he were standing in her way.

"Dearest one. I know. I know what you have been through. I ... am ... going ... to ..."

His words began to thicken, as did his tongue and lips. Communication between his mind and body disintegrated. He tried to take a step toward her but nothing happened.

"Did you not realize that I was aware of your suspicious nature?" she asked dryly. "You were quite correct when you thought you saw me outside of Menes' place when you went there to betray me. Of course you know what happened. You could not destroy me and take my baby without that information. But it is I who have destroyed you. You should have noticed the flavor of kimomo beans in your tea."

"Kimomo beans!" Lima thought to himself. That was the familiar flavor. They were used in surgery as a local anesthetic, and chewed for the same purpose during dental work. But they were used with great care. To swallow the juice of the kimomo bean was to induce paralysis to the entire body.

"You have always been such a magnificent swimmer. Let us see how well you swim with a belly filled with kimomo bean tea!" she shrieked as she pushed her helpless husband into the river.

Lima's dying vision was of the woman that he loved more than life itself, laughing hysterically as the current pulled his leaden body into nothingness.

6

"I would not be against a burnt offering to appease the wrath of the Megalight. Something must be done." The speaker was Nebuchan, Lima's bereaved father.

"Nebuchan, we all want to do something. That is why we are all here. But if our more than four-hundred years of history has taught us anything at all, it has taught us that we cannot act for the sake of acting. Whatever we do, must be done thoughtfully and intelligently. This is the small price we must pay for our linkage to the Megalight. But to address your point specifically, in the first place, we cannot assume that the Megalight is angry. I doubt very seriously if the Megalight even experiences anger as we know it. Secondly, burnt offerings were rendered obsolete when we learned to use our minds to pay homage to the Megalight."

"But Menes," another interjected. "Was it not you who reported strange occurrences in Zambutu when you were there recently?"

"Yes, that is so. There were a few pregnant women who became mysteriously and fatally ill, shortly before they were to deliver. I spoke with some of the Zambutu council members, and they have agreed to share whatever information they can gather. They know as well as we do, that there are no circumstance that will excuse rash behavior. We must study this situation very carefully, and come up with a strongly concerted effort that will produce the results we seek."

The atmosphere in the meeting of the Council of Elders was charged with an unprecedented sense of urgency and frustration. The drowning of Lima, an expert swimmer, coming on the heals of Basalt and Nizinga's deaths, especially in light of Basalt's expertise with limpins, had left the village in a state of confusion and near panic.

"I wonder," Menes paused, weighing the gravity of what he was about to say, "if the forbidden fruit may be involved. It is the only substance I know of, that could produce the kind of havoc we are experiencing."

The forbidden fruit. The rash of mysterious deaths had left everyone searching for answers, but the forbidden fruit? No one had dared even think of it.

"May I address the Council?" a strong female voice rang out before the members had been able to react to Menes' bold suggestion.

It was Chuka.

The council members were stunned. She had appeared briefly at Lima's memorial, but little had been seen of her since then.

During the memorial, she had displayed neither joy or sorrow. In fact, she had almost appeared to be bored. Eventually one of the members regained enough composure to invite her to speak.

"I have not been among you since the mysterious drowning of my beloved husband because I have given myself to meditation, in the hopes of gaining some understanding as to how these terrible things could have happened. Unworthy though I am, the Megalight has blessed me with a small bit of understanding."

Chuka had gained their attention. The only member she had to worry about was Menes. She knew that he would be trying to pierce her armor; to discern her intentions. "Let him try," she laughed to herself, knowing there was just enough of the old Chuka left within her to be used as a shield so that no one could peer into her true motivation.

"We have experienced so few major problems over the past century that we have come to believe that it is our right to live blissfully. We have arrived at the point where we have forgotten that a stagnant pool is a poisonous pool. It has been revealed to me that these deaths have been a wake up call from the Megalight. They represent the Megalight's way of getting our attention. They have ocurred the way that they have, persons dying the most illogical deaths, to make us rely on faith, and not information. We must simply redouble our efforts. Increase our fasting and praying. If we do these things, I am sure that these strange deaths will stop."

Although he could not pierce her facade, something about Chuka made Menes feel uneasy. If only there were some grounds on which to challenge her. He looked around the council and saw the others nodding their heads in agreement with her. He would have to go along with her until something happened to prove her wrong. He only hoped that if she was lying, the proof would not come after some tragic disaster had already hit.

The council members thanked Chuka for her information, then continued to meet among themselves. No one could present a plausible alternative, and they certainly had no desire to go back to the idea of the forbidden fruit, so they decided to follow Chuka's counsel.

7

The truthfulness of Chuka's words was borne out as the days turned to weeks, the weeks to months, and the months to years without further incident. Chuka moved from the home she had shared with Lima, citing unpleasant memories, into a much larger, abandoned hut-actually it was a series of huts connected by passageways-on the periphery of the village.

She so thoroughly dissuaded the early would-be suitors that after two years, no one else came to call on her, which was exactly the way she wanted it. As was their custom, many of the villagers quietly left baskets of food on her doorstep in the evening. For the first few months she would retrieve the food from the basket, then return the empty basket to the doorway.

Then she began to ignore the baskets. If the donor did not return quickly enough to retrieve what he thought would be an empty basket, the food would simply rot.

No one knew where she was getting her food, and Chuka had developed such an icy stare that no one dared ask her. Some said they had seen the same caped figure that was suspected of bringing Basalt to Menes around her hut when it was dark. But the accounts of a figure dressed in black that moved only in the shadows were so sketchy that it was difficult to say that he was not the figment of some overactive imaginations. After all, Chuka's behavior had become so strange that it fueled enormous speculation about her. Most folks guessed that she had never really been able to cope with Lima's tragic death. Those who had incurred her wrath-a sizable number to be sure- figured she had been touched by the dark side of the Megalight. While no one knew if the Megalight actually *had* a dark side, Chuka's behavior certainly provided fuel for those who argued It did. While the cause of Chuka's transformation may have been the subject of differing opinions, there was no disagreement on one point; it was best to leave her alone. Even her son's grandparents began spacing their visits further and further apart.

Caught in the center of the controversy which surrounded Chuka was her little son, Nagap. The community wanted desperately to reach out to him as it always did to fatherless children, but Chuka always kept it at bay.

Gradually a truce evolved. If Nagap came to visit, he was always welcomed, but no one ventured to go get him.

Menes was among the last to try to re-establish some sort of bonding with Chuka. Shortly after Nagap's seventh birthday Menes came to call on Chuka. It was customary for fathers to take their sons on walking trips once they had lived through seven rotations of the seasons.

The initial walking trips were something special for the young boys. It marked their official entry onto the path toward manhood. The trips were usually to one of the other cluster villages and involved at least one night in the wilderness between villages. Since he was already taking Jawala, Menes thought he would include Nagap in the trip. Chuka lied so badly in response to Menes' offer that it appeared that she did not care whether he knew she was lying or not.

"Yours is a most generous offer," she said, smiling with all of the warmth of deep space. "Did you say that you were going to Milanhi? Oh, that is too bad. His grandfather has already asked to take him to Zambutu. I would have loved for him to travel with you, but his grandfather sees him so rarely. Even though he would never admit it, he would simply die if he did not have the opportunity to reach this milestone with him. You do understand, don't you?"

Menes could only smile sadly at her. He knew she was lying, and he was sure that she knew that he knew she was lying. He had already checked with the child's grandfather to make sure that it would be all right to take him on the trip. He wondered why she would tell a lie that could so easily be uncovered. He knew that confronting her would accomplish nothing. She looked as if she would welcome a confrontation; like she wanted an excuse to bare her fangs.

It was obvious that she could no longer feel his love for her. She no longer cared. He found himself wondering as Lima had wondered about whatever could have destroyed the beautiful girl he once cherished and replaced her with this utterly disconnected monster. He thought of how his Megalight connection functioned; how no matter how tired he might have been, or how filled he might have been with his own problems--like coping with life without Lakwanda during the first few seasons after her transition--his connection always made room for the feelings of another. The great thing about being connected to the Megalight--of having the power, will, and compassion of the Megalight flowing through you--was that even when your own will had been exhausted and you wanted to just wrap yourself inside of yourself so that no harm, no activity, could reach you, the link to the Megalight forced you to appreciate the feelings of your fellow man; and that somehow always kept your own feelings from overwhelming you. The kind of insensitivity Chuka had shown could not possibly exist within the same soul through which the Megalight flowed. The flow of the Megalight through his spirit would not allow him to be angry at Chuka, or even to regard the hurt she inflicted on him, for it was nothing but a scratch compared to the deep abrasion that surely existed in her soul.

He wondered about life without a strong Megalight connection: without that inner sanctum, that pure place within oneself where fears and anxieties could be examined without fear of condemnation. Somehow, Chuka had lost hers. Poor child.

What of little Nagap? Chuka's disposition almost gauranteed that the boy would grow up disconnected from the village as well as the Megalight. The boy deserved a chance not to become a fool. Although their numbers were small, it seemed to Menes that he had met every fool who lived within a thousand-mile radius of Saroppo. In every instance, fools had become fools based on their own decisions. They had rejected the opportunity for connection. No one knew why some people were unable or unwilling to develop the most precious gift the Megalight could grant, but everyone was entitled to a chance. Now this child would be reared in a home in which the Megalight would seem a stranger. It just did not seem fair.

Nagap appeared just as Menes was about to leave. He was unaccustomed to having company, so when he saw Menes, his shoulders drooped forward and his little chest fell into his stomach, as it always did when he was afraid. He knew who Menes was-someone who was supposed to be important in the village- but that mattered less to Nagap than it would another child his age. Nagap knew, because Chuka had told him enough times, that he was special, and he was angry that he had allowed this man to make him afraid. "I am not afraid of anyone!" he proclaimed to himself as he sucked his little chest out, and pulled his shoulders back as far as they would go. He marched boldly past Menes, giving the man a slight sideward glance, called his mother by name, and declared that he was hungry.   Menes' eyes quadrupled as he stared incredulously at Chuka.

"Where are your manners?" she asked. Her voice was like silk draped over ice. "Did you not see the Mashari?"

The boy looked like his mother had spoken to him in a foreign tongue. But the ice beneath the silk told him he had better say something to this intruder in his hut.

"Greetings to you, Mashari," he responded with just enough civility to satisfy his mother.

"I do not know where you got the idea of calling me Chuka, but it is an idea whose time has come and gone. Do you understand me?"

It would have been clear to the village idiot that he did not understand

and that he probably called her by her first name all the time. It had been more than twenty-five seasons since Menes had seen a child address any adult, not to mention a parent, without using the proper salutation of respect that was demanded from children to adults. That boy would have been shipped to live with relatives in another village, had not cooler heads prevailed. He was let off with having his chores tripled for a month. His parents were so embarrassed that they secluded themselves until friends and relatives coaxed them back into society some eight months later. The boy eventually went on to fail manhood training, to the ultimate disgrace of his family, and was officially deemed a fool.

    He pondered Nagap's situation for the duration of his long walk home, and continued after he got home. He thought about going to the Council of Elders. But what could they do? Take the child away from his mother? Such an action would be unprecedented, but then Chuka's behavior as a mother had lacked precedence. Even if they *could* take the child, would they? The Council had had so few occasions to meet, and when they did, it was never to discuss unfit parents. There was no criteria. Besides, the judging of others had always been considered one of the swiftest ways to impede the Megalight nexus.

    After much brooding, Menes decided to call a meeting of just a few key council members, along with the child's grandparents. Surely, there could be no harm in coming together to see if Chuka and the child could be helped.

    The next day Menes made his rounds in recruiting participants for the meeting. He had little explaining to do, since Chuka's behavior had already become a source of concern for all of the parties he visited. Otumba would be more than happy to keep Jawala while they met. As he was about to leave the last home, he saw him. For the first time, he could confirm that he was no figment. The caped man was real. Menes called after him, but he seemed to vanish before Menes could catch him. He wondered if the man he saw was actually the same man who brought Basalt to him so many years ago. Though Menes only glimpsed this man, he could see that the fellow had but one eye. There was no mention of that when people spoke of him so many years before. "Be patient," he thought to himself, "The Megalight will see to it that all will be revealed at the proper time." The key phrase for Menes was "proper time." When he was younger he marvelled at how the Megalight always seemed to be on a timetable that could never be understood. As he grew older, he learned to be content with the knowledge that the Megalight understood timing far better than any mortal creature.

    The meeting had been called for the time between dinner and studies, when the sun would expand itself into a bright orange ball just a few feet above the horizon. It mattered little that they measured time imprecisely. They always knew when something was to occur, although they seldom gathered precisely at that time. There were some, like Finola and Alikum, Chuka's mother and father, who always arrived at events or affairs quite early. They were sociable people who enjoyed the extra minutes of socializing that preceded any event that was not immediately life threatening. Lima's parents, Nebuchan and Doramo, like most of the villagers, tended to arrive at some time past the understood arrival time. This evening would prove no exception.

"How did I know that you would be the first ones to grace my humble abode?" Menes asked mirthfully as he greeted Finola and Alikum.

"It must be that the Megalight has decided to increase your powers to the point of omniscience," Alikum replied. The three of them laughed heartily.

"I have cool tea for you," Menes said before disappearing into his cooking space. Below the water pump was a spot in the earthen floor that obviously had been plugged. Menes removed the plug. It was about a foot and a half in diameter, and three-fourths of a foot thick. At the bottom of the plug was metal ring, to which a rope was attached. He pulled up the rope. At the other end was a sealed jug, glistening with moisture.

"I also have cool wine for later this evening. I see that you are not eating the fruit that I have laid out for you. Must I *beg* you to eat my food?"

Etiquette demanded that whenever a meeting was held in someone's home that it be preceded and followed by social intercourse. To do otherwise would mean to disrupt the vibrations of the home. A person's home had to emit feelings of comfort. Meetings, no matter how serious, had to be tempered with sharing emotions or else the home would lose its warmth. Every occasion demanded a social element because each person was considered a gift from the Megalight, and one never knew when the Megalight might decide to retrieve one of its gifts. While humor was considered a powerful tool for the never ending task of emptying self to make room for the Megalight, Menes' lighthearted banter had a forced quality that only served to underscore the seriousness of the situation.

Finola and Alikum glanced knowingly at one another. They knew, along with everyone else in the village that, beneath his serious exterior, Menes had a fine sense of humor. He enjoyed laughing as much as the next person, although he was not the type who initiated humor unless he was ill at ease. The last time he had made three consecutive jokes had been during the memorial for Basalt and Nizinga. He had tried twice to be funny, and they had barely had a chance to sit down. They decided to concentrate their thoughts on their faith in the Megalight. Even when thoughts were neither probed or projected, they would still impact on the atmosphere.

Gradually the others began to trickle in. Next came Eloshima, second only to Menes in terms of influence on the council, and one of only four men in the entire village to achieve the title of "mashari." Then came Beliasan, who had received acclaim during the great debates many years ago, shortly after he had become a man. Euramus, known for his ability to instill humor into the most difficult situations, came next. Salikma, the most travelled woman in the village, followed Euramus. Lima's parents, Doramo and Nebuchan, came; and when Volarno appeared, the assemblage was complete.

Menes thanked each of the group members for coming as he distributed the cold tea; and they, in turn, thanked him for his hospitality. Once the proper time had been allotted to the social amenities, Menes officially opened the meeting with a short invocation which sought the guidance of the Megalight. The prayer was followed by a few moments of silent reflection. Then Menes opened the discussion by carefully detailing his observations and experiences with Chuka.

As he spoke, the people nodded their heads in affirmation of what he said. They issued a collective gasp when he told them that the child not only had walked past him without speaking, but also had proceeded to address his mother by her first name.

"The long and short of the matter is quite simply that we can either attempt to change Chuka's behavior, we can try to take the child from her, or we can continue to ignore this situation," surmised one of the council leaders. "What are your feelings?" he asked, turning to Chuka's parents.

"I believe I can speak for both of us," Alikum answered, "when I say that we have been quiet because we do not know what to say, think, or do. We feel as if we have already lost our beautiful daughter, yet we cannot surrender hope for her. We pray constantly about her, but it appears that the Megalight is preoccupied at those times when we do try. We are afraid that *if*-and that is a very large 'if'-we take the child we will forever lose Chuka. Yet if the child remains with her, we may lose our grandson as well. We must, at least for the moment, surrender ourselves to the collective wisdom of the group before we can give an meaningful input."

"The input you have already given, both the love and the torment that you have expressed, has been extremely meaningful. As you already know, much of our motivation stems from our love for you as well as Nebuchan and Doramo," Menes said, gesturing toward Lima's parents.

"We must fully analyze each of these options," said another. "Does our council even *have* the authority to take someone's child? It would be an unprecedented action. If that authority does exist, upon what grounds would such an action be taken? Do we *dare* to establish criteria for such an awful action? Would not the very act of establishing such a criteria strengthen the possibility of having to use it again? Could we take such an action without such criteria? The implications' implications have implications."

"Your points are well taken," said Doramo. "And we have not even addressed the question of to whom the child would be given, and upon what basis would that decision be made. Perhaps, our purposes might be best served by approaching this situation from another angle. The most perfect solution, of course, would be if there were some way we could determine what has brought these changes on Chuka, and how can we help her get back to the young woman we all cherished and adored."

"Thank you, Doramo," Chuka's mother sighed. For a moment it seemed as if the two women were not speaking to each other, so much as Motherhood was having a conversation with itself.

"Could this drastic change in her personality be completely attributed to the loss of Lima, or is there something more?"

"There is more," Menes responded. "Before he died, Lima confided to me that he was concerned about Chuka. She had already changed, and that change had taken place on the very same day that Basalt and Nizinga died so mysteriously."

"Why have you not brought this information to us until now?"

"What I have told you is really no more than bits and pieces which, until this meeting, were in need of some sort of context. Even now, we still need to know what the source of Chuka's change is, and how to counteract it. It would have served no purpose to mention it before."

"You are quite correct. I guess the question that we must address now is whether we can make her submit to a mind probe."

"A forced mind probe would constitute an extraordinary violation of our most fundamental right of privacy."

"Yes, but this is an extraordinary problem."

"Can such a probe be effective when the subject is unwilling?"

"If enough people are involved, and they have prepared themselves properly, it can be done. The preparation would be crucial and very difficult. We would be seeking the Megalight's aid to do something that is fundamentally against His way of doing things, even if our intentions our noble."

"Is there any way that we can persuade Chuka to voluntarily submit to a probe?"

The meeting grew silent. Collectively, They knew that they had worked their way around to the best possible procedure. Individually, they wrestled with possibilities for implementation.

The bell at Menes' entry way rang as they pondered the issue.

"Who could that be?" Menes asked aloud as he headed for the entry way.

It was Chuka.

"Oh, I did not mean to interrupt something," she lied as she surveyed the packed main hut of Menes' home, or being space, as they were sometimes called. "I had baked some bread as a peace offering. I am afraid I was a bit rude when I saw you yesterday. I wanted to apologize, but I can come back another time," she said without moving a muscle.

Menes marvelled at Chuka's timing. It reminded him of the time when she addressed the emergency meeting of the council following Lima's demise. Had he lived in a different kind of society, he surely would have been suspicious.

"No, do not go away. Please come in. We were just talking about you."

"I am sure you were, you bastards," she thought, but she said: "I am honored to have been a topic in such a prestigious gathering. Hello Mother, Father, Nebuchan, Doramo." She nodded to the others.

"I am afraid," Menes continued, "that our discussion of you has not been a pleasant one. We all love you dearly. But we are terribly concerned about you."

"You have always been the greatest blessing any man could ask for," Alikum spoke. "Since the day you were born, I have found it so hard to believe that the Megalight would actually use *me* to bring you into this world. When you were little, your mother and I kissed your scraped knees, cared for you, and worried over you. Now that you have a child, you will learn that this sort of commitment does not end when your child grows up. But I do not know who you are anymore, and that sickens my heart and grieves my soul."

In the seven years since she had eaten the forbidden fruit, the new Chuka had steadily grown to achieve almost total mastery over the old. The old Chuka had not died; she had become a slave to the new. Now her father's words breathed a tiny bit of life into the old Chuka, and almost shamed the new. He provided a bit of fuel for the war between the conquering new Chuka and the vanquished old. But it was too little, too late. The new Chuka thrived on fear and had been well sustained for the past seven years, while her sustenance had come at the expense of the old Chuka.

"I understand what you are saying. Try though I may, I cannot dispute the merit of your words. There is a story that I must tell all of you. It is a story that I have been carrying around for seven years, even though I should have known better.

"You see, on the very day that Basalt and Nizinga died from limpin poisoning, I too, was picking limpins. I ate one that had a strange effect on me. I did not get sick, but I became quite dizzy. I passed out. When I returned home that evening, Lima told me that he had not been able to feel my vibrations while I was gone." She had to make sure that whatever she told them matched the information Lima had shared with Menes.

"I was about to tell Lima what had happened to me, when someone came to our entry way with the horrible news about Nizinga and Basalt. I was so afraid that something may have happened to my baby that I could not bring myself to tell Lima after we received that news." Despite the fact that her story had been carefully planned, she was venturing into dangerous territory and she knew it. She *had* worried about her baby that day. The closer she came toward telling the truth, the more vulnerable the new Chuka would become.

"My cup became filled with the very emotions you taught me that I must constantly discard. Then, as you all know, I had a very difficult delivery. I think it must have been because of those emotions. Anyway, by the time I had gotten over the delivery, Lima was taken from me. A terrible pattern had built itself into me, and every time I tried to break it, something else happened. I guess I just got to the point where I stopped trying.

"What would you have me do?" She was almost sincere. When she planned her story, she had overlooked the cathartic aspect of telling it. She had been filled with tremendous pain for seven years and this was the first time she had spoken to anyone about being in pain. While deception had been her intent, a certain amount of sincere sharing also took place. If she had been completely honest, she probably would have erased the effects of the fruit she had eaten so long ago. Yet this combination of deceit and honesty produced an even more remarkable change within her. A sort of melding of the two Chukas transpired. Where there had been two almost completely separate entities within her, with one subjugating the other, there was now a certain blending of the two. She had come perilously close to the road to recovery. If only her faith could have pulled her through, but her fear remained as a thin, yet impenetrable, barrier to that faith.

She studied the gathering and could detect not a single dry eye among them. Her parents rose and embraced her. Shouts of praise for the Megalight rang out spontaneously. The others also rose and formed a circular line. Each of them hugged and kissed Chuka, telling her how much they loved her and how much they had been praying for this moment. With each embrace, each kiss, the old Chuka became stronger and stronger. Not only had she not anticipated the catharsis, but she had not considered the power of the love these people felt for her. She had forgotten about their love, and, having been disconnected, could not have anticipated it anyway. For the power of love was then, as it shall always be, the province of the connected.

If a diagram had been drawn of Chuka, it would have shown a continuum. On one end, would have been the purest of the old Chuka, in the middle, the combination of Chukas. At the other end would have been the most disconnected of the new, previously ruling, Chuka. It was the ability of this last bit of Chuka at the farthest end of the spectrum to interpret love as weakness, while the rest of her was being transformed, that kept her from being completely healed in this onslaught of love. It was this bit of her that knew that if the catharsis were to be completed, she would have to confess to the murder of her own husband. She had invested too much of herself in her illness to allow herself to be completely healed. Eventually, the new Chuka would regain firm control of her life. But for now, the change that *did* occur was so truly remarkable that she was forced to fight the tears that doubtlessly would have cleansed away the last vestiges of the new Chuka had they flowed.

Chuka's partial re-integration into society did not come without its perils. She had told Nagap that she, and only she, would be his source of information concerning his father. When the child related this information to Nebuchan, he immediately confronted Chuka.

"I am sorry. I truly meant no harm. It is just that when I relate stories about Lima to Nagap, it is almost as if the three of us are together again, as one normal, happy family," she lied. "Of course, you can tell Nagap about your son."

"I understand. Perhaps, I reacted a bit rashly. I have been so overjoyed at our relationship having been healed that I suppose it frightened me that something else might have gone wrong. I will leave now, but please remember that there is nothing that you can ask of me that, if it is within my power, I will not do for you, Daughter." It felt so good to call her daughter again.

Lima's death remained the single most painful secret that Chuka knew she could never divulge. Regardless of the changes that had been wrought within her, she would forever have to believe that Lima had been a threat to her and her baby.

8

"Sound the Drums! Evacuate all women and children! Let the weak-hearted take shelter, and the strong cling to one another. The greatest display of physical prowess ever to be witnessed is about to take place. Even the coming rains must wait, for the outcome of this titanic battle will determine ..." Jawala shouted in mock amazement.

"What will it determine?" asked one of the boys who had gathered around him.

"You mean you do not *know*?" Jawala asked incredulously. "Do you believe that he does not *know* the importance of this amazing contest that is about to take place? How can that be? Someone please come and explain to this poor lad the importance of the issue that is at hand. An issue that is so great, so important, that it cannot be chanced to reason. This is an issue that can only be determined by the most careful and sophisticated method we have available! Come, oh great gladiators," he gestured to the two boys who were about to fight, "explain to the unenlightened among us, the true importance of what you are about to do!"

The two boys looked at each other, at Jawala, and at each other again. Sheepishly they grinned at one another. In another minute they were hugging and apologizing. Jawala had done it again. While there was no room for fighting of any kind in Zarkonian society, the boys, particularly while their connections were still developing, would occasionally get into little fights. That is, if Jawala was not around.

"I will tell you what," he said after it was clear that there would be no fight, "I would like to have fish for my dinner. And since I am the only one here who knows how to fish, I may catch a lot of them, so that the rest of you will not have to starve this evening!"

The rest of the boys grabbed Jawala and playfully pulled him to the ground. "We will see who knows how to fish around here," one of the boys challenged.

"The last one to the fishing spot is the son of a zhybongo monster!" Jawala squealed, as the boys ran helter-skelter to the river.

Jawala was about to run off when he noticed that there was someone standing behind him, half-hidden behind a tree. It was Nagap.

"Nagap! It is so good to see you. You have been such a stranger. We are about to catch some fish, or at least we are about to try. Please join us."

Jawala's sincere offer caught Nagap off guard. While he had spent some time playing with the other fellows, most of the time he had been around them, he had done so secretly. He liked being able to see what the others were doing without being seen himself. Sometimes he would watch them play. In his imagination, he would join the games and win every time. When the games were over, they would hoist him on their shoulders and carry him off. Back in the real world, he had spent so little time around other children that he did not know how to act around them. He kept his distance and played the games in the safety of his mind, where he would never have to worry about losing.

Wherever there was a game, a dispute, or any activity involving his mates, Jawala could usually be found in the midst of it. They called him 'Little Beetle' when he was younger because of the way he scurried about the village, involving himself in just about everything that a young child could. He loved to visit, going from hut to hut, drinking in the stories of his elders, memorizing them as best he could- changing what he forgot- and then regaling his friends with his grown-up sounding stories.

He inherited his mother's musical talent, and her gift with numbers, although he looked more like his father. He had his father's impishness, and his smile. It was almost the identical smile that had rescued Basalt on any number of occasions.

When he was about five years old, he developed the same allergic reaction to going to bed that is common to all children that age. Sometimes he would sneak out of his room, behind Menes, into Menes' room. He would reappear draped in one of Menes' robes, his face scrunched up, and in his deepest voice announce that he was not really Jawala, but someone else, who had come to tell Menes that Jawala had left the hut, but not to worry because he would find Jawala for him. He would not allow the fact that Menes never believed him to slow him down. In fact, his failures added to his determination. If simply wearing Menes' *tshamos* did not work, he would add Menes' shade hat. But when he reappeared wearing Menes' robe, shade hat, and a beard and mustache drawn with ashes, Menes acknowledged that he was a stranger, asked him to stay for a moment, then went howling to Otumba's hut. Jawala's costume was simply too much not to be shared.

There were times, however, when Jawala's cheerfulness abandoned him; when there was nothing to fill the empty spot he felt within. He wished he could have at least seen his parents, heard their voices, known their smells. He had never seen them, but he still missed them. Sometimes Menes would point out someone who looked like Basalt or walked like Nizinga, or laughed like her, but that information only made him hunger for more.

He once asked Menes if there were other little boys who had lost their parents. Menes told him about Nagap. Then he showed him the figurine Lima had carved for him, telling him he could receive it at the proper time. Although he barely knew him, Jawala's heart swelled with love for his kindred spirit, Nagap.

While Jawala had been interacting with just about everyone, Nagap's only flesh and blood companion was his mother. He created imaginary friends. He liked the friends he made up because they were docile, and would do whatever he told them to do, whenever he told them. They knew that he was the boss, and he never let them forget it. When he tired of an imaginary friend, he would pretend that his friend disobeyed him, then stomp him into the ground. He could always make up new, more obedient friends.

He stayed away from the center of the village because it was frightening. How did all of those adults know him, when he did not know them? He knew no more how to handle the villagers friendliness than he knew how to handle Jawala's fishing invitation.

He ached to spend time with his peers, to do something different. But what if he was the only one that did not catch anything? What if the others caught more fish than he, or bigger fish? The risks were just too great. He disappointed himself when he told Jawala that he could not go with them.

Later that evening, Chuka, sensing he was upset, tried to get him to tell her what had happened. He opened his mouth, only to hear himself breathe. There was no way he could have explained having been gripped by fears which he did not understand himself.

"Eat your supper, Dear, and when you have finished, if you eat all your food, I have something to show you that will make you feel better."

There was something in the way Chuka spoke to him that piqued Nagap's curiosity. Whatever she was going to show him would be special. He could feel it. He wolfed down his supper, barely taking time to taste it, and waited impatiently as she cleaned up. He was so impatient that he almost offered to help, but did not wish to set a dangerous precedent. Finally she disappeared into her sleeping quarters and returned, holding a small booklet.

"You may see this now," she handed the pamphlet to her son, "but it is not yet time for you to read it. I have been saving this information for you since before you were born. When the time comes, I will give it to you. It contains information that will someday make you the greatest of living men. Always remember that you have this information, and you have me. As long as you remember these things, nothing will get so bad that you will not be able to look past it to the time when you will be able to use this pamphlet. But you must remember, I am the only other person that must ever know about this pamphlet. You must tell absolutely no one, no matter how close you think you are. Do you understand?"

"Yes, Mother," Nagap answered with reverence. Chuka had told him all along that he was special, that a special destiny awaited him. Yet here, for the first time, was tangible proof. The secret pamphlet with the frightening title told him that someday all of Chuka's promises would come true.

9

*N*agap sat quietly on a hill overlooking the other boys and debated whether or not he would join them. They were playing Sklomb, and while he had never played the game, it seemed like something he could do well. Sklomb was a game that the adults organized for the children until they were old enough to play by themselves. They would sit in a circle and take turns thinking of a number. The other children would try to guess the number. Sklomb was designed to develop and enhance the young people's powers of empathy and telepathy.

In the months that passed since Jawala's fishing invitation, Nagap vowed that he would not be found unprepared again. He began spending more and more time watching the others in the distance. He would note whatever techniques were involved, whether it was sklomb or wrestling, then practice what he had seen with one of his imaginary friends. Having watched the others play Sklomb, Nagap had found that if he waited long enough, he could guess the correct number more often than most of the other children, with the possible exception of Jawala. Nagap's Megalight connection had been so badly damaged when Chuka ate the forbidden fruit that he had almost no powers of empathy. Chuka's inability to bring the problems she and Nagap encountered before the rest of the village left him groping to compensate for his lack of spiritual powers, while hoping that he would not be discovered.

The idea behind playing Sklomb was to make mental contact with the person who had thought of the number. When Jawala and the others played sklomb, they would close their eyes, roll their heads around and try to relax until they had forgotten themselves and could feel only the number being projected. They rode the soft psychic emanations as if they were zephyrs. Nagap had to wait until the game was well underway before joining the guessing. His mind was so mathematically analytical that, after he had observed the same person for a while, he could perceive patterns and predict numbers based upon mathematical probability. Only Nagap's sincere love of winning could justify the mental strain he endured to correctly predict the numbers.

"Perhaps, if you could just learn to relax," Nagap taunted after a particularly successful game, "you might be able to feel the number in question. You must learn to lose yourself in the mind of another. It really is quite simple, once you get the knack of it. Why, I would be more than happy to help you chumps oh, did I say *chumps*- I'm sorry, I meant to say *champs*. I..."

"Nagap!" one of the boys could stand it no longer. "There is no denying your skill, but your boasting contradicts the very idea of playing the game in the first place."

"I have contradicted nothing. The only contradiction I can see is between what the rest of you say that you feel about the game and how you react because you cannot stand the idea that I am the best."

"I am not normally prone toward violence, but you may prove the exception," another boy grunted through clenched teeth while pound a fist into a palm.

Briefly, the idea of allowing one of the boys to pummel some humility into Nagap found acceptance within Jawala's breast. He even considered doing it himself. But his instincts and training prevailed:

"If a single game of sklomb can create such intense friction among good friends, then perhaps we all need to re-examine our connections. Maybe it is time we went our separate ways, that we may contemplate what has happened here today, and what could have happened."

The boys quietly dispersed. Three weeks would pass before they would play another game of sklomb, five before Nagap would play with them. When the entire group had finally gathered to play another game, they tried to erase the embarrassment of the last meeting by de-emphasizing the competition with silliness. The tactic worked beautifully for everyone, except Nagap.

Nagap's method for Sklomb had one major flaw: it depended on the underlying logic of the person who thought of the number. The group's silly mood removed that logic. As each player took a turn thinking a new number- Nagap was careful never to be the one who projected the number- he tried harder and harder to discern some pattern and failed miserably.

"Nagap, since you are the one who always has to know who

got the most correct answers," one of the boys with whom he had feuded before said to him following the game, "Tell us who got the most correct answers today?"

The youths were astounded as Nagap, eyes filling with tears, fists clenched, and body almost shaking with rage, stared angrily at the boy for a few seconds, before running away. The boys stared slack-jawed at one another as Jawala followed Nagap.

"Please, little brother, do not make me run so fast, or I will have no energy when the time has come for us to undergo our manhood training," Jawala gasped, referring to the one event that dominated every male child's thinking once he had reached the age of twelve. "Tell me what is bothering you. I may be able to help."

"You cannot help me. I thought you understood! But you know no more about me than the others. You will not understand until you are forced to understand. Now, leave me alone. I did not ask you to follow me."

"When I was much younger," Jawala answered, "I would ask Mashari about my parents. I asked all kinds of questions. But the one question that brought the answer that has always made me feel close to you was when I would ask if other children had their mothers or fathers taken from them also. Mashari told me yes; that such a lad lived right here. You are the lad that he told me about. He would talk of how close our parents once were.

"I want that closeness to exist between us, if it is possible. Please, tell me what is troubling you."

"Leave me alone!"

"Not until you tell me what is bothering you. Do you not realize that you and I are drops from the same ocean; that we both draw our breath by the Megalight's grace? We are different, but we are also the same. Why are you so angry? You must tell me."

"Leave me alone!" Nagap shouted as he struck Jawala in the chest. Jawala's eyes widened as he looked quizzically at Nagap. The punch did not hurt because Nagap was small for his age. But he startled Jawala so much that he could not react.

Nagap came to within six inches of Jawala and began pummelling him in the chest and screaming that he be left alone. While Nagap's punches did not bother him, Nagap's agony was more than he could bear. Almost as much for himself as for Nagap, Jawala put his arms around him and gently repeated to him that he was his friend, that he was not alone. Nagap's wailing turned to sobs.

"Sklomb is the only thing I can beat you at." he moaned.

Nagap's outburst was even more startling than his punches. Nagap's pain sprang from a terrain which Jawala had never traveled: jealousy. As a connected person, Jawala had always shared in the successes of others, rejoiced in them, because success was not something an individual could accomplish alone. Success, like pain, was like the air or the soil; it was community property. Jawala recognized that Nagap's pain was intense. He wanted to ease it, to take it away, but he could not understand it. He rocked the sobbing boy in his arms, little realizing the impact this physical contact would have on Nagap.

Not since he had been a toddler, had Nagap been held by anyone other than his mother. There had been a few embraces after she had somewhat reconciled with the community. But nothing had ever really been exchanged during those embraces. There was more than just physical contact being made now that Jawala had embraced him. Jawala seemed so strong, so comforting. Nagap wanted to squeeze Jawala, but he had to settle for allowing himself to be held. He felt ashamed for wanting the hug to last forever. He could not understand Jawala's feelings any more than Jawala could understand his, but he knew that Jawala was not experiencing their encounter the same way he was. As he gathered himself to withdraw from Jawala, Nagap promised himself that someday, he would make Jawala understand. Jawala would recognize that he was special. Regardless of what the others might think, there would come a day when Jawala would bow down before him. When that day came, he and Jawala would be able to become friends and brothers; but it could not happen until after Jawala had been humbled.

When he returned home that evening, Jawala was so quiet that it took Menes only a few moments to recognize that something was wrong. His suspicions were confirmed when Jawala said that he was not hungry. Menes knew that Jawala was about to enter puberty, but he could sense that whatever was bothering him was something out of the ordinary.

"How was your day today?" Menes opened the forum.

"Mashari, it was ... Well, something happened today ... I mean, well, there is something that I would like to talk about, but I do not know how to talk about it, or even if I should talk about it. Do you understand?"

"Yes. But the only way to determine if it is something that we should discuss is for us to discuss it. Of course if it is something that should not be discussed, by the time we determine that, it will already be too late, because we will already have discussed it. I would say that you have quite a dilemma there. But perhaps, there is another approach that we may take. Suppose you tell me the criteria that would establish something as being inappropriate for you and I to discuss, and then we can see whether or not this particular subject fits that criteria. If it fits, then we will not discuss it. That way we can at least determine if we should discuss it, without betraying it, if we should not." Menes could barely resist smiling to himself, as he tried to remember if he had ever gotten caught up in such gobble-de-gook when he was Jawala's age.

Jawala related his experiences with Nagap that day. As he spoke, he peppered his report with phrases like "I just do not understand it," or " I have never seen anything like it before."

Menes began to realize the seriousness of Jawala's concerns. He stopped smiling, and began to nod his head occasionally, trying to encourage Jawala.

"How do you feel about what happened?" he asked once the story had been completed.

"I wish I knew. He was in so much pain. I never thought anyone as young as me could be in that much pain. I do not understand where the pain came from, or why he was in it. I always thought that when the Megalight smiled upon you, you were not supposed to experience pain."

"My son, I do not know where you got that idea, but it certainly did not originate with any of my teachings. Pain is a fundamental and necessary part of life. When it is shared, it connects us. Those who do not understand pain and how to handle it, allow it to isolate them. They put it on a plane that is even above the Megalight, and it becomes their god and their curse. Yet pain is so necessary that people have been known to concoct their own, out of their imaginations. That fact not withstanding, it is quite clear that you have every reason to be concerned about Nagap. There is something very unhealthy about his actions. While I cannot fathom all of this mystery, I can identify some of its components."

"Mashari, you know that there are times when I have difficulty following you."

"Very well. However, the time will come when you will fully

appreciate the fact that I have never spoken to you as if you were a child."

"You probably could not, even if you wanted to," Jawala thought to himself.

"I heard that!" Menes bellowed with mock indignation.

"Mashari, you said you would never probe me without my permission."

"I did not *have to* probe you. Your facial expression told me more than any probe ever could. Now, back to the subject at hand.

"It is obvious that Nagap admires you a great deal. But if he does not possess adequate self- awareness, then his admiration may take the form of a poison upon which he may gag himself."

"I still do not understand."

"You may have to trust me on some of this, for I, myself, have a difficult time understanding it. But when a person is overly competitive, it is usually because that person is seeking self-esteem outside of himself. He does not know how to feel good about himself. He is competing against someone else when he should be competing against his own potential.

"You see, before this lamp came into existence," Menes motioned toward one, "there had to exist the *idea* of the lamp. Before anything can be created, there has to be an idea about that thing. You cannot make a lamp before you get the idea of a lamp. Do you understand?"

"I think so. Just as I cannot go fishing until after I think of going fishing?"

"Close enough. Anyway, when we strive to know the Megalight, and to be all that the Megalight would have us be, we are, in reality, striving to become like that perfect idea of us that already exists in the mind of the Megalight. Of course, we never really become completely like that idea, or picture, but we strive to become as close to it as possible. As long as we are in touch with the Megalight, this striving is instinctive."

"Has anyone ever become the same as the picture in the Megalight's mind?"

Menes grew silent. He answered affirmatively in a voice so low that Jawala strained to hear him. He stared at the floor, gathering his recollections. Although it seemd for a moment that he was about to cry, when he raised his head he offered a bittersweet smile.

"What is it, Mashari?"

"Oh, I was just thinking of how I wish you had been able to know your grandmother."

"Do you think that you will ever love another woman?" Menes was about to say 'no,' when someone flashed Otumba's picture right into the middle of his brain. Something within him declared that the time would soon be near when his tangled feelings would become clear, maybe even too clear.

"It is entirely possible," he amended his answer. "But let us return to our original discussion. We are straying," he added gruffly.

It seemed that no matter how pressing the issue, Menes and Jawala always strayed a bit during their discussions. Menes usually encouraged a little meandering because it afforded him the opportunity to impart more knowledge than otherwise would have been possible. This time, however, they wandered into uncomfortable territiory.

"The point I was trying to make," Menes continued," is that when a person has no link to the picture of himself that is within the imagination of the Megalight, then that person will choose someone whom he feels he can admire, and try to compete with that person. Now, do you understand?"

"Yes. And your explanation may explain the pain that I felt coming from Nagap. But I still do not understand why Nagap would be so out of touch with the Megalight's idea of him."

"Perhaps, it is because he has never received the proper instructions. Whatever the reason, I am afraid that our little friend Nagap is in danger of becoming the consummate individual."

"Consummate individual?"

"That is a person whose roots begin and end within himself. The consummate individual is almost completely dependent upon self. Fear prevents him from reaching out to others. He is in constant fear of being loved, and of being rejected. The consummate individual stands just outside of life's most meaningful realities and substitutes his own definitions for true meaning and understanding. He has to, because he lacks the Megalight's nourishment, which is required to sustain him through life's ups and downs."

"But Mashari, what is the difference between a consummate individual and a fool?"

"Excellent question, my son. No boy will be declared a fool, unless he fails manhood training. There is more hope for the consummate individual, than there is for the fool. Nagap is still too young to be considered a fool. You may be able to help him."

"How?"

"Love him as much as he will allow, but do so very carefully. You must not intrude upon his psychic space, and unfortunately, he probably requires quite a bit of space. Never try to force anything upon him, even if you know that it is for his own good. That is, of course, if you want to help him."

"You know I do, Mashari. But tell me, did you not say that Chuka had become much closer to the community than she had been? Then why do we not try to involve her in our efforts to save Nagap?"

"Another excellent question, the Megalight has gifted you with an exceptional sense of understanding for one your age. But I am afraid that Chuka has grown as much as she can for the present. There is still something that stands between her and her potential. Whatever that something is, it is something that she is not yet ready to deal with. And until she can further liberate herself, there will be no point in trying to work through her to help Nagap."

10

As the parents of the boys in Jawala's peer group surveyed their sons' half completed chores, they were forced to console themselves with the knowledge that the boys' distractions would soon be over. The time for their sons' manhood training was drawing near, so the boys could hardly be blamed for being preoccupied.

Two full cycles of seasons had come and gone since Jawala, along with many of the others, had first experienced those physical changes that herald that mystical period of metamorphosis between boyhood and manhood. Each change, whether it was the deepening of the voice or the appearance of pubic hair, served as a reminder that many other important changes would have to take place as well. Every relationship, be it with parents, older or younger siblings, youths who had already passed the manhood training or those yet to complete it-would be different once the training had been completed.

To become a man was not something that was taken lightly. Manhood was neither conferred automatically with the arrival of a certain birthday, nor was it accepted without an understanding of the cost involved. Once manhood had been conferred, the individual had to adopt a certain bearing, and remain ever mindful that one did not bring shame to the almost holy title of man.

Of course, the most obvious changes were in their bodies. Menes once spied Jawala trying desperately to wash out his sleeping robe and bed without being seen. When Menes asked him why he had suddenly become so concerned with laundry, Jawala confessed that he had had an "accident" during the night. Jawala's confession of the "accident" gave Menes the opportunity he needed to console his young charge. It was important for Jawala to learn that what had happened was not an accident, and that he had nothing for which to feel ashamed.

"How do you feel about girls, now?" Menes asked.

"Well, I used to like them as friends, except that they cannot run very fast; and they sometimes get hurt too easily. I like them, I guess, but I know that they are different from boys."

"Are your feelings toward girls changing?"

"I think so. I am not sure. I am confused."

"You are entering a very confusing period. What happened to you last night was your body's signal that it believes it is grown-up and wants to explore the female body. It is something that happens to all males as we begin the transition from boyhood to manhood."

Jawala's heart leapt into his throat. For the first time, Menes had actually acknowledged that he was becoming a man.

"Manhood is something that comes in stages, it does not arrive all at once. Do you remember the ways in which one strives to become a man?"

"Spiritually, mentally, emotionally, and physically?"

"Correct. And of the ways in which we become men, the least important way is also the first way. Why do you think that is?"

"Because the more value something has, the more difficult it is to accomplish, and the more time is involved."

"Excellent. Now, once you have become a man physically, spiritually, mentally, and emotionally, not only will you have acquired the understanding of yourself, including your body, but also you will have acquired the kind of discipline that is necessary to have a proper relationship with a woman."

"What kind of discipline is that?"

"The kind that will allow you to love fully, to give yourself completely to another person and at the same time, remain ever willing to lose that person if it be the Megalight's will or if it is in her best interest. When you can do this, my son, you truly will be a man."

Jawala's heart sunk back to where it had been before Menes had acknowledged that he was becoming a man.

At about the same time that Jawala began struggling with his emerging manhood, so too did Nagap enter the same struggle. He asked his mother if he should talk to his grandfather about the changes that were taking place in his body. Chuka told him that he had her permission to ask his grandfather, but that, even though she was not a man, she could still tell him anything that he might have wanted to know about becoming a man. She claimed to have that knowledge based upon mind probes she had shared with Lima. While she answered him, she pressed her hands around his and gave him that same controlling look she had used on him since he was a small child. The look said that although I give you my permission to discuss this with your grandfather, I would *strongly* prefer that you discuss it with me.

Nagap's coming into puberty represented one of many potential problem areas that Chuka had always known she would someday have to deal with, but for which she could never quite prepare. She listened patiently as he explained to her the strange feelings that were going on in his body. He was struggling with many of the same feelings she had crushed within herself, feelings the old Chuka had thoughtlessly indulged with Lima. Where the old Chuka had been weak, the new Chuka was strong. She reflected on the many suitors she had rejected following Lima's demise. A few had been quite appealing. As she had rejected the suitors, she had also rejected a substantial part of herself. She recognized that the need to share could seriously hamper her plans for herself and her son; so she regarded her decision as a triumph of discipline, rather than the emotional amputation that it was.

She would never take another mate simply to relieve some carnal craving. And love was certainly out of the question. Her mate would have to possess something truly unique, something special, something compelling. When Nagap finished describing his emotions, Chuka answered by explaining what she thought was the basis for a relationship.

"Love is fine," she counseled, "but it should not be the overriding factor in your relationships. You will hear many things from some of the elders in the village. They will tell you that when you take a woman unto yourself, you will be engaging in the ultimate act of communication, and for them, that may be true. But they do not have your destiny ahead of them, and they do not understand power. When you take a woman unto you and, even more importantly, when you learn to decide when not to take a woman unto you, you will be engaging in the ultimate act of power! Within your own body lies the seeds of your own destruction. When you have learned to beat your own sexuality into submission, you will have begun to achieve the power to place everyone else in submission as well."

In the following two years, Chuka would provide dozens of lectures on the proper attitude toward sexuality. She warned him never to repeat her instructions to anyone, because no one else would understand her message. She became so intense when discussing sexual matters that Nagap often felt embarrassed by his feelings. He had failed to stop his nocturnal "accidents." Chuka had told him innumerable times how superior he was, yet he still longed for physical contact with another human being. He liked the secure feeling of unconditional acceptance a warm embrace could provide. There also was the time when Jawala had hugged him, and he had felt shame for having enjoyed the embrace so much. Chuka's teachings caused that memory to grow more painful and embarrassing with each recollection. He had not asked Jawala to embrace him. Jawala was the one who forced the issue. Chuka's lectures served to strengthen Nagap's resolve that someday Jawala would be humbled before him.

Now the manhood training and ritual would be upon him soon. All of his peers knew it was about to happen, but no one knew exactly when. He had almost pleaded with Chuka to find a loophole to get out of the training, but even Chuka could not remove that obligation. He had always been able to fake psychic transmissions when playing Sklomb, but there were any number of activities that he knew he would never be able to fake if called upon during the training. If he failed, he would have to leave Saroppo forever. He would be too humiliated to try again with the next group of young men. Although she could not get him out of the training, Chuka had promised him that she would always be nearby; that she would not let him fail. He was hoping she would be able to deliver on her promise and was taking aim with his slingshot to kill a squirrel for sport; when Shobogun, the biggest man in the village appeared.

"I have come for you," Shobogun boomed.

Nagap's shoulders drooped and his chest fell, but not just into his stomach; this time it seemed to split at his pelvis and finally land at his knees. His lip quivered, and his palms rained sweat as he implored Chuka with his eyes. She stared back fiercely. Without a word, she told him that he would, just this once, conduct himself nobly. He straightened himself up and followed Shobogun.

They walked silently to the center of the village. Nagap was relieved to see that the rest of the fellows in his age bracket already been gathered in the village center. Other than the three men who watched over the boys, and of course the boys themselves, the village center, which normally would have been bustling with activity by now, was completely deserted. Nagap searched the eyes of the other boys, trying to find a glimmer of the same fear that he felt, or some sort of recognition. The other boys stared blankly into space. Only in Jawala's eyes did Nagap find a bit of solace. He cursed himself having sought it there, and Jawala, for having provided it.

"You will follow us," Shobogun barked once the boys had been fully assembled. "You will not stop nor will you speak. You will do exactly as you are told. No more, and no less!" With those instructions, he began a slow trot into the dessert.

Excitement and fear had so consumed the boys that they could not have noticed the shade leaves fluttering in their parents homes, as mothers and fathers said their own silent farewells to the boys they knew they would never see again. When they returned, they would be men.

As the sun approached its zenith, the boys found their feet sinking deeper and deeper into the burning sand. The men appeared to run across the top of the sand, hardly making any impressions at all. The boys tried desperately to keep up as the sand burned their feet and sweat stung their eyes. Just when they were sure they could go no further, the men directed them to an oasis to rest.

"When your training is completed, you too will be able to cross the sands without sinking into them," Shobogun offered as encouragement.

They drank their water, and soaked their scorched feet in silence. The boys knew better than to ask about food.

The men allowed them just enough time to refresh themselves, without letting their muscles get too relaxed, before resuming.

They marched another four hours along the periphery of the desert until they came to a low ridge of mountains. They stopped at the mouth of a cave.

"You will stay here tonight," one of the other men spoke for the first time. Shobogun disappeared into the cave and returned several times, carrying huge sacks. The men of the village had already stocked the cave in preparation for the boys training. The sacks contained breads, meats, cheeses, vegetables, and containers of water.

"You will also need these," Shobogun said as he pulled several *chackons* from his robe. Chackons were pieces of metal that were used like flint to start fires, and burned like charcoal.

"The night gets very cold out here, so you must learn to use the chackons wisely. You have enough provisions to get you through one more day. We will leave you now. You must find us in exactly seven days, and you must find us before the sun reaches its zenith. You are not to come to us before the seven days are up. You will have to find food and water and sustain yourselves during that period. You must not begin to look for us before five days has past. May the Megalight shine upon you all, until next we meet."

Shobogun and the other two men disappeared into the darkness of the night before the realization of what was happening had been allowed to sink in. The boys stared dimly at one another in the darkness, each feeling almost as if the quiet was a sacred vase that could not be broken.

"We had better build a fire," Jawala said as much to end the silence as to communicate the need for warmth; although it had gotten quite cold. Another boy began to rub the chackons together. They retrieved their rations and ate in silence. They would soon be men. After all the anticipation, the excitement, the waiting, and the dreams, the time had finally come. Each boy began wrestling in his own mind, with those aspects of boyhood that would no longer have a place in his life. When they returned they would begin building the single unit huts that new young men live in. As a man took a wife, and had children, the huts would be expanded with new additions being made to reflect the additions to the families. They would now be called upon to render opinions in matters that concerned the community, and they would no longer be allowed to answer frivolously. What they would say would carry a certain amount of weight, so that their answers would have to be considered carefully. They still would not enjoy the respect that was afforded to the elders; but getting this close to manhood, they were beginning to understand what their elders had been trying to tell them all along: that each gift or honor carries with it corresponding responsibilities- the greater the honor, the greater the responsibility.

They covered the cave entrance with leaves to eliminate the cold winds, and took turns acting as sentry at the mouth of the cave. Although they did not know exactly what it was they were guarding against, they thought it prudent to be cautious. When their training was completed, they would be able to scan an area for danger. For the time being, the sentry system would have to suffice.

The next morning they all awakened at the same time, except

for the boy who had pulled the next to the last sentry duty.

"We need to decide on a plan of action," Nagap spoke up, trying to sound authoritative.

"That is true. But we cannot begin to plan together, until we have each completed our morning meditation. We must make no decision to which the Megalight is not a party," one of the boys accidentally dashed Nagap's ego to the rocks.

The boys gathered into a circle, with each member sitting in the lotus position. They closed their eyes and meditated for what seemed an eternity to Nagap who had never really understood why they always made such a big fuss over that meditating business in the first place. He risked a few glances around the cave, fearful that someone might catch him with his eyes open. He tried to focus his mind on the prestige that would follow his declaration of manhood, but all he could think of was the knife. As part of the purification for manhood, the foreskin of each boy's member would be cut off. Nagap, like the rest, had heard that it could be very painful unless one knew how to use the mumbo jumbo sort of tricks that came with meditation. Since Nagap had never developed any of the psychic abilities of the others, he reasoned he had more than sufficient cause for alarm. He hoped that Chuka would find a way to keep her promise to be nearby, although he could not imagine how. Finally, the others stopped their infernal meditation. Nagap could not understand how it was that they all stopped together, but he figured it was either a coincidence, or something that did not merit any more thought than a coincidence, anyway.

The boys discussed food and water gathering. They debated whether they should try to kill any animals for food. They decided that they would not rule out meat, since they were unfamiliar with the vegetation of the area, but that they would pray so that if they did kill something, at least they would not be making animal orphans somewhere in the wilderness.

The boys practically amazed themselves with the knowledge they already possessed about survival. They were able to find vegetables, and they made crude but effective traps to catch small prey for food. They took turns bathing and fetching water from the oasis they had passed when they left the village. On the fifth and final day, they decided that they should fast so that they would be as sharp as possible for homing in on the vibrations of the men. There was only one dissenting vote against the fast, and Nagap quickly capitulated when he saw that he could not sway the group.

They stayed relatively close together on the fifth day, keeping their minds focused on the sight, smell, and general aura of the men they were seeking. Only Nagap ventured away much that day. When the others asked him where he had gone, he muttered something about being able to meditate better in seclusion. It was none of their business, he reasoned, if he had the good sense to find something to eat while they starved themselves.

When they arose on the sixth day, there was no need to discuss any plans. They knew where they had to go to rendezvous with the men. On the seventh day, more than three hours before the deadline, they found the men in a temporary barracks.

"You have done well," Shobogun greeted them. "We hope that you enjoyed your rest in the wilderness. The next few months will be the toughest of your lives."

Truer words could not have been spoken, had they come directly from the mouth of the Megalight.

Their regimen began with the first rays of the morning sun. Each day began with instructions in meditation, ethics, philosophy, secrets of manhood, and history. Perhaps the most intriguing element of the history lessons was the explanation of the Great Bang theory. It held that the current Zarkonian society could not remember any of its history beyond four hundred years ago because that was when it began. Before that time, there was a different society, one filled with almost magical devices and capabilities. The Great Bang theory said their highly advanced predecessors eventually developed weapons so fierce that they were able to annihilate themselves.

"Nagap!" Shobogun called crisply after unveiling the Great Bang theory. "Could such a thing have happened? If so, why? If not, why not? Should we even care if it happened?"

"I believe that it probably did happen, Mashari." The manhood training could only be supervised by one of the few men who had attained the rank of mashari.

"It may have been that they had limited resources and fought over them until they extinguished themselves. Maybe they had different racial groups like we have, but they did not understand each other."

"How could different racial groups have destroyed each other through lack of understanding?" Shobogun was genuinely curious about this strange idea.

"Of course, I am only guessing," Nagap warmed to Shobogun's interest. "But if they had had a long enough history, the tribes could have grown to outnumber ours by ten, twenty, even a hundred or a thousand fold. If the resources became scarce, they might have needed something to determine the make-up of the groups that fought over those resources. Race would probably have been an easy way to determine sides," Nagap discreetly beamed.

"Fascinating," Shobogun said softly. Nagap's answer had been so completely different from anything he had ever heard of or expected, that he decided he would have to share it with some of the more thoughtful village members, especially Menes, who would have been conducting the training, had Jawala not been one of the boys.

"Jawala, what have you to say on this subject?"

Jawala was hardly prepared to answer. Detached listening had always been difficult for him. He always tried to place himself inside any situation that had been described to him. How *could* a people destroy themselves? What could they have been thinking? Were they thinking? They must have done some kind of thinking to have even devised the means to wipe themselves out. Much to Nagap's delight, Jawala struggled to collect his thoughts.

"I do not believe that whether or not the story happened is important. I think the fact that the story even exists, whether it was thought up by some creative person or reflects the truth, tells us that it was possible, and that is what I find most frightening."

"If it *could* have happened, then *how* could it have happened?" Shobogun asked.

"Well, I do not believe that it would have been because of scarce resources. Even now, we have seasons when our resources are in short supply, but everyone who wishes to eat, does. And those who share the most always seem to have the most left over.

"The real issue would not have been limited resources, but the people's attitudes towards those resources and each other. It could only have happened if the people competed over resources instead of sharing them, and that could only have happened if they were almost completely disconnected from the Megalight."

Shobogun could barely contain his smile. Where Nagap's answer had been intriguing, Jawala's response carried an almost spiritual authority.

"How could an entire people lose their connection to the Megalight?"

"Maybe they did not know about the forbidden fruit, and ate it."

Nagap shivered as Jawala answered. He could not have explained why if his life depended on it.

"On the other hand," Jawala continued, learning from himself as he spoke, "I really think that if they lost their Megalight connection, it probably happened over a period of time. Probably centuries.

"If each generation passed on only ninety-nine percent of what it knew about maintaining a Megalight connection, then each generation would lose one percent of its connection. While a one percent erosion does not sound like a lot, if this occurred over eighty or ninety generations, there might not be a lot of linkage left."

"What does your theory suggest to you?"

"It makes me appreciate even more the training I am receiving now, and that I have already received. It makes me realize how I must not forget anything when it comes to the training of the children that I hope to have someday."

Shobogun could contain himself no longer, and in a rare display of pride, beamed that Jawala had just related the true significance of the Great Bang.

Jawala felt a cold blast of negative energy, but never considered that it had come from Nagap.

Their lessons were followed by chores and exercises. One of the more interesting exercises was the "becoming" exercise. The boys were instructed to start out by becoming whomever the person next to him at the time might have been. They moved on to becoming their parents. Their instructors were very clear in distinguishing between "becoming" and "pretending to be." In order to become someone else, one first had to cease being oneself. Once a certain proficiency had been achieved in becoming other persons, they were instructed to become various animals.

At first, Nagap found becoming animals easier than people. Pretending to be a different species-he did not care what they said, pretending was about the best they were going to get from him- did not involve dealing with personalities and shades of feelings he would rather not have to deal with in the first place.

But as the training progressed, it became increasingly difficult to fool the others.

By the end of the training, when a boy had become an animal similar to an otter, he would also be capable of diving into a stream and catching a fish in his mouth. If he became a gorilla, he was capable of lifting many times the amount he would have been able to as a person. He could use an animal's sense of smell to determine what other wildlife was in the vicinity, and sometimes, not only identify a species, but also the gender of an animal even after it had gone away. They never acquired *all* of the properties of the animals they became, but they came remarkably close.

Nagap usually managed to eavesdrop on his instructors enough to have an idea of what the next exercise would be. The night before he was supposed to catch a fish in his mouth, he went to the stream to catch a fish and keep it trapped in the water until his turn came. But he found one already trapped. When he was supposed to demonstrate the strength of an enormous animal, he used a sharp knife to carve a ring around the trunk of a small tree. He used mud to pack the bark chips back into place so that the tree looked normal. When his turn came, he pushed the tree over.

When they had mastered animals, they moved on to becoming inanimate objects like trees and rocks and streams. They learned how to blend their minds in with the elements so that if it was cold, they did not feel it, because they became one with the cold. They would march deep into the desert in the middle of the night. If one of the boys spoke out of turn, another hour was added to the march. While Shobogun and the other men walked effortlessly upon the sand, the boys continued to struggle in the granules that gave way like soup beneath their feet. Each night, they walked a bit further, only stopping at the point of almost total exhaustion.

"I have seen old, toothless women march better than that!" Shobogun would deride them as they sat, forming a circle in the dark and bitter cold of the desert night. "You sink into the sand because you allow yourselves to sink. When will you learn that you weigh only as much as you allow yourself to weigh?" he would ask, his question dripping in disgust. They did not know that Shobogun was intentionally keeping their minds from the cold when he yelled at them.

He would tell them that walking on the sand was the same as

becoming one with the cold. They had to learn that they were one with the air, to allow it to pass through them, instead of trying to block it. "The fish does not fight the water, nor does the worm fight the ground. You must learn not to fight the air you live in, no matter what its temperature, unless you wish to prove that you have less sense than the worm!"

The youngest of the boys giggled at Shobogun's last statement, catching himself a second too late. The other boys-especially Nagap-stared daggers at the offending lad, knowing they were all about to be punished for his transgression.

"I see that our lessons are amusing," Shobogun said, pronouncing the last word *a-meeewwwww-zing*. "Perhaps they will be even more a-meeewwww-zing," his words were soft, pregnant with threat until he snapped, "on one foot!"

The boys leapt to their feet, each holding an ankle by the hand behind him. "If anyone sinks beneath the ankle, you will stand there until the sun has reached its highest point!" Shobogun knew that, by now, they should at least be able to keep themselves from sinking beneath the ankle.

Nagap wanted to strangle the boy who had giggled, but he knew that if he were to have any chance of not sinking, he would have to forget about the boy and concentrate on standing on the sand.

It was times like these that Nagap hated the most about the manhood training. Although he lived in constant fear that they would find out that he lacked their psychic powers, he found that since the training had begun, he had more potential than he had ever realized. Had he applied himself diligently, he probably could have done almost all of the things the others did. But he enjoyed cheating. There was something safe-while at the same time quite risky- about cheating. He enjoyed the secret edge it gave, the delicious secret that could be shared with no one. When he cheated, he outsmarted them, and that was about the best feeling he could imagine. When they were told that they had to be able to allow pain-like cold-to pass through them, he had packed soil and leaves together between the wedges of his fingers and passed a long thorn through the mixture. Cheating made him feel so smart. But out here in the desert, there was nothing he could do, but act like the others and try to follow the instructions. Like everybody else.

Nagap promised himself that if he ever survived this horrible manhood training, there was one word he would never utter again, and would not allow it to be uttered in his presence if he could help it: harmony. When they were not told how to be in harmony with the air, or the sea, or the plants, it was with the animals. And when they were not being in harmony with the animals, they were in some kind of harmony with the soil! Even Nagap recognized that harmony with the soil was useful-it enabled them to instantly identify which crops would be best suited for which type of soil-but he figured he would find a way to have others plant his food for him, anyway. Especially, if it meant he would not have to deal with any more *harmony*.

When they were not involved with being in *harmony* with something, they had to participate in physical exercises: running, swimming, or maybe gathering logs. Their instructors took great care to make sure that the physical exercises were done as persons, so the boys would not take advantage of the physical skills of the animals they could become. Whatever they performed as animals was of no benefit to them as persons.

Once their body strengthening exercises had been completed, it was usually time to gather food. The teachers would tell them what the menu was to be, and it was the boys' responsibility to fill it. The meal was followed by quizzes covering material they had already been taught. The quizzes were followed by new lessons. As time went on and the boys were allowed to relax a bit more, the lessons provided increasingly lively discussions and debates. Like the time Shobogun started the session off by asking:

"Does a real man know fear?"

Nagap, thinking he knew the answer to be "no," fought off the urge to answer first, just in case he might have been wrong.

"Well?" he continued when no one answered. "What do *you* say?" he gestured to a boy named Guntamo.

"I think a man may know fear, so long as he does not show it."

"Are you telling us that a man must hide his emotions?"

"Not necessarily all of the time. I think it may depend upon the circumstances."

"Are there circumstances under which a man might show his fear and be justified; and if so, what would those circumstances be?"

The boy stared blankly at the mashari. His mind raced feverishly, but in circles. He prayed for either an answer, or death.

"If a man is teaching his son to overcome fear, then it might be proper for him to let his son know that he too feels frightened," Jawala offered somewhat timidly, for he was not at all sure of his answer; he just wanted to get the pressure off Guntamo.

Guntamo's eyes signalled his appreciation.

"Then you are saying," Shobogun turned his attention to Jawala, "that a real man may know fear."

"I do not think that it is possible for anyone to be alive without knowing fear." The boldness of his words struck him after they had escaped. By then it was too late to do anything but follow through.

"That idiot has put himself into a trap that he will never get out of," Nagap thought warmly to himself, as he smiled for the first time since the training had begun.

"Are you saying that *I* am fearful?" Shobogun challenged him.

"No, Mashari, I meant no disrespect. I just meant that there is just so much that we can never know. We try to do what the Megalight would have us do, but we cannot be sure that everything we do is correct. We learn fear at the same time that we learn pain, and both stay with us throughout life."

"Menes has taught the boy well," Shobogun thought to himself. But he wasn't ready to concede. He would make Jawala work; it would be good for his debating skills.

"What do pain and fear have to do with each other? And what does any of that have to do with being a man?"

"We usually experience pain at the same time we experience fear. When we are little, we may go to close to the fire and get burned. We learn fear as a reaction to pain. Sometimes we have pain without fear. I have been taught that if we are wise we learn to use both our pain and our fear to make us better people."

"You still have not told me what pain and fear have to do with becoming men," Shobogun pushed him, well aware that Jawala on the right track.

"When a boy is in pain he tries to hide it, because he thinks it will make him appear unmanly. When a man is in pain, he tries to find ways to use his pain to understand the pain of others. The Megalight uses shared pain to help bring us together.

"There are two kinds of fear," Jawala paused, trying to remember all that Menes had taught him, while adding his own interpretation. "There is good fear that makes us use caution when large predator animals may be around.

"Then there is the bad fear that separates fools from men.

When we came to manhood training, we were all afraid that we might fail although none of us would have dared say so. But that fear did not stop us from trying. If anything, it made us try harder. But sometimes a person may be so afraid of failing that he may fail to try. That is what makes a fool."

"You have given me pain and manhood, and you have given me fear and manhood. You still have not given me pain *and* fear *and* manhood."

Jawala ransacked his memory, trying desperately to find some nugget there that Menes might have left, that he had overlooked. Then he realized that he was trying too hard. He forced himself to relax a bit. Maybe one of the other boys would rescue him as he had done for Guntamo.

No one said a word.

"So, this is the extent of your debating skills." Shobogun said, trying to sound disappointed. For in reality, Jawala had already displayed more understanding than he had any right to expect.

"Maybe," Jawala started again, very slowly. "Maybe it is the fear of pain that keeps some from becoming a man."

"Continue."

"In order to discover our true selves, we must make a pilgrimage to the innermost parts of ourselves. We must dig into ourselves through layers of thoughts and feelings. The journey will always involve going through parts of ourselves that we do not like, parts that are painful. We must be willing to push ahead, beyond the painful parts, even though we do not know if what lies ahead is even more painful than what we have already passed. Going inside ourselves is frightening, because it is painful. But when we realize that everyone must undergo this pain, then the fear becomes manageable. Men overcome this fear. Fools do not."

"Why are some able to overcome, while others cannot?" Shobogun saw that Jawala was stumped again but decided not to push him any further. "The question is for everyone."

No volunteers.

"It is a matter of faith, and a matter of vision. You must be able to see that only at your core can you be connected to the Megalight. You must be able to realize that knowledge of yourself is the only door through which knowledge of the Megalight can be granted, that the blessings that come from union with the Megalight outweigh any slight discomfort you might encounter along the way. Now, sleep on tonight's lesson."

That night, as he lay awaiting sleep, Nagap tried to imagine Shobogun in the midst of one of the Great Debates. Since he was only in manhood training because he had no choice, he learned to listen selectively: picking out those bits and pieces of information that he felt might prove helpful. He had no desire to understand the rest, since he wasn't going to deal with it anyway. But debating techniques ... Though, like the others he had never been; he knew about the Great Debates. They represented the biggest single event in all of Zarkon. During the debates, if a man handled himself well enough, he could build a reputation that could spread across the continent. Someday, everyone would know the name, Nagap.

As the training progressed, many of the tasks that had seemed impossible at the beginning became increasingly doable. By now, almost three months into training, they could walk upon the sand almost as well as Shobogun. All but Nagap could project thoughts. He managed to hide this shortcoming by sneaking into a boy's sleeping quarters and repeating a phrase over and over while the boy slept. The next day he would pick that boy and transmit him. The boy would remember the phrase Nagap had whispered during the night. It worked well enough most of the time for Nagap to be passed along with the admonition to spend as much of his time as possible practicing his transmissions.

Most of the boys progressed at about the same rate. While Jawala excelled in the spiritual exercises, his physical conditioning tasks were often interrupted by some menial chore. He frequently wondered about being removed from the physical activities: was there something wrong with him? He would have to keep his musings private. Orders could not be questioned during manhood training. Despite their growing pride in their accomplishments, the boys eventually began to wonder if their grueling training regimen would ever end. Then one day as they awaited their instructions, the men told them to rest. Their training had been completed, and all that remained was their purification the next day. They had spent so much time in anticipation of that announcement that when it came, they were too numb to celebrate.

The moment had come to mean so much more than they had ever dreamed it could, that they savored its impact; soon they would be returning to their village as men. The only test that was left was the simple removal of a piece of skin that had never served any purpose anyway, except to make the cleansing of that area a bit more difficult. Only one of the boys held any reservations about the minor operation.

    Nagap cursed himself for having been so smart when he cheated in the examinations involving physical pain. Who knows? Had he tried harder, maybe he would have been able to pass them honestly. The purification ritual was done without anesthetic. If only he had some kimomo beans! Where was his mother now that he needed her most? Those thoughts haunted him as he went to sleep, so much so that he dreamed that Chuka came to him in the middle of the night. In the dream she handed him a small gourd of kimomo-bean salve, and instructed him to apply it to himself just before his operation. She told him to apply it thinly, so that it would not be detected. When he woke up the next morning, he found a small gourd that contained what appeared to be kimomo bean salve.

11

"The Megalight smiles brightly upon you today," Bolemus, one of the men whose son was also away at manhood training, greeted Menes.

"You are too kind," Menes replied, "For we both know the glow that you perceive is but a mere reflection of your own Megalight glow."

"That could be, except that the reflection can never shine more brightly than the original, so it must be your light against which our sun dims by comparison."

The two men paused to smile at one another. Such greetings/contests were enjoyable only if they were not carried too far.

"I have a problem that I had hoped I might seek your assistance in solving."

"I am honored that you would even consider me in a matter grave enough that you should seek consultation."

The evolution of the greeting/contest into the dinner invitation/ritual had begun. Menes, who favored the direct, simplistic approach, had learned to tolerate such rituals as tools by which civility and the proper perspective were maintained. As a child he had been told that "tasks were for people, and not the other way around."

On this particular day, Menes was surprised to find himself ever so slightly tinged with impatience at Bolemus' dalliance. He had been feeling impatient since Jawala had gone. He knew there was more to his agitation than Jawala's absence; certain feelings that could no longer be shunted behind his involvement with Jawala began to assert themselves.

"Menes."

"Forgive me. I am afraid I have been a bit preoccupied today. Where was I? Oh yes, I had just expressed my honor at having been ..."

Bolemus' cocked eyebrow told Menes that the conversation had progressed further.

"I had just told you that since my son has been away at

manhood training, my wife had been unable to adjust her cooking habits. Scold her though I may, she continues to prepare too much. I am afraid that we may waste food this evening."

"The Megalight frowns upon the wasting of anything, and that certainly includes food."

"Perhaps, if you could join us this evening, this pending transgression might be averted."

"I will be delighted. Thank you."

"May the Megalight continue to shine on you until then."

"And you, also."

With Bolemus no longer there to hold them back, Menes' personal demons threw themselves upon him with all the force that had accumulated while they were held at bay. Menes was so engulfed by his thoughts and feelings that he unconsciously negotiated the trees, stones and other obstacles that lay in his path by way of that special radar that only the connected have.

True. He missed Jawala. Dinner invitations filled the air like moisture during the rainy season because the other parents missed their sons too. A melancholy had beset the entire village when the boys were taken away. Even the air, without the boys' laughter to support, turned its energy to the trees, bowing their limbs almost to the point of submission. Streaks of gray crept into the bluest skies. Yet there was something more, something intensely personal that bothered Menes. He tried to shift gears, to find refuge in matters of great universal concern, but was reminded of the story of the simpleton who scratched his arm when he could not reach the place that itched.

"The Megalight shines upon you!" the signature barrel-filled-with-flower-petals voice of Otumba yanked him from his trance and back into the world of substance and time.

"What brings you to my humble corner of the village?" she asked, filling a gap that, if left open, would have signalled another greeting/ritual/contest.

Menes rolled his eyes from side to side in search of the written answer. Surely it must have been written somewhere in the air, for he certainly had no idea of how he had wandered to the front of Otumba's hut when he had originally been headed in a different direction.

"I, uh," the man known for his eloquence muttered, "I was about to look for limpins."

"But it is not limpin season."

Menes narrowed his eyes impatiently at Otumba and she retreated accordingly.

"I have cool tea inside. Do you wish to come in? Or shall I bring a cup to you?" she asked demurely.

"Please bring me a cup. I would consider it a great kindness."

She returned shortly with two large cups of tea. They sat upon the tree stumps that had been left for that purpose when the land was cleared, sipping the tea in silence.

"Will you be dining alone this evening?" she ventured hopefully.

"I have accepted an invitation from Bolemus."

"Oh."

They stared into their tea cups, remembering how freely conversation had always flowed between them.

"This tea is excellent."

"Thank you."

"I had better be going."

"There is always much work that must be done."

After several unsuccessful attempts--the stump had some sort of extra potent gravity in it--Menes managed to stand up. He took a few steps before his feet rebelled. Otumba remained on her stump.

"There is business to which I must attend near here this evening."

"It will be a clear night," she answered, trying to be helpful.

"It has been said that it is better to drink wine alone, than to drink in the stars by oneself."

"I too, have heard this said."

"Perhaps, you will be about when I pass this way?"

"It is entirely probable."

"Then I shall bid you farewell until next we meet."

"May the Megalight continue to shine on you."

"And you."

Menes wandered back to his hut, guided by the same radar that led him to Otumba's.

When the day had finally whittled itself down to the dinner hour, Menes, dressed in one of his finest robes, prepared to leave. Absent mindedly, he placed his marriage necklace in one of the folds of his robe. It was the same necklace he had given Lakwanda. He had never dreamed that another woman might someday wear it.

The dinner engagement passed uneventfully. The food was

tasty, and the conversation passable. As soon as an acceptable amount of time had passed following the consumption of the meal, Menes excused himself.

He bounced along with the gait of a teenager until he had gotten two-thirds of the way to Otumba's. Earlier in the day he had decided that he would not try to analyze his own behavior: that he would simply enjoy the feelings he was experiencing. He had been fairly successful until now. His lifelong tendency to know himself, to understand every knowable nuance of himself was beginning to reassert itself. After all, it was only through intense self knowledge that one could begin to develop the kinds of powers that led to the title of "Mashari."

He tried to understand why his feelings, feelings he had first experienced some seventeen years ago, were now suddenly running amok. Why should he, of all people, exhibit instant impatience after seventeen years of virtual nonchalance in this matter?

If the feelings had been there all along, and he was supposed to be in harmony with himself, how could he have allowed them to build to this point of near eruption? He began to weary himself by wrestling in this territory, which, after so many years since Lakwanda's death, had become unfamiliar. He decided that there were areas concerning the emotions that were as unfathomable as the Megalight itself; and that some things happen simply because it is time for them to occur.

He did not take time to notice that, although he was anxious to see her, he did not feel the kind of queasy nervousness that had plagued him earlier in the day. The earlier meeting had signalled that this evening would be different. His intentions had been made known, and received warmly.

Then he saw her. She wore a robe Menes had never seen before. It was silky-shiny. It must have required many hours to make, because it was covered by intricate patterns, filled with many different colors. Her hair had been pulled back and treated with oils so that it captured every available drop of moonlight. She had combined oils from flowers and herbs with her own body secretions- from her underarms and between her legs- to create a musk fragrance of unbelievable attraction.

He wondered how he could have seen her so many times, talked and laughed with her on so many occasions, without ever having really seen her until this moment. This was no buddy with whom to be pals. This was a queen, to be adored, honored, and loved. Whatever it was that had caused such a dramatic change in his feelings toward her (or perhaps, it was his *awareness* of his feelings toward her) must have affected her at the same time. How else could she have blossomed so spontaneously?

When he had come close enough, Otumba radiated a smile at him that spoke with an eloquence that could never be captured in words. Her smile reassured, invited, complimented and complemented. It packed information like no smile since Lakwanda's ever could or would. It was a giving smile that would tell him anything.

She had been aware of her own feelings, and suspicious of his, for many years now. She had not wished to yank him down from the intellectual clouds that had separated him from her all of these years. Those clouds were an important part of what she loved about him. She had always thought it strange that the very things that people loved in each other were often the things that kept them apart. No matter, her life had been full, and she knew that eventually the veil would lift from his eyes; she just did not know that it would be raised by the departure of the second son that he had reared.

"Truly, by your beauty, you have justified the existence of the moon this evening."

"You are much too kind. But I must say that you do indeed present an image of manhood that no small group of females would find more than appealing."

Menes dropped his head, kicked at the dirt, and gave an "aw shucks, Mam" gesture with just enough twinkle in his eye to convey a joke. They both laughed heartily.

"Would madam care to go for a stroll?" he asked extending his arm with just the right touch of panache.

"I would be delighted, kind sir," she answered as she slipped her arm through his as if she were putting it back in its rightful place.

The moonlight created soft shadows that blended the trees and grass into a pleasant dream. Unlike earlier in the day, they glided easily through long periods of wordlessness. There was no pressure to speak.

A wild quiphar strolled by them. Quiphars were similar to giraffes, except that their necks were much shorter, and they could run with the speed of a cheetah. Quiphars, like any wild animal, could be dangerous, but only to the unconnected. For the connected, the linkage which began with the Megalight, extended to all things that were considered the handiwork of nature.

"Would you like to ride him?" Menes asked, sounding like a boy seizing an opportunity to show off.

"No. I am enjoying your attention entirely too much to allow some quiphar to divert the tiniest bit."

He smiled and squeezed her arm a bit more firmly. When they returned to her hut, she invited him in for cool wine. They could not know that the same Time that had been on vacation the entire afternoon was now forced to work twice as fast to compensate for its earlier dawdling. In so doing, it transformed their few minutes into hours and brought light to the sky almost before the darkness had a chance to settle in.

"I must be going. I had no idea it had gotten so late. In another moment, we will both be meeting ourselves getting up, when we go to lay down!"

When her laughter subsided, Otumba agreed that it had gotten late.

"Could I trouble you for another cup of cool wine before I leave?"

"It would be no trouble at all. But you do seem to be a bit thirsty this evening."

"Perhaps it is the dust."

Once she turned her back, Menes pulled the marriage necklace from his robe and placed it on her floor pillow. Casting about for some sort of covering, he eyed one of her *arafahos*-kerchiefs the women sometimes used to tie their heads-hanging from a hook across the room. The *arafaho* had barely covered the necklace when Otumba returned with the wine. She glanced furtively between the *arafaho* and Menes, but said nothing.

Because no cat can speak clearly when his mouth is stuffed with canary feathers, Menes mumbled something about not being that thirsty after all, and the lateness of the hour, and he who sleeps late missing opportunities, as he bolted from her hut.

Under different circumstances she would have enjoyed a good chuckle at Menes' hurried departure. But there was nothing funny about the object which she knew was covered by the *arafaho*. So, in the twilight of this unforgettable evening, she could only stand, rooted in her spot, and stare at the *arafaho*. She could see the form of the necklace protruding through the cloth.

She stared at the *arafaho*, using her eyes to anchor it so that the necklace would not be able to fly away or disintegrate or something. So long as the necklace remained under the cloth she *knew* it was safe, but she was afraid that if she touched it, it might vanish.

Eventually, in direct response to a need for movement, her muscles carefully set the cups down and moved her to the *arafaho*. She kneeled before the pillow, and using only the thumb and forefinger of each hand, gently lifted the kerchief. Not only was the necklace still there, but it was gorgeous! Finely carved wood, shell and bone, interspersed with polished blue, red, green, and clear stones. Through her tears, she watched herself finally touch it, then hold it to her bosom. She would not wear it until the next morning, when Menes would be able to see her proud affirmative response to his marriage proposal.

12

"So, tell me, how do I look?" Jawala asked as he whirled stylishly, showing off his best new robe. "I do hope that you will tell me that I look every bit the new eligible man about town," he continued jokingly.

"What I will tell you is that you need to go back to training and refocus yourself on your mind, and not how you look. And while you are back there, maybe you might find out that just because you have become a man, that still does not mean that I may not exercise my option of teaching you a thing or two!"

"That vote of confidence was all that I needed," Jawala pursed his lips and looked Menes straight in the eyes. He would hold this pose for as long as he could, because in a moment he and Menes would both be awash in laughter and embracing one another. In less than an hour, they would be at the ceremonial dance.

The ceremonial dances were held to commemorate a number of special occasions, including harvests, new births, and new graduating classes of men. Sometimes if too much time had elapsed since the last legitimate occasion, they would simply have a Megalight celebration dance. One of the many advantages that came from having their lives so thoroughly wrapped up in the Megalight was that they could always justify a good time by dedicating the event to the Megalight.

For the recently anointed men, the ceremonial dances served a function even greater than their formal introduction to the community: it marked the beginning of their participation in the mating ritual. The adults who already had found their mates danced indiscriminately with one another. But the new adults used the undulating rhythms to send and receive countless exploratory mating messages. They had been taught to speak and listen with their bodies and the ceremonial dances were the best testing grounds for how well they had learned their lessons.

"I will have a surprise for you this evening," Menes told Jawala slyly as the approached the dance grounds.

"The only surprise will be if you do not announce the wedding, or go through with it tonight."

Menes eyebrows leapt toward his increasingly evasive hairline.

"Now, what makes you so smart?"

"I was taught by the master."

"I too, will be surprised if a certain light-eyed, dark-complexioned girl does not receive more than her share of dances with you!" Menes could not resist the competitive urge.

"How could you? I have not even mentioned her or been around her in your presence," Jawala stammered.

"You have become a man, but remember, that is but one milestone in your educational journey."

When they arrived at the ceremony, Jawala tried to be inconspicuous as he searched for the girl in question: Osheara. She was no where to be seen, but Nagap was. He greeted Nagap with a wave of the hand. Nagap nodded back. Nagap seemed confused, like he wanted to embrace him, and at the same time to ignore him. Jawala had felt similar conflicting vibrations coming from Nagap during the manhood training, when he appeared to want to answer a question while shrinking from being called upon.

Despite all of Menes' counseling, and all the time he had spent with Nagap, Jawala still found him to be a mystery. He had witnessed Nagap reward his kindness with indifference, or at best, transparent feigned appreciation. He had seen Nagap bitterly criticize others for doing things that Nagap, himself did without a second thought. Nagap possessed enormous sensitivity- his feelings were easily hurt- but his sensitivity did not extend to others. There were so many things about Nagap to dislike: things that made almost all the other boys dismiss him as not being worth the effort. And yet...

There was something within Nagap that made Jawala reach out to him. There was the hole: that bit of emptiness resulting from the lack of a father, and the lack of community nurturing. As much as he loved Menes-no one could have asked for a better guardian-there were times when he wondered what his life would have been like had his parents lived. Not having known them created a permanent void in his being-a void that somehow recognized its cousin in Nagap.

When he looked at Nagap, he did not see his misbehavior. He saw the void behind the misbehavior. He knew Nagap lacked the spiritual maturity to help him with his pain, or maybe to even care about his pain, but he also knew that in his very strange and ambivalent way, Nagap had reached out to him, too.

In the days between the manhood training and the ceremony, Nagap had confided to him-after considerable hedging and beating around the bush-that the reason he was not thrilled about the ceremonial dance was that he could not dance. After overcoming the initial shock-everyone from the toddlers to the elders could dance-Jawala convinced Nagap to let him teach him.

They spent hours and hours together in their secret sessions, with Jawala pounding a drum until his hands were numb and his shoulders ached, shouting encouragement and instructions: "No. You are working too hard! Do not fight the rhythms. Let the drum do the work. Listen to the beat and allow it to carry you."

Stripped to their loincloths, their bodies glistening with sweat, Jawala would set the drum down and loop his arm around Nagap's shoulders while looping Nagap's arm around his.

"*One*-two, *one*-two," he would chant, kicking his feet into the air in pronounced steps with each beat. Nagap would mimic him, keeping perfect timing as long as Jawala held him. But as soon as Jawala let him go and retrieved the drum to resume the *one*-two, *one*-two beat on it, Nagap floundered. He wheezed and stamped angrily as he tried to force the drumbeat to conform to his awkward gyrations.

On the third and final day of the lessons, Nagap flounced and jerked as awkwardly as he had on the first. "Surrender to the beat, and the beat will be yours!" Jawala shouted as he banged the drum. It was then that Nagap understood. The word, *surrender* tore through his flesh until it reached his heart, where it engorged itself. Surrender. His father, Lima, had been a renown swimmer, yet Nagap could not swim because he could not surrender to the water; he could not trust it. Now, he would not be able to dance because he could not yield to rhythms beyond himself. The envy and the jealousy of Jawala would return later, but for now, for the first time in his life-maybe the manhood training had some effect after all?-Nagap accepted responsibility for his own failure. He stopped his thrashing about and through tears so thick he could barely see him, he thanked Jawala for his efforts and walked slowly into the forest.

This time Jawala knew better than to follow. He sat on his haunches and sucked hard on the wind, pulling it through his teeth. He accepted the feeling of failure. Out of kinship for Nagap, he welcomed it, as if he deserved punishment for something.

That was the last time Jawala saw Nagap before the ceremony. He would try to keep an eye on him, from a distance, of course.

As he scanned the crowd, he began to pick out some of the others who had been through manhood training with him. The sharing of manhood training had formed a bond among them. As they spotted one another, they embraced and exchanged congratulations.

All of the young men were in their finest robes. They wanted to look good for a while, because once the dancing had begun in earnest, the robes would be doffed, and only the most essential undergarments would remain.

Jawala allowed his mind to drift away from Nagap and savor the event. The endless marches, the exercises, the memorizing, never seeming to be able to do things exactly the way Shobogun had wanted them, it was all over now. He inhaled the area. There were three ceremonial fires: a large one in the center of the area, and two smaller ones. Soon, dancers would ring the three fires, forming, breaking, and re-shaping configurations. But the dancing would have to wait until the new young men had been formally introduced to the community.

When it was time for the introductions, all of the young men formed a single line behind the main fire. Each young man would walk through the blazing fire when his name was called. He would be greeted by thunderous applause upon his exit from the fire. The firewalks were always done fully clothed. The undamaged clothes served as testimony to the young men's abilities to project their minds beyond their immediate bodies.

Although Nagap had not mastered the techniques involved in walking, fully clothed, through fire, he remained the picture of utmost confidence. He really had no need to fear. Chuka had coated his robe with flame-retardant oils.

13

"What are you two doing here?" Nagap snarled, his words oozing contempt.

The men cowered, having been caught completely off guard by Nagap's challenge. Yet within seconds the thin angular man had composed himself enough to respond.

"These ceremonies are open to anyone who wishes to attend them," he shot back, failing miserably at sounding brave.

"Well, just stay out of my way! And stay away from all the real men here!" he commanded. Turning sharply on his heals, he marched away, leaving his dumfounded victims in disarray.

The tall thin one, Rollof, and his roley-poley companion, whose name was Ondorf, stared blankly at Nagap as he disappeared into the crowd. Twenty seasons ago, they had been in manhood training together. Sharing Nagap's distaste for pain, but lacking his guile-not to mention his helpful mother-they were the only two males from Saroppo to fail the manhood training in at least the last fifty years.

Since no one else cared to have much to do with them, they became inseparable - most would say insufferable -companions. They shared a cave outside of the village, and ventured into Saroppo only on special occasions when they knew the food would be plentiful. While they were hardly welcomed, Zarkonian compassion dictated that they at least were tolerated.

Rollof and Ondorf tried to blink away the fear that Nagap had left lingering. Once they had calmed themselves, they were able to resume the activity Nagap had interrupted: pilfering free food. They always wore oversized robes on these occasions, lining them with all the food they could carry.

Dismissing the two fools whet Nagap's appetite for other manly things to do. The problem was he couldn't think of any. He had carefully avoided the dancing fires and was trying to find some other way of attracting the attention of one of the eligible females to his new manliness.

He surveyed the crowd. He caught sight of Chuka and their

eyes met. She had told him she would come, but that it would be painful for her. There was no way he could understand how this type of event could stir up the war that lurked beneath her surface: how the old Chuka, who refused to die, would gain just enough sustenance to make life difficult for the new. The old Chuka was her unwanted conscience.

He had not wanted to hear about her pain when she tried to tell him before. This was his day- the day he had spent so much time fantasizing about-the day the young maidens would notice him; really notice him. Whatever problems Chuka was experiencing, she would just have to cope with them, he thought coldly to himself. He averted his eyes, ever searching for some new way to assert his manhood.

He scoured the crowd in search of the girl in whom he was sure Jawala was interested. Jawala would never have mentioned her directly, but during the dancing lessons, He had admitted that there was someone about whom he was curious. Nagap had a pretty good guess as to whom that person might be. The he saw them, and sure enough, they had paired off as the dancing configurations had changed. Damn! The music, especially the drums, was so loud he could hardly hear himself think. He amused himself at Jawala and Osheara's expense, and bade his time. When Jawala went for refreshments, he scooted over to Osheara.

"A word with you, fair maiden," he smiled as gallantly as he could.

"Well, I had promised this next dance to someone."

"The night is young, there will be plenty of dances. Surely you cannot deny me a moment of your time on the night I became a man," he sounded convincingly wounded.

"Very well, but just a few minutes."

"Let us get away from this noise so we can hear each other better."

Nagap's reference to the music as "noise" puzzled her, but she said nothing.

When they reached a more quiet spot, Nagap told her how beautiful he thought she was, and how much he appreciated her taking this time out to spend with him.

Osheara strained to be polite, despite the discomfort Nagap's overture inflicted. She knew him only casually and yet he was speaking to her as if they had been courting for more than a year. An unwritten law stated that a man only made such personal statements to a maiden after an extended period of discreet inquires to determine that the feelings were mutual.

"Your lips are so full and sweet, I bet if I squeezed them, alaber berry juice would come out," he continued, feeling his confidence soar, despite the fact that she gave no indication of reciprocity.

Osheara looked nervously at her hands, which she wrung in her lap.

"You are very kind to say these things to me. I really do not know what to say, except to thank you for the compliments. But I really must be getting back now."

"It is Jawala that you must get back to. Isn't it?" he demanded angrily, his tone and mood was like a sudden thunderstorm on a bright sunshiny day.

Osheara stared at him blankly. She had seen this type of behavior before but only in young children, never in someone who had passed manhood training.

"I had better leave," she said flatly.

"I am sorry. I do not know what came over me. Please stay with me a bit longer," he pleaded. But Osheara walked back toward the others as quickly as she could.

The chest Nagap had puffed all evening deflated into his gut. He tried to pull himself back together- to claim that it was her loss and not his- but the encounter had sobered him. It was not until he saw Osheara later that evening, laughing and dancing with Jawala that Nagap was able to regain the anger that had protected him in the past. It was also the point at which he plotted his ultimate revenge against Jawala.

There had to be some way he could get back at Jawala. If only Osheara had not spurned him for Jawala, this revenge would not be necessary. But she had, and the list of grievances had grown. Now, only public humiliation would do. He racked his brain for a plan, when like a thunderbolt, it hit him. The Great Debates would be coming to Saroppo soon. It would be the perfect opportunity for the ultimate humiliation. Nagap began to feel relieved. Once he had publicly humiliated Jawala, the rivalry would be over. Then they could be brothers.

14

*T*he air cackled with excitement and Saroppo buzzed with anticipation as it prepared to host the Great Debates. While minor debates occurred frequently, the Great Debates took place only every five seasons. Menes, Shobogun, and some of the masharis from the other cluster villages had done a remarkable job in lobbying to have the Great Debates in their cluster. Menes and Shobogun had done an even more remarkable job to get the debates held in Saroppo. Menes' work received particular acclaim, considering that he had to leave his new bride.

Bringing the Great Debates to Saroppo had been no small task. In all of the hemisphere, there was no more prestigious event. The debates represented an opportunity for a man to make a name for himself throughout the entire continent, but more importantly, they represented the single greatest opportunity for the exchange of knowledge. The very wise and the not-so-wise traveled the length and breadth of the continent to attend. Sometimes entire families made the trek. Just about everyone who could come, did, except the fools; for the Great Debates were the only events at which fools-with their self-important, shallow rhetoric- were not welcomed.

There had even been talk of holding some sort of joint debates with the people of the western hemisphere. So little was known about them- the continents were connected by only a small isthmus- that travel between the continents was limited. Yet the hope remained that someday the Great Debates would involve both continents.

Jawala appeared to be as excited about the debates as the next person. It had been more than a complete cycle of seasons since the manhood ceremonies. He had his own hut and plot of land to farm. He knew about Nagap's thwarted advances toward Osheara. He strongly suspected that Nagap knew he was interested in Osheara when Nagap approached her, but he could not be sure. He wasn't sure of how he would react, even if he could confirm his suspicions. Why would Nagap try something like that? He would have pursued the matter further except that something held him back.

Whatever it was that held him back from exploring Nagap's intentions toward Osheara seemed to slow him down regarding everything else. He had planned to "happen" to bump into Osheara on a number of occasions, but had not. His occasional encounters with her lacked premeditation, and she knew it. When he did see her, the disappointment in her eyes caused him to look away.

He tried to psyche himself up for the Great Debates. He was fully aware of their significance, yet he moved like a robot and his declarations of excitement lacked conviction.

Jawala's cheerful exterior was so firmly in place that only Menes-and to a lesser extent, Otumba-noticed anything peculiar about him. Menes- knowing that if Jawala could work through his problem, he would; if not, he would visit him- said nothing. One day, less than a moon before the debates, Jawala made that visit.

"Greetings, Mashari," he said, his smile coming exclusively form his lips.

"Greetings, my son. Otumba, would you ..."

"I am drawing tea for you now," she cut him off. "And if you do not mind, once I have drawn the tea, I have matters that require my attention, elsewhere!"

Menes looked lovingly at Otumba. She recognized as quickly as he had, that this was no ordinary visit. Sometimes, when he needed privacy, she would leave quietly, as he always did for her. At other times, like today, she would make an "I have to leave my own home" type of fuss. It was a good-natured fuss. Just her way of keeping things interesting.

"You look well, my son."

"As do you, Father."

"The Great Debates will be upon us soon. How are your preparations?"

"They go well. Except."

"Please continue."

"I recognize, as do even the smallest children, how honored we are to have the Great Debates here. I know it will probably be two or three more lifetimes before Saroppo is so honored again. And yet ..."

"You can find little enthusiasm in your heart."

Even after having been reared by Menes, Jawala could never get over the feelings of awe the man could inspire. He seemed to always know what a person was thinking, feeling. Jawala wondered if his own Megalight connection would ever grow to afford him that kind of insight.

"I am an old man. I am supposed to be able to discern certain things for myself."

Menes did it again! But the time had passed for marvelling at Menes' quickness.

"I have been unable to generate very much enthusiasm about anything lately, it seems. I had wanted to spend time with Osheara, but something has been holding me back. I have this horrible feeling that I cannot afford to get too deeply involved in anything, or anyone, because I am supposed to be someplace else, like I am about to be sent away."

Jawala noticed that the old man's face tightened visibly, though Menes continued to listen attentively.

"I feel that I am being pulled someplace, but I do not know where or why. It is almost as if I am in my own home, in my own village, by mistake!"

Menes sat expressionless, his mind sifting through feelings and thoughts, trying to place mental innuendoes in their proper perspective. Despite the thousands of people who had sought him out over the years, he still felt that being asked for advice- even by one's own child- was one of the highest compliments one could receive. He always wanted to be as sure as he could, that his response would be the best one possible.

"The first thing you must know," Menes spoke slowly, not wishing to divulge suspicions he was unsure of, "is that the feelings you are experiencing probably signal that your Megalight connection, your intuitive ability, is greater than you realize. I have suspected for many years, that the day might come when you would come to me with something of this nature. I am still waiting for that final confirming sign. When it comes, I will explain everything-at least as much as I understand. In the meantime, know this, the Megalight continues to smile upon you. Go about your activities as normally as possible, but do not try to force any feelings that do not exist. This too, as all other things, will be revealed to us at the proper time."

There were times when talking to Menes gave Jawala a great sense of security, of knowing that everything was going to be alright. This was not one of those times. Menes' calmness meant nothing. The man would be calm in the middle of stampede, a flood, and a raging forest fire. He would probably say that the flood and the fire would cancel each other, and the steam would scare off the animals, AND help his complexion at the same time! The mere fact that Menes' facial muscles tightened, no matter how slightly, meant that whatever Jawala was experiencing must be something of enormous consequences. But what could he, Jawala, have to do with anything big enough to make Menes almost twitch?

He was still fighting this avalanche of thoughts when he passed Nagap.

"Good day to you, cousin," Nagap beamed at him.

Although Nagap had become increasingly friendly since the manhood ceremony, this marked the first time he had ever ventured so familiar a greeting as "cousin." Nagap's burgeoning warmth had made Jawala think Nagap knew about his former interest in Osheara. But it had since become painfully obvious to the most casual observer that Jawala had since expressed little interest in anyone. He began to realize that Nagap's sudden congeniality had nothing to do with Osheara. Could it be that passing the manhood training had somehow removed some of the doubts that Nagap had allowed to stand between him and others all these years? That was the only answer that made sense. Even if it was the correct answer, Jawala decided that it was time that he put his problems first, and let Nagap worry about Nagap.

In the following weeks the travelers began to arrive. Some had walked for more than a moon to get there. Others had ridden quiphars or horses as long as two moons. From the jet-black Numations, famous for their work in physics and mathematics, to the pink-skinned Airopins, known for their work with metals, they came, wearing exotic garbs and bearing exquisite gifts: hand-carved flutes, drums, masks, mugs, and jewelry, which they exchanged for food and lodging along the way. Those who traveled the greatest distance usually ran out of gifts before reaching their destination. It did not matter. They were treated as warmly as those who brought gifts. When they left bearing no gifts at all, they would exchange news from the debates for food and lodging. Of course, any traveler was always welcome at any village. The exchanging of gifts was simply a courtesy: the kind relatives often extend when they have not been home for a while.

Jawala watched and listened to all the excitement through the eyes and ears of a total stranger, a stranger he was not particularly fond of. Of the men in his age bracket, Jawala seemed to be the most sought after when travelers needed information on who had food or lodging, or when communication was a problem because the language variations were so sharp. Sometimes, when the language of Saroppo was right in the middle of the variations, he could translate. When he couldn't, he could find someone -- usually Menes, if he wasn't already tied up -- who could.

There was so much work to be done! Debaters had to registered according to rank, from the most recent adults to the elders, subject matter, and position on said subject. Two debaters of similar rank but opposite positions on the same subject constituted a match. When someone, almost always an elder, presented an uncontested position- it could be on the rotation of the planet or the stars- that individual could be granted a period of uncontested floor space. There was no way, even given the Zarkonians' incredible mental capacity, to ensure that everyone who wished to debate was evenly matched. Yet, somehow, the mismatches tended to be rare, while genuine issues, espoused by authorities, tended to be the order of the day. Of course, everyone who had a genuine position could not be slated; but minor debates would arise outside the hall, where, provided the issues bore sufficient weight, provisions could be made to have the contestants invited to the main debating arena. Flexibility was the key.

The sights and sounds of Saroppo, freshly scrubbed and bustling with entertainment, discussions, and most of all, new people, had to be seen and smelled for Jawala by the stranger. The stranger watched as the travelers wandered from hut to hut, in search of food. No matter how much food had been prepared, some huts would run out. When this happened, they would find food in another hut. It was not unusual for a husband to come home and find that some visitor had eaten his dinner. He would usually stay long enough to chat politely with his guests before sauntering to someone else's hut to eat. If he ate his neighbor's dinner, the cycle would continue. Remarkably, no food was wasted and no one went hungry.

When Jawala ate, the stranger had to taste the food for him, because he couldn't. The stranger made polite inquires of the travelers, gathering news from far-flung places and exchanging information. The stranger laughed for him, even rested for him. Somewhere in his psyche he understood that his absence was ordained;

his separation the result of being called upon by the Megalight. Yet, to dwell on this understanding would have constituted bragging that the Megalight had chosen *him* for some deed. Besides, no amount of understanding could really soften the pain of isolation - of fragile wisps of thought and feeling that came and went like a breeze, but left lingering aftertastes which dulled his appetite for life itself. He knew the stranger would have to leave soon, and that he would be back. His return would be marked by at least some answers to his puzzle. Whatever those answers were, he would have to face them. He prayed the Megalight would give him the strength he knew he would need.

15

Nagap could hardly contain his excitement. The debates were finally about to begin. No one had prepared more diligently for the debates than he. He had pestered almost everyone that was regarded as knowledgeable about almost any subject. He had made himself appear cordial, sometimes almost humble, in the search for the ammunition with which he could destroy Jawala once and for all. Ever since Osheara had spurned him, he had lived and breathed for the debates. They would bring his moment of vindication.

The debates, like everything else, were organized around age groupings. Those of Nagap's peer group, the young adults, were scheduled to debate on the first day, the elders on the last. His heart soared as he watched Jawala merely going through the motions of preparing for his debate. Though Nagap could not fathom why Jawala's performance had been so lackluster, so lacking in conviction, he rejoiced in Jawala's mediocrity. Defeating- no, crushing- Jawala would be easier than he had anticipated. Oblivious to the villagers' curiosity over his new gregariousness, and encouraged by Jawala's dismal showing, Nagap continued his quest for the ultimate argument: the argument that would truly unite him and Jawala on his terms, and provide the respect that had wrongfully been withheld from him all these years.

At last, the final day of the debates arrived. Each day had seen the village swell with new travelers, but on this day, it swarmed with people. Only the wisest and most knowledgeable of men dared to step into the debating circle on the day of the finale. What better forum for Nagap to claim his true birthright as the favorite son-not just of Saroppo- but of the continent? People would carry his praises to every nook and cranny of the hemisphere by the time he had finished with Jawala.

He paced nervously about his hut, waiting for the lazy, good-for-nothing cock to crow. Finally it shattered the silence. The debates would soon begin. His chest swelled as he imagined the crowds chanting his name, declaring him the most outstanding young scholar to come along in the century.

He forced himself to stay inside the hut, even after the others had begun stirring about. He did not want to look too anxious. Everything had to be just right, down to the last detail.

The ringing of his entryway bell interrupted his reverie. Who could that be?

It was Chuka.

"Chuka, what are you doing here?" he asked nervously. He had never stopped calling her by her first name when they were alone.

"You are flesh of my flesh and blood of my blood. And SOMEDAY you are going to realize that I know you better than you know yourself. You have something very big planned for today. I can feel it. I came by to tell you that I know your day will end in victory. I see you have laid out your finest robe to wear today," she pointed to the finely embroidered robe Nagap had lain aside.

Quietly he studied his mother. She was still quite beautiful and looked more like his sister than his mother. He had often worried that she might someday allow another man into her life, although that day had yet to come. Yes, she was right. In the whole wide world, she was one person who truly understood him.

"You are right. I do have a big day planned. I did not wish to say anything until after I had secured my victory, but I might as well tell you that the victory is as good as secured right now. I ... what are you doing?"

"I was inspecting your robe, and I am happy to report that there are no stains or loose threads. I must be going, but you will appreciate my visit much more before the day has ended than you can right now."

He gave a moment's thought to his mother's last words before returning to his ritual. He washed himself meticulously. He rubbed fragrant jubi leaves over his arms and neck. He dressed himself slowly, with the deliberate motions of a man trying to capture the last moments before greatness would change his life forever. Once he finally completed his inspection, he forced himself to casually saunter out beyond the village to the debating arena.

Although he had been around the arena since the debates had begun-trying to soak up any information that might help his cause-it seemed to Nagap that he was seeing the debating arena for the first time. It looked so much bigger than it had just yesterday! Having helped erect it, he viewed the structure with pride. It was circular, about eighty yards in diameter. It stood ten feet high around the edges, but rose to a height of more than twenty feet at its center. The arena consisted of a bamboo skeleton with huge leaves folded accordion style at specific intervals which could be stretched in a matter of minutes to provide shelter in case of rain. He had been happy to help construct it, despite the near backbreaking work involved. After all, he had been working to build the place that where his greatest triumph would occur. He could see the actual debating area; a flat topped circular mound, about twelve feet in diameter and five feet high, with steps carved into opposite sides. The debating mound came alive as he watched it and saw himself, once again, utterly destroying Jawala before Chuka, Osheara and everyone else.

The first event of the day was an elder who had been granted time to present a position by himself, for lack of an opponent. As far as Nagap could tell, the old fool was droning on about changing the planting cycles for certain foods to be more closely aligned with something Nagap did not understand anyway. Where was everyone? Though arena was almost filled, he could not spot Jawala or Chuka. He had to restrain himself from visibly fidgeting when the next event was introduced-- a discussion of the relative merits of different methods of probing.

By the time the next debaters began, Nagap was in a state of near frenzy. Where was Jawala? By the Megalight's eyes, surely he would not be cheated out of this one chance to square his accounts and claim his birthright. He had waited too long, prepared too diligently- even seeking advice from that pompous Menes- for Jawala not to be here.

He eyed Jawala. Apparently Jawala had been on some sort of errand. Well, when Nagap finished with him, he would wish he had never completed that chore. He looked around and made sure he could make eye contact with Chuka. Although he had not told her what he was going to do, he wanted to know that she was available, should he need her help for any reason.

At last, it was time for the intermission. As a young adult, Nagap could not formally challenge anyone while the debates were in session. However, once the intermission came, the arena simply became free space.

As many of the people began to file out in search of refreshment, or simply to stretch, Nagap bounded onto the debating area.

"I declare that the greatest gift the Megalight confers upon us is our intelligence!" he shouted, waving his arms like a circus ringmaster. "Furthermore, I dare anyone of my peer group who disagrees, to debate the matter here and now!"

He succeeded in keeping some of the audience from leaving. Many, taken aback by the rashness of this young man, remained in their seats.

Nagap's eyes swept across his peer group in the stands. Another fellow who had gone through manhood training with him was about to accept his challenge. He had not figured on that. For a split second, he wondered if there was anything else he had not taken into account. No, this was the only possibility for which he had not prepared.

As the young man began to rise, Nagap thrust an almost accusatory finger at Jawala, who was about to leave with the others.

"Surely, Jawala, you must have *some* thought on the Megalight. You have *heard* of the Megalight, have you not?"

Nagap's taunt almost jarred Jawala enough to bring him back, not just into the arena, but from the clutches of the stranger as well. He ignored Nagap's challenge and continued to leave. Chuka blocked his path.

"My son has challenged you to a debate," she said loudly. "You bring dishonor upon him by refusing to respond. And you bring dishonor upon the name of the Megalight by refusing to indulge in a debate which might bring greater understanding of the Megalight."

Where Nagap's challenge failed to bring Jawala back, Chuka's succeeded. He *really* came back. The nerve of the two of them challenging him, while he was minding his own business, wrestling with his own absence, made something snap. He had spent time with Nagap, trying to help him when no one else would. How dare he AND his mother challenge him at this kind of event? When Jawala felt the anger for himself, the stranger vanished.

"I will contend," he exclaimed loudly, months of frustration about to be released as he leapt to the debating mound," that the greatest gift the Megalight bestows upon us is our connection to the Megalight."

Jawala's answer sent people scurrying to retrieve those who had already left for the intermission. It also came close to inducing cardiac arrest in Nagap. He had expected Jawala to say that the greatest gift was something like compassion, or health, or even love. Nagap was prepared for any of those answers and a few more. But connection itself? Linkage to the Megalight was talked about so much, that it seemed too obvious an answer for anyone to think of it. No matter. He had still spent more time preparing for these debates than Jawala could have imagined. The victory would just be that much sweeter.

"It is our intelligence that separates us from the animals; that enables us to walk upright. It is only our intelligence that gives meaning to the writings which state that we are made in the image of the Megalight."

The crowd applauded Nagap's opening remarks. He was grateful for the applause. It helped his confidence.

"Separation from the animals is not the issue," Jawala countered. "Knowing what we are not is valuable, only when we cannot say what we are. Our connection to the Megalight enables us to say what we are. Our intelligence allows us to think that we are in the image of the Megalight. Our connection allows us to *know* it."

Like two verbal gladiators they argued back and forth, each point and counterpoint bringing more applause that the previous one. Although their debate spilled over beyond the point of intermission, no one stopped them. No one could remember when men so young had argued so powerfully and passionately. Each challenge brought forth a more powerful response, and each response a stronger challenge.

"Without intelligence, being connected to the Megalight means nothing, for we would have no way of knowing of our connection. We could not thank the Megalight for our existence because we would not even be *aware* of our existence. A mindless being has nothing with which to bring glory to the Megalight."

The applause began to heal the tightness in Nagap's throat and the throbbing in his head. His chest began to swell of its own volition, as it always did when he was feeling proud of himself. And he had never felt more proud. A smile began to fidget with his lips and his eyebrows raised themselves in triumph. There was no way Jawala would ever be able to come back from his latest argument. It had been brilliant if he did say so himself.

He had finally defeated Jawala in public. All the frustrated years of waiting had been well worth this moment. He looked to Jawala for a sign of concession as the applause began to die down.

"I will submit," Jawala stunned Nagap as his voice rang out with an authority seldom displayed, even by elders, "that as creations of the Megalight, it is not our intelligence which magnifies the Megalight, so much as it is the intelligence with which the Megalight makes us that brings honor. The flower, the butterfly, the tree and the stream, all pay homage to the Megalight without showing any intelligence.

"Flowers and butterflies can do no wrong, because they cannot think. We *can* do wrong, because we *can* think. No gift, whether it is intelligence or love, can have any real meaning unless its purpose is understood; and the mind can only understand so much. It is our connectedness that enables us to feel with our thoughts and think with our feelings. These are the things that bring purpose, that enable us to say, without fear of hypocrisy, that the will of the Megalight be done!"

The applause was deafening. Nagap tried desperately to think of a comeback. If only they would stop that infernal clapping, maybe he could think of something. But the applause grew louder and his damnation more certain. Jawala had won.

That terrible sinking feeling returned as his shoulders drooped and his chest fell beneath his stomach. The air, which had been plentiful mere moments before, evaporated, leaving in its wake smoldering cut glass, too large to be consumed by Nagap's laboring lungs.

He searched for Chuka, but when he found her, the look of pity on her face repulsed him.

The applause still ringing in his ears, he raced from the debating arena. He ran until he could run no further and collapsed under a tree. He swung back and forth between fighting the pain and wallowing in it. His struggle could not have mattered less, for everywhere he turned, in every nook, cranny and crevice of his being, the pain was there. If there was a Megalight, then that Megalight be damned. What had it ever done for him, other than cause him grief and misery?

He crumpled against the tree and cried himself to sleep. When he awakened, it was dusk. He could not decide what to do or where to go; he only knew that he was not going back to Saroppo, at least not yet. If and when he did return, it would be triumphantly, or not at all.

Something was chafing him. It had been doing so all day, but in his excitement, he had ignored it. He reached deep within the folds of his robe and found the pamphlet Chuka had shown him so many years ago. That was why she had come by earlier, so she could slip the pamphlet to him.

His mind reeled as he consumed a portion of the pamphlet's contents. It felt like it had been written specifically for him. The ideas! There was so much in the pamphlet that he knew he would only be able to consume a small bit at a time. Yet the billowing ideas he received from what little he read almost completely erased his pain. When he had taken his fill from the pamphlet he carefully placed it back inside his robe.

The dusk had turned to dark. He saw a campfire, not more than three hundred yards away. While he was in no mood to be around people, *especially* anyone who might have witnessed his humiliation, his lack of options prompted him toward the distant glow.

As he drew nearer the flame, he discerned two figures who were obviously in a heated argument about something. Great. After the day he had endured, the last thing he needed now was to run into people infected with the debating disease. Calling upon what little he retained from manhood training, he approached the campfire stealthily, making sure he could leave without detection if necessary. The nearer he got, however, the more he understood that something was not quite right about the argument that was in progress. He could tell that two men were arguing earnestly, yet there was something comical about the pitch of the dialogue, even before the words became clearly perceptible.

At thirty yards, he was able not only to make out the words, but also the voices. They were familiar. Then he could see who they were. The pamphlet would come in handy sooner than he could have dared hope. Like two gifts from the dark side of the Megalight, the perfect objects of his revenge sat blithely insulting each other, just waiting to be put to use: Rollof and Ondorf.

"Greetings to you, my elders!" he smiled broadly at the men as he entered their campsite.

"Y-Y-Y-You h-h-have n-n-n-o r-reason to b-b-b-bother us! W-We are j-j-just m-m-minding our own b-b-business. W-W-We st-st-stayed away from the d-d-d-debates s-s-s-so w-w-we w-w-wouldn't have any tr-trouble." Ondorf huddled next to Rollof as he tried to ward off Nagap.

"No, my good fellow, I believe you misunderstand me. You are probably thinking about that brief discussion we had at the manhood ceremony last year. You took me too seriously. I was only *joking*. I *admire* you men!"

Rollof and Ondorf blinked at each other, trying to digest Nagap's overture. In their hearts, they knew that *no one* admired them, but that was not the kind of admission that fools readily make.

"I knew you were joking all along," Rollof replied. "I tried to tell this frightened old fool that, but he would not believe me!"

"Who are you calling fool, fool?"

"You're the fool. Don't call ME a fool. Why, I ought to ..."

"Gentlemen, please! I was fortunate enough to overhear some of the discussion you were having just prior to my arrival, and I can assure you that each of you handled himself with more eloquence, wit, and knowledge than any five participants at the Great Debates combined. Pray that I may stay just a moment or two with you, so that I might soak up some of your wisdom."

Rollof and Ondorf stared stupidly at each other for several seconds before Ondorf found his voice: "We would be delighted, good sir, to enjoy your distinguished company. We have plenty of fruit and rabbit meat."

While the idea of eating with these buffoons repulsed Nagap, he could no longer deny the hunger that gnawed at the pit of his stomach. Then he thought of something that would solve several issues at once.

"Thank you, good sir, for the invitation. This repast looks absolutely scrumptious. I wish I could contribute something, but I am afraid that all I have is some wine that is back at my hut, and I do not have the energy to retrieve it," he said, knowing no true fool could ever pass up an opportunity to get drunk.

Wine. He could almost hear their minds humming the word harmoniously together.

"We could go fetch it," one of them- it did not matter which- said.

"If it is not too much trouble, my hut is the last one in the southeast quadrant of the village. I will wait here, and tend you fire until you return."

Once the two fools had left, Nagap was free to eat and think in peace. He needed to tie together the knowledge in the pamphlet with his good fortune in finding Rollof and Ondorf. Finding them had indeed been fortunate because, even after reading some of the pamphlet, he would never have thought of the two repugnant fools.

When he had eaten his fill, he laid back against the ground and allowed his thoughts to circulate. Gradually a plot began to fall into place. He became excited, agitated, and more than a little frightened as the picture in his mind began to fill out. The plot hatching in his brain dwarfed anything he had ever dreamed before. He found himself actually anticipating the return of Rollof and Ondorf.

16

"You know, I have noticed, Rollof, that you hold your wine as well as you hold an argument. And Ondorf, you seem to have the perfect ability to interpret the will of the Megalight. It is absolutely shameful that those idiots in the villages do not have the good sense to appreciate the genuine treasures that you two men are," Nagap lied as he pretended to drink deeply from the wine jug.

"You know, I was just thinking that some day, someone like you would come along a appreciate us for the men we truly are. All that nonsense about the manhood training is absurd. We could have passed if we had wanted to; we just did not want to show anybody up. Isn't that right, Ondorf?"

"Indeed, you are indispudabobaly correct," the drunken Ondorf slurred.

"The thing I admire most about the two of you is that you share the same quality that has historically separated the great men and women from the rest of the crowd: fearlessness. Others follow the rules. Men such as yourselves break the rules and make your own."

"Truer words were never spoken," one of them hiccupped.

"Why, these other idiots are afraid to go into the forbidden caves. They lack the courage and the intellectual curiosity of great prophets such as yourselves. Rather than explore, they allow themselves to be shackled by silly superstition."

The essence of Nagap's words sliced through the wine induced fog that shrouded Ondorf and Rollof, sobering them a bit. Great guffaws of laughter were aborted in mid-throat.

"Of course we are brave! We could not live out here in the wilderness if we were not brave! But the forbidden caves ... I am not afraid, but I know poor Ondorf here has a bad heart, and ... Perhaps, you should say something, Ondorf."

"Well, I uh,..."

"Please, gentlemen, do not worry yourselves about the caves. I know you have the courage to enter them. There is no need to prove your bravery to me. I was simply making conversation. Here, have some more wine." Nagap knew that with a bit more wine, and a few more compliments the men would follow him anywhere.

Another jug of wine, and several sweet words later, Rollof and Ondorf found themselves, in the middle of the night, following Nagap toward a forbidden cave.

"Gentlemen," Nagap said as they approached the mouth of the cave, "While I know that either of you would gladly be the first to enter, perhaps it might be best if I go into the cave alone. If it is truly dangerous in there, Zarkon will suffer far less from the loss of me, than if anything were to happen to either of you. Please, allow me to enter alone."

"Well, I really was looking forward to entering the cave first, but if you insist; we do not wish to stand in your way. Right Rollof?"

"Right!"

As he entered the cave, Nagap felt an indescribable tingling sensation. The deeper he progressed, the stronger the tingling grew. It was especially strong along his spine, which felt like it was growing hair inwardly. With each step, some portion of his brain demanded that he retreat. But a larger part of him was being inexorably drawn inside. His destiny was inside this cave. He could feel it. It was an eery feeling, something akin to *déjà vu*. Or maybe more like a homecoming. There was a familiarity wrapped inside the strangeness of the cave, like the feelings which exist between twins, reunited after having been separated at birth. His fear peaked, and the cave enticed him even deeper into itself. He became so confident that he extinguished his carrying light.

The darkness welcomed him. Had his seduction not been so overwhelming, he might have wondered why the cave was so familiar. A gentle aroma wafted to him, filling his nostrils, encircling his head and guiding him into the cave.

Eventually, he detected a small orange glow. By now he had begun sipping the air for the taste of the intoxicating fragrance. He plucked one of the glowing spheres and gently caressed it. The sphere was as pleasant to touch as it was to smell. The sight, smell, and feel of the fruit seduced him, promising pleasure beyond any he could have dreamed. It was good, he thought, that the fruit was forbidden. He could see how it could suck the brains out of the wrong person. The fruit *belonged* to him. In his mind's eye he could see his reflection in the fruit, and the fruit reflected in him.

Oblivion claimed his memories and all else that did not originate with the fruit. Gently he fondled the fruit and felt its energy rippling through him, creating unheard of ecstasy. Ever so slowly he brought the fruit to his face. He rubbed his lips with the fruit, allowing his desire to build until he could no longer contain it. He fell to his knees and bit violently into the fruit. The sweet sticky juice splattered his nose and beard. Hungrily he bit into the fruit again and again, chewing and biting, trying to suck all the meat out of the fruit. He revelled in the thick juice that clung to his cheeks. He plunged his face into the fruit until he could hardly breathe. Suddenly he stopped.

He leapt to his feet. He felt his body whirling. It whirled faster and faster until he was still within the whirling. Energy flowed into him, around him, through him, out of him. It fed itself while depleting itself. He saw himself stepping out of his skin and into vapor. He watched himself regurgitate a putrid liquid which turned into a vapor which, in turn, turned into him.

Finally, he stepped back into himself and was still. For the first time in his entire life, he was truly still. He began to see things with a clarity that he never knew could exist. He understood why he had never been a part of the community; why he had always thought and felt differently than the others. He recoiled at having ever been afraid of not measuring up. Meat had been put on the bones of promises his mother had made to him all those years.

He gathered as many of the fruits as his sack would allow, then proceeded- in total darkness and without the least bit of difficulty- back toward the entrance of the cave.

He found Rollof and Ondorf bickering as usual.

"Silence! You dolts!" Nagap commanded them.

Rollof and Ondorf cringed before the transformed Nagap. He *looked* the same, but he obviously wasn't. Quickly, they became sober.

"Take hold of this sack, and give me your empty sacks. I am going back into the cave."

Rollof and Ondorf tried to comply, but were frozen in fear.

"Do as I command you!"

Nagap's order broke the paralysis. They moved quickly to give him their sacks.

"You have nothing to fear. Swear allegiance to me and I will lay the world at your feet. Betray me and I will destroy you as the bugs that you are. Do you swear allegiance?"

"W-W-We swear," Rollof and Ondorf offered meekly in unison.

END OF PART I

17

"The Megalight must be smiling today!" cried one of the men in the crowd that descended upon Jawala.

"You were magnificent," added another.

"You debate almost as good as you look," chimed in a sultry young female stranger, obviously interested in more than Jawala's eloquence.

Jawala mumbled half-hearted acknowledgements as he stumbled through the crowd. He could hardly afford to indulge himself in their congratulations. He had returned from his psycho-spiritual limbo to face concerns far greater than defeating Nagap in a debate. The air turned dead and the crowd receded to a lower level of consciousness when Jawala spotted Menes. Their hearts and minds found expression in their eyes as they looked deeply into each other's eyes/thoughts. In a sea of jubilation, Menes and Jawala each saw deadly seriousness in the face of the other.

They would have to talk. As soon as possible. When, through their separate routes, they had escaped the crowd, they stood looking wordlessly at each other. They knew that time would be required to find words capable of conveying the meaning of the moment. Before, only Menes had understood that Jawala would not return empty-handed from his sojourn. Now they both knew the exile was over and the time had come for a different kind of exile.

Without exchanging directions, they walked to a nearby stream. The water would be soothing.

"What has happened to me? Where and why must I go?"

"The Megalight has called you into service. Trouble is coming. I have suspected since before you were born that something was brewing. I do not know the nature of the trouble, but I can only tell you that it is not unrelated to the strange deaths of your parents. There were a number of strange things that happened around that time--mysterious seeds planted that may just now be coming to fruition.

You must go away because the Megalight has ordained that you be involved in the preparation of the antidote to the poison that I feel is coming. You will not be the antidote, but you will be involved in its preparation. You have felt removed because the Megalight was working with you; stamping your best thoughts onto your heart so that you would be able to avoid some struggles between the heart and mind. What lies ahead will be difficult. It will require that you maintain harmony within yourself. Do you understand?"

"I know that when there is disagreement between the heart and the mind, the spirit rests uneasily. When I came back to myself I realized that some sort of mission was involved. The only reason I am not petrified with fear right now is that I am still too numb to feel it. I need as many details as you can supply for me."

"You shall have them. First, I must tell you of a dream I interpreted shortly after you were born...."

With the gurgling stream as background music, the two men talked until there was nothing left that could be said. They rose to go their separate ways when Menes remembered something.

"Stop by my place for a moment. I have something for you."

They walked silently to Menes' hut. There was no way to say goodbye. They could only pray that they would see each other again. When they reached Menes' hut- formerly Jawala's home- Jawala stopped outside. Menes went in and reappeared within moments.

"It is time for you to have this," he handed him the figurine Lima had carved for him so many seasons before.

After a brief history of the figurine was given, the two men turned from each other. Neither wished to have the other see his tears.

By the time the sun rose the next morning, Jawala was well on his way into the desert. There was room only for his most cherished possessions in the sack that draped his back. He had fastened the figurine Menes had given him onto a chain which hung round his neck. Later, after many days traveling, his mind would begin to unwrap and investigate the weight which Menes had placed upon it; it would long for the goodbyes that were never spoken to all the people he loved, and it would ache for companionship. But for now his mind was forced to adjust to the weight itself, and the adjustment was so great, the weight so immense, that carrying it left him numb.

Walking across the top of the sand, about the only thought he could muster was that he was thankful for his manhood training. He became one with the heat, as he had learned to become one with the cold, allowing it to pass through him.

The sunrises and sunsets began to blur together as Jawala lost track of how long he had been walking. He was in no hurry, for he needed time to allow the functioning to return to his brain.

Midway through the fortieth day of his journey, he saw fuzzy shapes against the horizon. He increased his pace, and in minutes could see that it was a person at a well. After forty days of isolation, he had grown weary of conversing with himself. He wondered if the person were male or female. If it was a woman, it might be the one Menes had spoken of. Burning sand swallowed his feet as he redirected his energy and focused it on the fuzzy shapes in the distance: it was a woman.

An inexplicable fear gripped him as he realized that this might be the woman of whom Menes had spoken. The images blurred once again as he rose to the top of the sand. By concentrating on breathing techniques, he was able to fight off the terror that grappled with him. Although he tried to slow himself to gain more time to think, he seemed to reach the woman in record time.

"Good Madam," he asked as gallantly as he could manage, "Have you water for a tired traveler?"

The woman turned to face him, whirling a blast of hideous energy at him in one singular motion. Only Jawala's quick reflexes kept him from being internally scalded. Again his feet sank into the sand as he allocated his energy for a wall of defense against the woman's onslaught.

"Horrified, aren't you?" she challenged him garishly, using the strongest thought projection possible. "Let down your wall so that your contempt may be seen. I will destroy you! You should thank me. By destroying you, I set you free from a fate worse than death: Me."

"Why must you fight.." Jawala's transmission died in midsentence as he caught his first full view of the woman. Her heavy eyebrows met in the middle to form a single unbroken strip. Her teeth were jagged. Her skin was sprayed with horrible blemishes. Her eyes could not agree upon a single focus. Even in a land where physical beauty was given the lowest priority, this woman was undeniably the ugliest person Jawala had ever seen. None of the scary creatures he had drawn as a child even came close!

"*You must master the reality of this woman,*" Menes words haunted him. He took a deep breath and tried to calm himself enough to regain his composure. "*If this woman's looks are any indication of her health, she cannot possibly have very long to live!*" he thought to himself, then felt embarrassed by the cruelty of his thought. With all the things he had learned to overcome, surely he could get beyond her physical appearance.

Desperately, he searched her face for some redeeming quality: a hair that was in the right place, a tooth with a round edge- ANYTHING. But everything about her seemed intentionally to have been thrown together to achieve the worst possible effect. Then he realized that the beauty he sought lay not *on* her face, but *behind* it. As he wrestled with his perception of her, he was able to gradually turn his psychic forces from defense to a little offense. He thrust his energy at her, and felt her relent just the slightest bit.

Like two rams locked in mortal combat, Jawala and the mystery woman threw a steady stream of energy at each other. Under normal circumstances the expenditures of energy that these two made would have resulted in the complete depletion of both. But each had an adversary that inspired new energy from some previously untapped source. So much energy became locked into the battle that it took on a life of its own. Jawala and the woman began to watch as much as participate in the showdown. As the energy pool grew, it also became increasing mystical. The union of the two energies, locked in combat, evolved into a higher form of energy utterly unlike what had begun in their minds. As the great swirl of energy grew, Jawala and the woman became increasingly disconnected from the fray. It was like staring at a dot until everything else fades, only a hundred times stronger.

Though the energy continued to flow from them, they became increasingly involuntary spigots. Eventually, neither of them knew what was going on, they just faded as the swirling energy became increasingly material. Jawala's energy took on his form, as the woman's took on hers.

Arms extended, legs spread apart, Jawala's spirit and the woman's spirit circled each other warily. He lunged at her. She ducked and kicked him, sending him sprawling. She tried to stomp him, but he grabbed her ankle and flung her to the ground. Like rubber, she bounced from the ground into a full somersault, landed behind him, and put a choke-hold on him.

He freed himself with an elbow to the ribs. Before she could recover, he flung her to the ground again. This time he stayed with her to prevent another bouncing-ball act. He tried to pin her arms, but felt them grow cold and slimy. She transformed herself into a python. The snake coiled itself around him, forming an ever tightening grip. She brought her reptilian head up to his and hissed telepathically, *Kiss me NOW!* She summoned all of her strength for one great fatal squeeze. The man spirit vanished. The snake found itself wound in knots. The man spirit reached for the snake's tail, only to be kicked several yards by a horse's hoof. A giant mare, almost the size of a quiphar, replaced the snake.

The mare breathed fire and bared teeth that only a piranha could love. She charged him. He dived to the side a split- second before impact. She kicked and snorted, sometimes she snorted and kicked, keeping the man spirit turning cartwheels and other acrobatic manuevers to avoid the deadly hooves.

The man spirit grabbed her mane and was able to pull himself onto her back. Wildly she turned, bringing her sharp teeth within inches of his arms and singeing his hair with her breath. The horse's body contorted as she flew into the air, bucking and stomping to rid herself of the unwelcome passenger. She twisted this way and that, but the man spirit held more firmly than before. Finally she reared on her hind legs for several seconds until she could feel his weight shifting down her back. In one fluid motion she landed on her front legs and kicked her rear legs to an almost forty-five degree angle. The man spirit sailed magnificently through the air.

"Do you want to make love to me, now?" She snorted as she tried to sit on his face. Again he dodged her, and again he grabbed her mane before she could regain a fully upright position. For what would have been hours- had Time been invited to the rodeo- the horse bucked and kicked and the man held on. The horse tried the violent weight shifting trick again, but this time the man adjusted his grip.

Energy was expended, replenished, diminished, recycled, transformed, reborn, and channeled: everything but justified. An agreement had to be reached, or else the ride would last through eternity. Each combatant was forced to review the other's application for admission into their private world. The stalemate changed the applications from ludicrous to possible to quite attractive.

The energies, having no other recourse, began to untangle as a first step toward returning their respective homes. The flesh-and-blood Jawala, and the physical woman began to regain their senses.

Jawala and the woman opened their eyes. Jawala was forced to blink a second, third, and fourth time; for in span of his initial blink, the hideous creature he thought he had seen was gone. In her place stood the most beautiful woman Jawala had ever seen.

"Indeed, I have water for you, Sir," the vision of loveliness replied to Jawala's request as if he had just asked, which, in the realm of time, he had.

"When I first approached this well, the thirst for water was the utmost matter on my mind. I must say now, however, that water has fallen to a minor priority when compared to my thirst for your name." Jawala could not *believe* what he had just said. His words seemed preposterous yet they flowed naturally, and she seemed not to notice his verbal absurdity.

"I am called Kalimba," she said, as she drew a ladle of water. When he gulped it, she drew another ladle.

18

Like bothersome flies that have become fixated, the tears refused to stay away from the old man's eyes. She was back. His baby girl had really returned to the form which the Megalight had intended for her. This was the third miracle Godanza had witnessed in his life time, and were it not for the new possibility of a grandchild, he would have been perfectly ready to make his final peace with the Megalight.

It had been so strange to watch a dream come true in stages, to wait so long for the final chapter to unfold, and then to have it explode into reality when it was least expected. The Megalight did indeed work in ways unfathomable to mortals.

"Father, it has been more seasons than I can recall since we have received a visitor, and now that one has come, you leave us to drift to another place. Pray, stay and chat with us. The place that draws your mind from us must be horrible, judging from the expression on your face."

"I am sorry daughter. Please forgive me. Have you seen your reflection since you met Jawala?"

"Yes. And?"

"Does my daughter look any different to you than she did when you first met, young man?"

"Not that I can recall, Sir."

"It is as I suspected," the old man thought to himself. "My child has always seen herself as she truly was, not as the world has viewed her. This young man has seen her as she truly is as well. If only there were something worthy enough to give the Megalight to show my gratitude!"

The old man's thoughts spun rapidly. There was so much that he wished to share with his daughter and his son-in-law-to-be. But they could not know that they were destined to be married, and it would not be fair to burden them with the knowledge he held. Still, he needed space to deal with his thoughts.

"Please do not think me rude. I am not. I am overjoyed by your presence, young man. I built a hut for just such an occasion; it has been waiting for quite a few years to be occupied. When I built it, Kalimba thought I was crazy, but I knew what I was doing. Please, Kalimba will show it to you. Right now, I need time to dwell upon my thoughts."

Kalimba was dumfounded by her father's behavior. Jawala, having been told of the dream, understood.

"Perhaps, we can talk later," he said sympathetically.

Godanza breathed the night air as deeply as he could, hoping it would wash through his brain and help him digest the day's events. Kalimba went to fetch water. She left home alone and disfigured and returned with her natural beauty intact and accompanied by her future husband.

He allowed himself to drift back to the roots of the flower that had begun blossoming on this day. He wished his late wife, Ula, could be here to see their daughter now, and to see the fine young man that sat in their hut. He felt that wherever she was, she knew that the dream was coming true. Everything seemed to revolve around that one dream!

He and Ula had been happily married for years, their only problem being that they could not have the child they so desperately wanted. They had talked to every acknowledged, and some *un*acknowledged, healer and mashari, not only in their native village of Zambutu, but for miles beyond. They tried prayer, fasting, and just about every herbal concoction conceivable; yet they remained childless.

Then one night after they had been forced to abandon the dream of parenthood-they were now in their sixties- Godanza had a dream that could only have come from the Megalight.

In his dream a huge dark cloud hung over a dry and barren planet. The cloud was bursting at the seams with water, but could not rain. The cloud was more than condensed moisture. It was intelligent and it had feelings. It ached to rain, but it only grew bigger and darker. Finally the cloud resolved itself to forever holding its rain when another, smaller cloud began to form over another portion of the planet. Once the newer cloud had come to maturity, both clouds loosed torrents of water. The rain from the first cloud formed a stream which ran smoothly until it hit a portion of hot ground where it began to turn to steam. The cloud loosed even more water and the stream continued on, although it now lurched unevenly like a gel.

The rain from the second cloud also formed a stream. While the second stream did not encounter the hot ground, its cloud disappeared immediately after it fell. When the stream from the second cloud joined the stream from the first, the first stream reverted to its original form. The combined streams formed a river which eventually produced a lake. The lake abounded with all manner of life in the midst of the barren terrain.

The dream had been so real, and the remaining images so vivid, that Godanza roused Ula to verify that he had indeed regained consciousness. Once she confirmed that he was awake, and that she could offer no insight into the meaning of the dream, he dressed himself quickly to search out an interpreter.

He had dreamed countless dreams, some pleasant, some not so pleasant, but never had he encountered a dream that impacted him like this one had. He knew in the marrow of his bones that this had been no ordinary dream. He would not rest until he knew its meaning. He inquired of all who could reasonably be expected to interpret his dream, yet no one could fathom or discern its meaning.

Dejectedly, he was moping his way back home when he bumped into a stranger.

"Oh, pardon me, I am terribly sorry," Godanza apologized to the middle-aged stranger. "I am afraid I have allowed myself to become so engrossed in my thoughts that I was not looking where I was going. I do not believe I have seen you before. My name is Godanza."

The stranger introduced himself and explained that he was visiting Zambutu for no apparent reason, other than he felt he had been called to visit.

"It is obvious that your are carrying a weighty issue about with you. While my own shoulders are hardly empty, perhaps I might share some of your load for a bit," the stranger offered.

Godanza was about to thank the man for his concern and assure him that he could not help when something about the man stopped him. The man exuded a quiet reassuring strength that Godanza had rarely encountered.

"Are you a mashari?" Godanza embarrassed himself by asking.

"You are most perceptive."

"Perhaps you can help me. Even if you cannot, you would bring honor to my humble home if you would consent to have dinner with my wife and me. After we have eaten, I can explain this incredible dream to you. That is, if you have no other plans?"

"I have none."

"Excellent. I was about to head home now. My wife can be an excellent cook when she wants to. It will only take a moment to project home that company is coming."

Following dinner, the old man repeated his dream for the curious stranger.

"Can you make any sense of it?"

"Your home is filled with longing for a child, is it not?"

"Truly, you are a child of the Megalight, for indeed it is. We had longed for a child for many years until we became too old."

"The first, older cloud in the dream is the union between you and your wife. The rain is your child. There are two reasons why the cloud had trouble raining. First, it was trying too hard, and second (and this is the most important reason) the destiny of its rain is connected with the destiny of the rain of the second cloud. You and your wife will soon conceive a child that will mate with another child born around the same time. Had your child been born when you had wanted it, it would be old enough to be the parent of its intended mate. Both your child and its mate have a special destiny; for the lake which provides life in an otherwise barren setting is actually the offspring of your child, or your grandchild.

"You must know this: there is substantial adversity pending. The stream hitting the hot ground indicates that your child will come close to losing his or her life at an early age, but the additional water represents the power of the Megalight flowing through the two of you that will save it. The near brush with death will substantially alter your child- that is why the stream lurched along like a gel. But when your child encounters its mate, all will be restored to a level far greater than would have been achieved had your child not fallen ill. Your child's mate will have been orphaned shortly after birth, as evidenced by the cloud being blown away as soon as its rain ended. The barren nature of the planet reflects a spiritual barrenness. When the spiritually alive are surrounded by the spiritually dead they languish because of the ferocity with which the dead try to mandate conformity to their deathliness.

"I wish I could say how much of our beloved Zarkon will be affected by this spiritual death, but I cannot. Yet even if only one person is affected, we are all diminished by that person's loss. There is but one life force, from which we each draw our individual portions."

Godanza and Ula were stunned. Their world had been destroyed, resurrected, destroyed and resurrected again in a few minutes. They sat in silence until the stranger asked to excuse himself, and Godanza begged him to stay. There was so much to deal with that Godanza was forced to focus first on having a baby until the rest could be sorted.

"Ula, we are going to have a baby. We have more than a hundred and twenty seasons between us, and we are going to have a baby!"

"I heard," she whispered the only words that would come to her.

"Aren't you happy?"

"Sometimes joy and sorrow wear the same mask," the stranger interjected.

Godanza and Ula filled with emotional tension. Later that night they released it with each other. Nine months later, Ula gave birth to a beautiful baby girl.

From the moment she was born, it was clear that this was no ordinary child. She seldom cried, and when she did, she sounded melodious, like she was making a tune. She played like any other baby, but beneath her eyes was a calmness, a maturity. She gave the impression that if she could speak, great pearls of wisdom would pour forth.

Shortly after she entered her third season, she was stricken by the illness of which the stranger had warned. She looked like she had been bitten by a poisonous zhubu fly, except that her symptoms were too severe. She developed a fever and her skin exploded with horrible, puss-filled bumps. Godanza and Ula had taken care to rub her daily with alobo tree butter as soon as zhubu season came. The alobo tree butter instantly repulsed zhubu flies. In light of the prophetic warning they had received, they had taken every conceivable precaution to guard the child's health; and she still became deathly ill.

After three days, little Kalimba fell into a coma. Godanza and Ula could feel her spirit slipping from her tiny body. They pulled their minds together to form one mind with one thought and one purpose. Bravely they fought through the emotional hysteria that tried to claim them. They emptied themselves until they could feel their one mind lock onto the power of the Megalight. They voided themselves of consciousness until the only energy force that remained was that of the Megalight. They felt the Megalight force flow through them and snatch the last bit of remaining life in the child and then pull on it. Gradually the life force was pulled back into their baby. When it had completely returned, both parents collapsed from exhaustion. Godanza and Ula had always tried to live in harmony with the Megalight; but neither had ever called upon the Megalight so profoundly, or been answered so miraculously. Ula was the first to regain consciousness. When she inspected her child, she found that the fever had broken; but the little girl was horribly disfigured.

Ordinarily, Kalimba's physical disfigurement would not have created any insurmountable problems, but her Megalight connection was altered as well. Although it still functioned vertically, between the child and the Megalight, it ceased to spread horizontally to the other people. Her connection became self-contained. It had no outlet. She could neither send, nor receive thoughts, even though she was deeply united with the Megalight. Only her parents understood that she was connected, and only they had the slightest inkling of the pain the child's unexpressed connection caused her.

She began to withdraw from everyone except her parents. The others suffered her withdrawal gladly. For, without being able to feel her vibrations, they could only encounter her superficially. Her ravaged looks took on more importance than they should have, and the family was forced to draw their emotional wagons into a circle.

Shortly after Kalimba's thirteenth season, Ula died. She just laid down one day without any intentions of ever getting up again. Godanza shunned the customary memorial service and instead, prayed quietly at home with his grief-stricken daughter.

A week later, he packed his most cherished possessions and, with Kalimba in tow, left Zambutu to live in seclusion on the edge of the desert. Were it not for the remaining prophecy to unfold, he would have had no reason to continue living.

Now, finally, that prophecy was being unfurled. Only Kalimba's intended mate could have seen her for what she truly was, thereby releasing her from her physical bondage. Yet even this fulfillment of the ongoing prophecy carried with it cause for concern. The spiritual barrenness had to be forthcoming.

"Forgive my intrusion, but I wished to bid you goodnight before I took leave of my soul for the night," Jawala interrupted Godanza's reverie.

"Oh, by all means, please join me for a moment. I am afraid

I have so many things to think about that I do not know whether to be happy or sad."

"My father used to say ..."

"Your FATHER. Your father is alive?" he asked, remembering the part of the dream where the second cloud disappears.

"I call him Father, but actually, he is my guardian. My parents both died just at the time I was born. I am told that I was plucked from my mother's womb just before she breathed her last breath."

"I am so sorry. Please, continue with what you were about to say."

"Well, he used to say that joy and sorrow often wear the same mask."

"WHAT did he say?"

"That joy and sorrow often wear the same mask. He used to say a lot of things like that."

"Where did you say you were from?"

"Saroppo."

"Then, HE is your father! I should have known! My dear friend, Menes, the man who interpreted my dream for me!"

His eyes brimming with tears, Godanza wrapped his arms around the startled Jawala, whisked him into the air, and kissed him on both cheeks.

19

"Very soon, my faithful followers," Nagap smiled expansively at Rollof and Ondorf as they emptied the last of the powdery contents from their last sack into the stream. "Very soon, you will know power and prestige beyond your wildest dreams. You will owe fealty to no man, except me, and you will have to bow before no man, except me!"

Rollof and Ondorf could not have known- nor would Nagap have wanted them to know- that the pep talks he loved to give them were as much for his own benefit as theirs. Ever since his first trip to the forbidden cave, he had achieved a rhythm like a superstar athlete when all of the pieces of his game fall into place. Still, he had to become more accustomed to the new identity which he had found in the cave. Each day, a little more of the old fears and hurts gave way to his burgeoning confidence. Yet, he would cling tenaciously to much his pain. He needed it to fuel his malevolent scheme. Without his love affair with his own pain, he might have stopped to consider the true consequences of his actions. In the dungeon of his mind, he thanked Jawala profusely for defeating him in the debates. For without that defeat, he would not now be on the verge of conquering the entire world!

Nagap had dried the forbidden fruit into a powder and inoculated Rollof and Ondorf by forcing them to drink a weak tea made from the powdered fruit. The inoculations had been unnecessary since neither Rollof nor Ondorf possessed enough of a Megalight connection to have been harmed by the fruit in the first place. Still, Nagap would take no chances with their health. He needed their assistance, and he also had grown quite fond of his grovelling flunkies. They were his imaginary friends from childhood come to life.

Once the fruit had been powdered, the three men used it to pollute the streams that fed the villages in the Saroppo cluster. They started with the Zambutu water supply and did not stop until the circle of their actions led them back to Zambutu. They spent three days outside each village, and each day they placed a little more of the dangerous powder into the streams. They were careful not to put too much powder in at first, for fear that the resident's Megalight connections would warn them. Each dose of powder would render the people's warning systems a little less effective.

They completed the circle of the villages three times. The second trip they stayed seven days at each location, and on the third, an average of fifteen days per location. Nagap just seemed to know how much powder to use, and for how long. By the end of the third cycle, it was time to test the effects of the powder.

Nagap could not bring himself to test the project in his native Saroppo, so Zambutu would be the initial site. He reviewed his instructions with Rollof and Ondorf until they could- and did- answer him in their sleep.

"My, that looks like awfully difficult work, " Rollof grinned at the stone mason as he approached him.

"It is," the man replied without lifting his head from his work.

"It obviously requires a great deal of skill, intelligence, and physical prowess; the very things which have made the Airopin race the greatest in history."

"What do you know of us? You are not Airopin," the stone mason lifted his head for the first time to look directly at Rollof.

"That is true, but I was raised by Airopins. Also, I was raised to believe in truth. No matter what race a man is, if he does not see that the Airopins are the Chosen Ones of the Megalight, then he is a fool. I can see that you are an honorable man, a man who probably tries to get along with everyone, regardless of race. Is that not so?"

"It is," the man replied as he set his tools down to give Rollof his undivided attention.

"Now, let me ask you this; have you been feeling unappreciated lately? Unfulfilled? Have you noticed how long it has been since anyone around here bothered to notice the quality of your work? Have you not noticed the Numations who live as well, if not better, than you do, and yet all they do is have a good time, while you are out here slaving for nothing?"

The man leaned thoughtfully on his fist and narrowed his eyes on Rollof.

"How is it that you know my feelings?" he asked when his voice returned.

"I know these things because of the master, whom I serve. I

am but a messenger of a messenger, for he who sent me, was himself sent by the Megalight for the redemption of all of us."

"Then, your master is an Airopin?"

"No. He is also Numation."

"I am lost. Why would the Megalight send a Numation when we both know that the Airopins are the Chosen People?"

"I am glad you asked that," Rollof paused to make sure he would say exactly what Nagap had told him at this critical point in the discussion. "My master is not like other men. He has the body of a Numation, but the mind of an Airopin. You know how difficult it can be to get people to accept the truth, especially Numations."

"Yes."

"So too, does the Megalight understand this. The Megalight wanted a messenger to whom all people could relate. Since we all know that the mind is more important than the body, the messenger was given an Airopin mind; it is just that it dwells within a Numation body. It is because of my master's Airopin mind that I am able to relate the frustrations of the Airopin people, even though I am not one myself, although I wish I were."

"I still do not like the idea of Numations speaking for Airopins; but since you seem to understand that *we* are the Chosen Ones, and *you* are not, then the very least I owe you is to listen to you. But tell me, why are you telling me all of this? As a Numation, there can be nothing in it for you."

"But there is something in it for me! As a messenger of the messenger, I long for an orderly society. I have been promised that when the will of the Megalight is done, I will reap enormous benefits.

"My master knows, not only what is happening now, but also what will occur in the future. In less than two months, a village council-meeting will be held. Ask around if you wish, but I can assure you that, as of this moment, there are no plans for a council meeting. Only my master knows this. When that meeting is held, there will be much bickering. He will come forth with a plan that, given the ingenuity of the Airopin people, will give you an excellent advantage in the management of the affairs of Zambutu and beyond. Tell no one of this plan, or of my visit. But when the time comes, attend the meeting, and listen to my master's plan. If you do not like the plan, then, by all means, do not support it. However, I am confident that you will endorse what he will have to say.

"Until next we meet, I will say goodbye."

"Thank you," the stone mason whispered, "thank you very much."

Had Rollof stayed a few more minutes he probably could have watched the man cry. As much as he might have enjoyed that spectacle, he was even more anxious to return to Nagap with the news of his success.

Strolling back to their campsite, Rollof could not have felt better had he tried. Not since he failed manhood training had anyone listened to anything he had to say except Ondorf, and although Ondorf had been his friend- his only friend- his listening did not matter. After all, no one listened to Ondorf either. Now, thanks to Nagap, he had been able to convince a complete stranger with the most preposterous tale he could imagine.

He felt he had a right to feel proud of himself; and even better, he knew Nagap would be proud. He wondered if Ondorf had done as well. He felt so good about himself that he would not mind if Ondorf had been equally successful, so long as he did not surpass him.

When the trio reunited at the campsite, Rollof and Ondorf bickered as to who would give his report first. Ondorf won. He reported his entire conversation, almost verbatim. He included a physical description of the man with whom he had spoke. He described the atmosphere at the man's work station. He drew detailed, elaborated word pictures of the man falling helplessly beneath his spell as he masterfully convinced him of the plague of the Airopins. By the end of his discussion, the Numation was ready to blame the Airopins for bad weather!

When Rollof's turn came, he made sure that he took more time than Ondorf to tell his story. His eyes grew wide and he spread his fingers apart as he told of the Airopin's confusion at being led by a Numation, and how he had overcome that confusion.

Nagap's puppies had grown teeth, and he was proud of them. He decided to reward them by telling them of his plans for the next day. He stretched out a large piece of parchment.

"Can either of you tell me whose face is on this paper?"

"It is you!" they exclaimed in unison, as they had so many times before. "It is a wonderful likeness of you," Ondorf ventured even further.

"Thank you. Now, I will tell you why I had it drawn." He

spent the next hour outlining his plans for the drawing. He was remarkably patient when one of them became confused, remembering that were it not for the pamphlet Chuka had given him, he himself might have had trouble understanding.

He also made a mental note that once Zambutu had been conquered, Saroppo would be next. He wanted to get Chuka involved as soon as possible.

The next morning, Nagap arose early and dressed quickly. He wore his second finest robe- he had been defeated by Jawala in his best robe and was not yet ready to wear it again. Shortly after approaching Zambutu, he spied a metal worker. He strode confidently into the man's work space.

"May I help you?" the man asked as Nagap approached.

"Perhaps, it is I who may help you," Nagap answered with the confidence of a tiger surrounded by zebras. "I am afraid," he continued," that I could not help but notice the precision with which you work your craft. Do you mind if I watch you for a bit?"

The man looked quizzically at Nagap then told him he was welcome to stay as long as he liked, so long as he did not interfere with his work.

After a few minutes of watching the sweat glisten on the man's arms, shoulders and chest, Nagap spoke again.

"The more I watch you, the more I can appreciate how truly difficult your craft is. It must have taken many seasons to perfect it to the degree that is evidenced by your magnificent work."

"Everyone knows that metal working requires many seasons of apprenticeship."

"Watching you work, I can see why. Tell me, are you making that piece of jewelry for a relative?"

"Only in the sense that we are all related. But there is no immediate blood relationship between my customer and me, if that is what you mean."

Nagap paused for a moment to study the man. Based on the reports he had received from Rollof and Ondorf, his encounter with the metal worker should have been progressing more smoothly than it was. No matter, the bigger they are ...

"How much will this person compensate you for your efforts?"

Again, the man peered curiously at Nagap.

"Compensated? I am not sure I understand what you mean. When I have finished this bracelet, I will give it to the person who asked me to make it. He will, in turn, offer what he has of value that he may think I might use. If he has nothing I can use, he will be obligated by custom to perform some service for someone else, without hope of compensation of any sort. But I am sure you must already know this. While I can see that you are not from around here, this is the way that things are done in every region in which I have traveled, and I must say that I have traveled somewhat extensively."

"Yes, I suppose that is the way that we have always done things," Nagap answered wearily, as if bored by the weight of senseless tradition. "But I was just thinking that perhaps it is time to consider a new way of doing things. After all, with all due respect, were it not for some forward thinking people in the past, you would not be a metal worker. We did not always have the mastery over metal which you now possess. What percentage of the people are metal workers?"

"About one in two hundred."

"How many of the people grow crops?"

"I do not know. Maybe, seven out of ten?"

"Yes, that sounds about right. Do you live any better than the people who grow crops?"

"Of course not. I depend on them for food, and they depend on me for tools and implements. What is your point?"

"Perhaps, I do not have one. It just seems odd to me, that one who possesses one of the rarest of skills should receive no greater rewards for his efforts than one who performs the most common, menial tasks."

"I am beginning to follow you."

"Excellent. Now, take this bracelet that you are slaving over as an example. If the recipient does not compensate you, and compensates someone else instead, what have you gained for your labor? I know the old way of thinking; I know about `what goes around, comes around,' but the fact remains that not only might you not be compensated, but you cannot be sure that someone else will receive something because of your labors. And, even if the man does a good deed for someone else, I doubt seriously if he has the skills to perform a task that would be the equivalent of this bracelet. I just feel that it is time that skilled artisans such as yourself be given their proper recognition."

"Sir ..."

"You may call me Nagap. And by what name are you known?"

"I am called Biloxin.

"Nagap, I must admit that I could not readily discern the

wisdom of your discourse; but after hearing you out on the matter, I can see that you have far more insight than anyone could rightfully expect from a man of your age, or from a man of any age, for that matter. I am in awe of your perceptiveness. For indeed, I have just recently been feeling unappreciated and unrewarded, but I could not say why; these feelings have been so new to me. Yet, I have just met you, and you have spoken the words that were locked in my heart, that even I could not have spoken for myself. I feel that you have another motive in telling me all of this. Even though I do not know you, I do know that anyone who can see better into a man's heart than that man himself, must surely be Megalight sent. If there is anything I can do to help you, please advise me."

"Now it is my turn to salute your perceptiveness; for indeed, I have been sent by the Megalight to know the pains that straddle good men's hearts and to correct whatever might be the source of that pain. That is the mission on which the Megalight has sent me. And yes, I do have plans in mind."

Nagap reached into the folds of his garment and produced three chunks of different metals and the parchment he had shown to Rollof and Ondorf the night before.

"They are not quite rare, but neither are they common, especially the yellow metal, the brinanium."

"Can you create these medallions I have sketched and to the specifications I have detailed?" he asked pointing to the parchment he had spread before Biloxin.

"Yes, I can do that. I can do them so well that people will talk to the medallions and expect you to talk back to them!"

"Great!" Nagap feigned a chuckle. "Make as many as you possibly can. I will have my assistants supply you with more of the metals as the need arises. But you must tell no one of your work. And you must work for no one else, so long as you are working on this particular assignment. I know what I am asking you may sound like a lot, but when the things that I foresee come to pass, you will be compensated beyond your wildest dreams.

"You see, I not only can see into men's hearts, but I can also see the future. Such is the burden of he who is Megalight sent. In the very near future, there will be a village council- meeting. Not even the village elders know this, because there are no plans for a meeting yet. At that meeting, I will lay the future before your feet. I will place you on the road to becoming one of the most powerful men in the history of Zarkon.

"But remember, tell no one of this visit. Also, remember, I have the power to make your life a mirror reflection of the Megalight's grace, or I can make you wish you had never been born. I demand unswerving allegiance. Do you understand?"

There had been no need for the threat, the man had already been won over, it was just that Nagap could not resist the opportunity.

"I understand, Messiah,"

"MESSIAH!" the word rolled around Nagap's brain and dribbled off his lips. "MESSIAH!" he repeated the word over and over again, changing the accent as his whim suited him mes*siah*. mess*iah*, *messiah*, me*sssiii*iah. Oh, it felt good!

The next six weeks found Nagap, Rollof, and Ondorf as raindrops are found during a monsoon: everywhere. They consorted, consoled, cajoled, and complimented. They serenaded and sympathized. They peered deeply into the scarred psyches of the people and applied the balm of appreciation to the newly disconnected. No one was appreciated, loved, or respected enough, and Nagap, Ondorf and Rollof understood; and brought with them the answers.

By the end of the six weeks, not even the Megalight could have convinced these people that their lives were not in ruins and that a council meeting was not absolutely crucial. A meeting was convened.

Nagap hurried his step as the damp air chilled and the rain began to fall. "Good," he thought to himself. The rain would force the meeting indoors, and he would have an even more captive audience. Not that it was necessary, given the people's current mood, nothing short of a flood would have stopped the assemblage, but every little bit helps. Rollof and Ondorf were already at the meeting, stirring and fomenting the people as if they were some sort of brew. As he neared the meeting tent, the raucous voices grew louder, and the words discernible. He could tell that the elders would not be able to control the meeting.

"I helped build your dwelling space!" a voice rang out.

"You have been living off my generosity for years!" cried another.

More beautiful than a thousand birds chirping in harmony, Nagap laughed aloud to himself, as he recalled his manhood training.

Nagap strode confidently to the center of the meeting area and majestically raised his arms, requesting silence. Rollof, Ondorf, and the others they had recruited, led by Biloxin, moved quickly to quiet the others. Nagap allowed the silence to settle in before he spoke.

"These are troubled times," he intoned. "These are confusing times. Everywhere we turn, we see nothing but confusion. Jealousy and envy are running amok. We are all working harder than ever before. We are sacrificing more than we have ever sacrificed before. Yet, what do we have to show for it? Nothing!"

Nagap paused to scan the audience. Every eye was upon him, every head nodding affirmation, and every ear cocked as they hung upon his every word.

"These are troubled times," he repeated. "And these are changing times. We have long been oppressed by a system in which no matter how hard a person worked, his neighbor could have just as much as him, even if the neighbor just sat around all day, watching him work. Is that not so?"

"It is so!" Biloxin was the first to agree, although the others joined him immediately.

"Times are changing. The time has come for us to stand up for our talents. The time has come for us to stand up for our time. The time has come for us to stand up for our children and our families and to stand up for ourselves. I am telling each and every one of you that can hear my voice that if you want to be a part of the future instead of being left behind in the past, then I want you to get out of those seats and stand up. Stand up! Stand up!"

The crowd rose to its feet, clapping and chanting, "Stand up, stand up."

Nagap basked in the chants, and the rhythmic clapping almost aroused him sexually. He wallowed in their approval for as long as he dared, before settling them down again. He could not allow their energy to be dissipated just yet. He called for silence again.

"Through the divine guidance which the Megalight has bestowed upon me, I have been chosen to devise a plan that will erase all of this confusion. You are about to witness freedom being born.

"My good man," Nagap indicated Biloxin, "will you come forward?"

Biloxin was so excited that he reached Nagap in what looked like a single bound.

"Will you bring forth the work you have done for us?"

Biloxin reached into his robe and brought out a handful of coins.

"These medallions are properly called coins. They are called money. Currency. They are the means by which we all will be compensated for our labors from now on. This large yellow coin is a Nagapine. The second largest, silver coin is a half-Nagapine. The smallest orange coin is a quarter Nagapine. One Nagapine is the equal of two half-Nagapines or four quarter-Nagapines. From now on, whenever you do something for someone else, they will have to exchange one, or several of these coins, depending on the work that has been performed. I have taken the liberty of drawing up compensation tables so we can see how much a given piece of work or item is worth in terms of these coins. Never again will you have to worry about your generosity being taken advantage of. No longer will your kindness be taken for weakness. Every individual and every family will be issued a specific amount of coins. Those of you who are shrewd- and who among you is not?- will be able to accumulate more and more of these coins. The coins will bring power and freedom. If you acquire enough of them, you will not have to work anymore, because you will be able to pay someone else to do your work!

"I have also worked out a plan where Nagapines can be loaned, and the lender makes even more money, just by lending them. For each Nagapine that is loaned for a full season, the lender must repay the Nagapine, plus a quarter-Nagapine. Those of us who have the industry and the ingenuity to acquire many coins will have no choice other than to become richer and richer.

"And I still have not told you the best part yet! These coins will not only be used in exchange for goods and services, they will also be used to purchase food and land!"

Nagap rode a high he had never known possible. The words pouring out of him sounded so good to him that he fueled himself. He could do no wrong, say no wrong. His triumph made him salivate, and his salivation triggered the hunger for more victory. Caught up though he was in his own glory, he was still able to detect that he might be confusing some of the people.

"The way things stand now, we sometimes eat foods that grow wild, and we sometimes eat foods that we plant. Often times, we invest our sweat and labor into planting food, only to watch some lazy stranger pass by and eat the food that we took the trouble to plant. And what do we get in return when someone else eats our food? Nothing! Nothing, but a `thank you.' Well, I do not know about you, but I have never been able to eat a `thank you.'

Under the present system all we get is confusion and cheating. The lazy eat as much as the hard working. Under my new system, distinct plots of land will be allocated to each family. Only that family will be able to grow food on that plot, or to eat anything that grows wild on that plot. If you grow more than you can eat, you can sell the surplus to someone else. Or you can have someone else harvest your crops in exchange for a portion of your surplus. When you develop a surplus and use it to acquire coins, you can then use the coins to acquire more land, with which you can develop even greater surpluses! All that nonsense we have been taught about the Megalight owning the land is just that--pure nonsense. The Megalight bequeathed this land to us. We are entitled to it. We have been chosen to own it. It would be sinful *not* to take ownership of the gift of land and make the very most of it.

Once the plots of land have been issued, you will be able to buy something else I have created: barriers to keep intruders off your land. These barriers are called fences. They will also be used to mark the limits of plots so you will not have to worry about someone else trying to encroach on your property.

What do you think of my plan? Are you with me?"

If there were any dissenters present, they had the good sense to keep their opinions to themselves. The crowd rose again as one, clapping and chanting. This time they chanted but one word: Nagap. The chanting continued as they carried their new savior into the night.

20

"Where is Godanza? Menes? ANYBODY? I have got to get some help!" Jawala swallowed hard, as if the fear that stalked him were located beneath his adam's apple. Godanza had left in plenty of time to have returned by now with the help they so desperately needed. Jawala and Kalimba had joined their psychic forces to reach Menes, but had not been able to lock onto his vibrations. Jawala had received instructions in subjects almost too numerous to mention, but delivering a baby was not one of them; and to make matters worse, this was not any baby, this was his baby. For the first time, in the two years since they had wed, Jawala was afraid to be alone with his wife.

Kalimba squeezed hard on Jawala's hand, forcing him to face her. "I NEED YOU," she sent to him as emphatically as she could. Her message registered. He could not afford the luxury of worrying about Menes, Godanza, or anyone else, at least not right now. If help came, fine; but in the meantime, he would have to face the situation as it presented itself. Jawala and Kalimba began to concentrate on breathing: he to clear his thoughts, she to ease the delivery.

They tried to meld their minds, but could not. He tried to send his energy to her, but he could not find the proper channel. He would have to leave her until he could gather his energy and focus it at her, but each moan that issued forth from her hooked him even deeper into the spot. The harder he tried to pull away, the more viciously the groans dug into him, yanking him into the abyss between purpose and chaos. When he realized he could no longer resist, he abandoned his strategy and allowed her pain to swallow him whole. It was amazing! Like a swimmer allowing himself to be swept by a current, once he gave up the fight, he found himself being carried to the center of the place he had been struggling to find.

His now unrestrained psyche touched hers and shared its calm. Both grew limp. They found the rhythm within themselves to coax the recalcitrant baby into the world.

It was a boy. A beautiful baby boy. The proud father was about to hand the screaming slimy bundle to its weary mother when he stopped in mid-gesture. The baby had a clubbed foot and a withered hand. In a land where birth defects were so rare the term did not exist, theirs had been born with two.

Kalimba lay waiting for her husband to lift his head and present her new baby to her, but he remained frozen in his half-kneeling position. Although the baby's wailing told her it was alive, she knew something was wrong.

"Give me my baby!" her gritty voice rang out impatiently.

Jawala still did not move.

She raised her fist, and with the little strength she could muster, hit him on top of his head.

He gave her the baby.

Maybe it was because Jawala's reaction had warned her, or maybe it was because of the trials her own illness had inflicted upon her; whatever the reason, she ignored the baby's deformities and squeezed it to her bosom.

"If it be the Megalight's will," she whispered softly as Jawala fought through his shame and cleaned the baby while preparing to cut the cord.

The increasing rumble of hooves insisted that Jawala and Kalimba acknowledge the advancing rider. Jawala left the tent and greeted his approaching father-in-law. Godanza dismounted before the quiphar could come to a complete halt. Neither man spoke as Jawala motioned toward the tent.

Twenty minutes later, Godanza returned to his confused son-in-law. "The child has an aura of strength around him. He is a beautiful baby."

"Yes, he is," Jawala answered tersely. "Perhaps he might have been even more beautiful if his mother had had more help than her ignorant husband."

"This is no time for self-pity," Godanza warned sternly. "Nothing in the delivery of the baby could possibly have had that kind of an effect. You did nothing wrong. As for the help I was supposed to bring ..."

Jawala's eyebrows rose inquisitively.

"If that child is to have the destiny your father spoke of, he certainly was not born a minute too soon. Wherever I turned for help, they showed me these small medallions- they called them coins- and asked if I had any. When I answered that I did not, they said that they could not assist me in any manner whatsoever unless I could exchange coins for their services. Even after I explained the urgency of the situation a dozen times, I was told a dozen times that no one could help me without the coins. It was as if the coins held some magic which they deemed more valuable than the grace of the Megalight!

I managed to get a few of the coins in exchange for my arm band, but I had nothing else, except the quiphar, for which anyone would barter. I saw people who used to be my friends. They just looked at me sadly and repeated what everyone else said. I tried to get some sort of feel, some kind of reading on them, but they were all blank. They were like empty scrolls, except nothing could be written on them. It was like they were full, and yet empty at the same time, like a dream that intrudes upon space normally reserved for reality.

I could not feel a single Megalight connection. It was like each person's spirit had some sort of individual wrapping around it. They were not connected to each other, nor could I feel any linkage with any of them. It was the most frightening, saddening experience I have ever encountered. I even pleaded with some of the people who had been friends at one time, and they laughed at me! They said I was uninformed and unsophisticated. But beneath their laughter I detected the most horrible fear I have ever encountered."

"That is amazing. The spiritually barren planet has already begun to assert itself. Whatever is happening in Zambutu may explain why we were not able to reach Menes in Saroppo. I will ride there tomorrow. I will need your quiphar."

"You shall have it."

"Tomorrow holds the promise of many challenges. But let us wait until tomorrow to deal with them. Now it is time we got better acquainted with the newest member of our family."

Jawala, oblivious to the hot sun, rode directly across the desert to save time. He was grateful for the long solitary ride. He needed time to sort things out. He had always been taught that worry was the absence of faith, and he had always believed it. Yet now he found it almost impossible not to worry. They had been unable to locate Menes; his baby had been born with strange physical problems he did not understand, and Godanza had returned with the news that people were refusing to help each other. Had Godanza returned with the news that the village was flooded and underwater, or completely destroyed by fire, or even if it had disappeared into thin air, Jawala would have felt more comfortable than an entire village of people refusing to help. The dream had presented a spiritually barren wasteland, but Jawala could never have imagined anything quite as extreme as people not helping each other.

It was obvious that something terrible had happened to the Megalight connections of the people of Zambutu, but what could it have been? He tried to think of the fools he had encountered growing up. He had not met more than five in his entire life, and of those, he had only spoken with Rollof and Ondorf for more than five minutes. He had not been repulsed by them, but neither had he enjoyed their company. They were not "real" enough-honest enough- to like. Though they were hardly trustworthy, he had not found them to be particularly evil. He had pitied them. Then it occurred to him that only two disconnected in the midst of the connected could not nourish evil; but if everyone was disconnected, then nothing could prevail *but* evil: evil he had no preparation for understanding.

He had always been taught that the Megalight brought order where there had been none. Yet all around him he could see nothing but chaos. How could the Megalight be ruling over such chaos? Could the Megalight have lost interest in the affairs of Zarkon? He recoiled at the thought and begged the Megalight's forgiveness for having indulged it in the first place.

As he approached the three-quarter mark of his journey, he spotted a small band of people- eight or ten maybe- walking in his direction. He began to detect powerful, familiar vibrations. He increased his speed until he could identify them. It was Otumba leading a band of his neighbors from Saroppo.

"The Megalight be praised! There was little doubt that I would find you, but I dared not hope it would happen so quickly," Otumba exclaimed once Jawala had reached her party.

"It is so good to see you!" Jawala answered as he dismounted. He embraced his step-mother then added, "But why are you out here looking for me? And where is the mashari?"

"There is much that I must share with you," she said softly as she squeezed his hand. Otumba's touch brought back memories of an almost forgotten sense of security. She had taken care of him so much that when her marriage to Menes was announced, Jawala wondered why it had taken them so long. It felt good to be in her presence again.

"There is much that I would hear from you, but first I must tell you that I have a son."

"The Megalight be praised again!" she exclaimed as she embraced him again. This time she released another forgotten memory: he had forgotten how strong she was.

"Obviously, there is much that we must share with each other. But they can wait until you have properly greeted your neighbors who have grieved through your absence with hearts almost as heavy as mine."

If it were not for the voice, I could have closed my eyes and sworn that was Menes talking, Jawala thought to himself. Menes had that effect on people.

Jawala released Otumba to engage the rest of the gathering. She was right. Had the choice been his to gather the most beloved of his neighbors, he would have selected the people who stood before him.

There was Salikma, the man who preferred travel to marriage; and Eloshima and his wife, who had given Jawala sweets when he was a child. Shobogun- his once feared, and now beloved taskmaster from manhood training- stood with his wife, Sheliabu. Nagap's four grandparents were also present.

Jawala kissed and embraced his neighbors individually, allowing each to transport him back through time to some special moment they had shared. His longest embrace would have been with Shobogun, whom he regarded with practically the same reverence as Menes, were it not for Finola and Alikum, Chuka's parents. He had already embraced each of them separately when, in tandem, they swooped him into their arms and held him so tightly- tears streaming down their wizened faces- that he looked curiously to Otumba for some clue. She blinked and nodded her head toward him with a look of compassion. Following her cue, Jawala held the tormented couple until they were ready to disengage. When they released Jawala, they huddled together and walked off a bit to comfort each other. Jawala surveyed the others and could feel each pulling a part of the pain that originated with Finola and Alikum. He knew that had it not been for the others shouldering some portion of that pain, its weight already would have crushed the trembling couple.

"As I said," Otumba spoke, "there is much to discuss. But first, there is work to do; it is getting dark."

They made camp for the night. They scrounged fresh roots and vegetables to stretch the provisions they brought with them. Throughout the meal, the conversation was kept light. Jawala sensed that the serious discussion would have to take place out of earshot of Finola and Alikum.

When the time came, he related the circumstances surrounding his son's birth to Otumba and a few of the others. He told her of the news that Godanza had brought with him from Zambutu, but he was careful not to mention not being able to reach Menes until after she had spoken.

"What you have told us about Zambutu could just as easily have been said of Saroppo. It is as if some great wind came along and blew everything upside down. What had been considered virtuous is now held in contempt. Wisdom and foolishness have traded places. Love and sharing have become obsolete, although anyone will do almost anything for those cursed coins. We have them too. What is most amazing is that the coins all bear an image that is almost the exact likeness of Nagap."

"Nagap? Godanza showed me some of the coins, but I was in no mood to examine them closely. Nagap? How could that be?"

"He disappeared right after you defeated him in the debates. No one heard from him, except maybe Chuka, and if she did, she was not about to tell anyone. Anyway, the seasons had completed one and one-half cycles since then, when tempers stared flaring and disputes became the order of the day for no reason that we could discern at the time. Almost everyone was so dissatisfied that a village council-meeting was called. None of us who are assembled here were present, because we knew that no good would come of the meeting; but we do know that Nagap was there. He resurfaced ..." she paused for a moment as the realization of her words came upon her, "right around the time the dissension had begun. I had never bothered to connect him with the bickering before."

"Do you remember Rollof and Ondorf, the two fools who used to come around only when there was some sort of ceremony, so they could stuff themselves with food?" Salikma asked.

"Yes, strange you should ask that. I was just thinking of them today," Jawala replied.

"They also appeared at the same time that Nagap returned."

"You know," Shobogun spoke, "I never really felt comfortable about passing Nagap through manhood training. Of all my students, I felt he understood my teachings the least. But I had insufficient grounds not to pass him. Perhaps, I could have held him back, but I was not sure enough to do something that drastic to the boy. I did not want to ruin his life."

"Apparently he has done that himself," Salikma added. "But we have veered Otumba's story far enough from its path. Please continue."

"Thank you!" Otumba bellowed with her signature look of exasperation. "If you continue to interrupt me, I will be telling this story to my grandson's child!

"Now, where was I? Oh yes, the coins were introduced at that meeting. Afterward, no one would lift a finger for anyone else unless they could receive a coin in exchange. Menes and Salikma were both away from the village when these strange things started happening. I am afraid that the rest of us were almost caught up in these affairs. Fortunately, Menes and Salikma were able to save us. The others were too far gone. What you see before you represents the sum total of former Saroppo inhabitants that have not gone mad. That is why we are out here. Menes sent us. He said the time had come for us to leave and look for you. He said something about your representing the focal point of a new beginning."

"But why did he not come with you?"

"The stubborn old fool!" Otumba nostrils flared, but her anger could not mask her concern. "He insisted on staying behind. He said it was important to gather as much information as possible."

"How was he going to get this information to us? He could overload and strain himself if he tries to send it all."

"He said you would know when to come for it."

"That sounds like Menes."

Jawala gave his traveling neighbors detailed instructions for reaching his dwelling space, as well as where best to look for food and water along the way. They said their farewells that evening, knowing there would be no time in the morning.

The following nightfall found Jawala approaching the outskirts of Saroppo. He spotted Guntamo, with whom he had gone through manhood training, as well as a few of his other friends from what seemed to be so long ago. He wanted to cry out to them and embrace them, and it felt strange not being able to do so. Sneaking into his own hometown- especially when he had left following his great victory in the debates- gave Jawala an eery, uneasy feeling. He moved stealthily through the shadows until he reached his old home. He peered through the sunhole. Even though he could see nothing but darkness inside, he knew Menes was there. He could feel his presence.

He rapped on the entry panel. Nothing. Gently, he eased the

panel open to allow a sliver of moonlight into the room. Still nothing. He whispered Menes' name as loudly as he dared. No answer. He crept further inside, whispering Menes' name, when he heard a faint groan escape from the corner. He lit a lamp. What he saw nearly took his breath away.

It was Menes. One eye and both lips hideously swollen, he lay huddled against the wall.

"By the Megalight's eyes! What happened to you? Who did this to you?" Jawala had never seen anyone badly beaten. He could never have imagined anyone hurting anyone else in that fashion, let alone Menes.

Jawala tore away a strip of his robe and started toward the water pump, but Menes motioned him away from the pump and pointed toward a gourd of water on the floor.

Jawala cleansed the old man's wounds then left. He returned within minutes with kukasia leaves to make a poultice. After attending to Menes' wounds, he made a second trip. This time he returned with herbs and roots. Quickly he brewed a thick tea which invigorated Menes almost immediately.

"Saroppo has been befallen by a great evil, my son. Several men were here looking for you. When they saw you were not here, they began interrogating me. They did not believe me when I told them I did not know your exact whereabouts. In all of my years, my word has never been doubted.

"But why would they be looking for me here? Everyone knows I left Saroppo right after my debate with Nagap."

"Yes, your debate with Nagap. I suspect that they wished to apprehend you in order to fulfill some moronic vengeance of Nagap's. Nagap is behind all of this."

"I know. I encountered Otumba and the others along the way. But I got the distinct impression they wanted me to learn most of the details of what has transpired from you."

"That is probably correct. As I was saying, they thought I might know where you were."

"So these men beat you because you would not tell them where I was?"

"That was just the beginning. I am afraid that I have yet to divulge the strangest elements of this encounter. When they realized I had no information about you, they wanted to know if I would swear allegiance to this new 'republic' they are building," Menes spat the word republic as if it were a disgusting bug lodged in his mouth.

"What is a republic?"

"I cannot say, exactly, except that it is one of those words that are bandied about whenever people speculate about the Great Bang Theory."

"What did you tell them?"

"The only thing I could tell them: that to swear was to take a holy oath, and that since the Megalight is the only entity that is truly holy, I could only swear allegiance to the Megalight."

"Only you would say something like that," Jawala said affectionately to the man he had known as father.

"What did they say when you told them that?"

"There was nothing they could say, so they struck me repeatedly. When they realized that force would avail them nothing, they tried still another approach. They asked if I believed that Nagap- NAGAP of all people, was the only begotten son of the Megalight!"

Jawala could scarcely believe his ears: "They asked you WHAT? I do not know if I want to hear your reply."

"As you know, I am not one given to frivolity or bouts of uninstigated laughter."

"Nooooo," Jawala thought sarcastically, though he said nothing.

"Well, when they asked me that, I had no alternative other than to burst into the most raucous laughter."

"How did they react?"

"They became enraged and struck me again."

"Describe these men to me!" Jawala screamed, the veins in his neck straining against this skin.

"No, my son. I know what is in your heart, and I love you for it, even though I know it is wrong. When you heard me groaning, it was not because of what they did to me, it was because of what I did to them. They acted out of fear and ignorance. I knew better, and yet .."

"What did you do?"

"I am sorry. I spent all of my life teaching restraint; self-control. But when they began striking me again, even though their blows did not hurt me, since I allowed the pain to pass through me ..."

"What did you do?" Jawala asked more insistently this time.

"I lost control," Menes answered remorsefully, "and sent worms into their brains."

"WORMS? How did you ... You never taught me how to send

worms into people's brains!"

"It is not something I wanted you to know. In retrospect, it is something that I wish I had not known. I behaved as badly as they. I could easily have dismissed them without taking such a drastic measure."

"Worms? What kind of worms? Were these real live worms?" Jawala asked incredulously.

"They were very real. Not in the physical sense that flesh is real; but as real as fear, jealousy or envy. I would say that they were quite real. And I am afraid that my visitors would agree."

"What happened next?"

"Well, there were five of them. They were taking turns beating me. I only got the worms into the heads of the three who were closest to me. The other two ran out before I got them. I could have sent the worms after them, but by then I had come to my senses. All of them ran screaming into the night. I was going to remove the worms, but I have been so exhausted, I have not had the energy. Perhaps, tomorrow I will retrieve the worms.

"But enough of this sordid affair for now. There will be plenty of time for me to share all the information I have for you. Have you news for me?"

Jawala told him about his son, and Menes assured him that the physical problems were nothing more than opportunities to build the child's character. Godanza had told him the same thing, but when they words came from Menes, they carried an air of reassurance that no one else could duplicate.

Then Jawala wanted to know how Menes and the others had been able to maintain their Megalight connections while everyone else's apparently had been severed.

"There is something in the water. That is why I directed you away from the pump earlier. While I was away, someone--I am sure it was Nagap and his cohorts--polluted the water with something. I would also guess that that something would have to be forbidden fruit, for that is the only substance I can think of which could have this sort of effect. Salikma and I returned at about the same time, and we noticed that everyone, even Otumba, was acting a bit strangely.

"My spirit warned me to sip the water very carefully in order to test it. The water produced a bizarre feeling of self-containment, as if my life mattered only to me, and the lives of others mattered only to them. Had I not just completed a fast, I might not have been able to detect the sensation, because it was extremely subtle. Do you remember how I often used to tell you that a person connected to the Megalight resembles a hollow tube through which the power and the will of the Megalight flows?"

"Many times."

"And that negative thoughts and doubts form layers inside the tube that can choke the flow of the Megalight and cause the person to be self contained?"

"Yes."

"Well, my encounter with the water was like having a thin layer painted inside my tube. Perhaps the strangest aspect of the experience was that I found myself trying to dictate what had happened, rather than allowing the truth to flow naturally from within. I realized then that everyone was in danger.

"Otumba and the others you encountered were the only people whose Megalight connections were not so far gone that they could still be restored to a state of good health. The others reacted with hostility when we tried to warn them, almost like they knew we were telling the truth but did not want it spoken."

"Come, my father, you have talked enough. It is time that you rested. We must prepare to leave this place as early tomorrow as possible."

21

"You cannot have him. He is mine!" the woman screamed passionately. She was beautiful, young, and naked.

"You lie! Nagap is mine!" another similarly attired and equally attractive retorted.

Soon the girls were shoving, pushing, and clawing each other.

"You both lie. Nagap belongs to me!" a third beauty cried as she joined the fray.

The fracas grew as new girls materialized-each more voluptuous, more beautiful and more intense than the previous one- and entered the fight. One girl's strong voice rose above the cacophony of the struggle:

"There is no need to fight. Nagap is more than a mere man. He is a god! We can share him. Come, let us satisfy ourselves with his touch."

The battle ceased abruptly. They turned from each other and converged into a living, flying carpet. A beehive. They swarmed about Nagap and descended upon him, smothering him in a sea of flesh.

"My Lord," the proclamation interrupted his reverie and brought reality thundering in upon him, "your servant, Konstine, awaits your pleasure," the young man announced stiffly.

"Have him wait for a moment until I send for him. Now, leave me," Nagap growled, irritated at the interruption.

Safely alone, Nagap reached for his sack of happy powder. He had found that by mixing the powdered forbidden fruit with finely ground pollen from certain plants, and then inhaling the mixture, he was able to achieve an indescribable state of euphoria. The powder vanquished any nagging doubts or worries, and solidified his claim of divinity.

On this particular morning, however, there were no doubts to banish. He had awakened with a sense of great anticipation. This time, the happy powder was used to enhance the enjoyment he knew was coming. Konstine had something for him to see that he hoped would elevate his leadership to a status of absoluteness.

After Rollof and Ondorf, there was no assistant about whom he felt better than Konstine. Thanks to his trusty pamphlet, he knew that the people had to be divided to be conquered, and united to be governed. As Nagap's VOCA- Vicar Of Church Affairs-Konstine had provided the people with a common, unifying fear.

His mind floating on a cloud of happy powder, Nagap decided not to return to the bevy of sensuous girls, and instead pondered his recruitment of Konstine. He had already had someone else in mind for the position when he happened to overhear Konstine berating a group of cowering men.

"You are all so intent on trying to be happy that you do not have the will to suffer in the name of the Megalight. You feel that you are blameless because maybe you have not sinned in the last five minutes. Perhaps, you have not sinned this entire day, though I seriously doubt that. But even if you have not sinned yet, the day is not over. And tomorrow you will arise and probably sin twice as fast to make up for today! You are lewd and weak. You do not desire a woman for purposes of procreation. You desire a woman for the sordid pleasures of the flesh. You let them tempt you with their soft flesh and their round curves."

Nagap enjoyed the way Konstine became frenzied, his arms waving frantically and spittle flying from his mouth, when he spoke of sexual transgressions.

"I have watched you watching the women of the village," Konstine continued zealously. "Your thoughts are not pure. You lust. You will never know salvation until you admit that you are evil, that you were born evil, and that only through the saving grace of the Megalight can you ever be saved! Repent your evil ways, my brothers! Repent your evil ways, my brothers! Repent your ..."

"Excuse me."

"Not now. Can't you see I ... Wait! You are the man whose face appears on the coins! Forgive me. Of course, I have time to talk to you." Konstine turned his back to his audience without a second glance.

"There is much that I would share with you. I observed you making that fine speech. Rarely have I heard a man speak with such courage, such conviction. I am an excellent judge of character, and it took me no time whatsoever to see that you are a born leader. You spoke the truth. But you only scratched the surface. I have the *real* truth. You will understand this, when you discover who I really am. Modesty does not permit me to tell you directly, but my assistants will be more than happy to explain who I am to you, for I am not an ordinary man. But then, you know that no ordinary man's face would appear on the coins.

"If you are willing to find out about me, and to work with me, I will make you one of the richest, most powerful men to ever walk the face of Zarkon. These people who bother to pray, pray incorrectly because they are strangers to the truth. I will give you that truth to pass along to them. I will establish you in such a way that you will be able to bring salvation, not just to a few insignificant men gathered here and there, but to everyone; even if you have to kick it into their teeth, which is a distinct possibility. Power. Wealth. Influence. I offer you all of this, and much more ... to be used for the glory of the Megalight, of course. In return, I ask nothing except that you be loyal to me and that you obey me. I will kill any man who dares to betray me.

"I have no desire for a hasty reply. Go. Think on what I have told you. There are two distinguished men in the village. They are called Rollof and Ondorf. Ask either of these gentlemen of me, and they will tell you what you must know. I will spend much of tomorrow in public places. Come and find me and give me your answer then."

The next day when Konstine finally caught sight of Nagap he raced to him, fell upon one knee, and kissed his hand.

"My lord, you do me honor to let me work with you. I shall do anything that you would ask of me."

In the five full cycles of seasons that had elapsed since then, Konstine had honored his pledge. He had worked tirelessly recruiting new assistants, implementing religious law, and, most importantly, promoting Nagap. He was just bright enough to be useful without being threatening. In fact, it was Konstine who initiated the idea behind the invention Nagap was to observe this day. It was called an ARI for Automatic Repentance Inducer.

When summoned, Konstine came for Nagap and led him to the small reviewing stand that had been built for his pleasure. He assured Nagap that the Holy Mother would also be present. As they climbed the stairs, Konstine explained the procedure. Chuka was already seated.

The ARI was a large tub, about five-feet deep and two yards

across. Above the tub was a seat, actually a plank, suspended by a wench. The tub was filled with water. Two hooded BORE men- the special assistants Nagap and Konstine had recruited formed a secret police type of unit called the Brigade Of Religious Enforcement- manned the winch controls on either side. Other brigade members glowered over the defendants who huddled before the tub. The rest of the villagers gathered as spectators beyond the defendants. Konstine, after genuflecting before Chuka, cleared his throat, called for quiet, then cleared his throat again. He surveyed the crowd, then cleared his throat yet another time.

When he had depleted his store of preliminary gestures, Konstine addressed the gathering.

"Neighbors. We are gathered here on this solemn occasion to witness, for the first time, the implementation of justice that has been so sorely needed. You see before you," he motioned to the defendants," your neighbors who have transgressed against the Republic and against the Deity. They have sinned. It is only proper that we should chastise them, that we should cleanse them, lest we too should be contaminated by their sinfulness.

"We would not have known about many of these transgressions, had it not been for the diligent vigilance of you good people. It is your solemn obligation, and it is your solemn duty to mind not only that your own lives are free of sin, but also that your neighbors live without the taint of sin. If you catch your neighbor transgressing against our holy laws, you must report him, or run the risk of being accused of withholding official information. When you turn the offender in to us, if he is found guilty, a portion of his goods will be confiscated; and a part of those confiscated goods will be awarded to the person who turned the guilty party in to us. This is the only way to ensure that we will all live righteously. That is why this holy court has been established: to see to it that we walk in the path of righteousness. To ensure that we live as purely as possible. To see to it tha ..."

Nagap tugged at Konstine's robe.

"Let us proceed."

Konstine read the first name from the list. It was a man who had taught Nagap how to hunt for berries when he was a child. The man's eyes pleaded with Nagap for a sign of recognition.

Nagap ignored him.

"You were observed praying out loud, calling on the Deity by name. It is further alleged that you prayed in your own name, without reference to our Savior, Nagap. How do you plead?"

"I do not understand," the man answered meekly.

"Ignorance of the law is no excuse. The Deity demands results, not excuses. In the name of His Holiness, Nagap, and the Holy Mother and by the power of this holy court, I do hereby confiscate one-fifth of all your worldly possessions and sentence you to as many visits to the automatic repentance inducer (Konstine would *never* abbreviate the name during an official ceremony) as will be required to restore your soul to a state of good health."

Two burly brigade members grabbed the hapless man and tied him to the plank over the tub.

"Now!" Konstine commanded.

The man was dunked into the tub and kept submerged for several seconds until Konstine ordered that he be raised from the water.

"Do you repent your sins?"

The man sputtered, gasping for air. Before he could speak, Konstine ordered him back into the water.

While a few of the spectators became fearful- one woman gasped, a man covered his eyes- that what was happening to this man could also happen to them, most of them cheered, waving their arms, indicating that the man should be dunked again. The poor man could not be dunked often enough or long enough to satisfy his neighbors and *friends*.

Again the man was pulled from the water, and again he was dunked before he had a chance to answer Konstine. After the third dunking, Konstine hesitated long enough for the man to shout his repentance. He was released.

Konstine called the names of the next two defendants together, this time a man and his wife.

"You have been charged with engaging in deviant sexual behavior."

Nagap's eyes widened. He bolted upright un his seat.

Chuka's hard glance settled him a bit before he could ask, "Tell me, how did these charges come to be placed?"

"A neighbor happened to be passing by the defendant's being space when he heard strange sounds coming from within. He did his duty and summoned a brigade member. The brigade member investigated."

"What kind of investigation did the brigade member conduct?"

"He removed a portion of their sunhole cover. He found them engaged in the most lewd and sinful behavior."

"Can you, ahem, be more specific? This is a most serious matter, and I must know all of the available details."

"I could not agree with you more, Messiah. That is why I instructed the brigade member to tell me every detail he could remember, and his memory was remarkable."

Konstine leaned closer to Nagap and gleefully whispered the intimate details of the couple's activities.

"Ahem, you may proceed," Nagap ordered sounding as authoritative as possible, considering that his voice cracked.

"How do you plead?"

Having witnessed the fate of their predecessor, the couple pleaded guilty and begged for mercy.

"Good servants. We find no pleasure in meting out punishment to the citizenry. We do what we must for the benefit of your souls, just as a parent takes no delight in punishing a child. But the parent knows what is best for the child even when the child does not understand."

"But what we did, we did in the privacy of our own being space!" the wife cried in terror.

"Silence! Do you not think that the Deity can see within the confines of your being space? If we servants of the Deity can uncover your transgression, then surely the Deity must know of it also. You have displayed a repentant spirit. Or maybe it was merely a frightened spirit? We wish to be merciful, but the gravity of your crime dictates that the Deity will not be appeased unless some form of punishment is administered.

"Therefore, in the name of Nagap, and by the power vested in me by this holy court, I do hereby sentence you to five visits to the Automatic Repentance Inducer and the confiscation of one third of all your worldly possessions. If you truly repent and return to the way of righteousness, the Deity will provide ways for you to gain greater wealth in the future than you have ever had."

Despite his satisfaction with the proceedings, or perhaps because of it, Nagap found himself wandering at one point:

"I meant no harm!" Jawala pleaded, sputtering, his lungs filled with water.

"You have been found in transgression. You should have given a thought to your actions before now. Do you repent?

Jawala thunked back into the water before he could reply.

"*Forgive me. PLEASE forgive me. You are the true Chosen One. Forgive me and I will forever serve you!" Jawala's words came haltingly as he gasped for air. Though he was drenched, his eyes begged sincerely. His repentance was real.*

The brigade members were about to dunk Jawala yet another time, when Nagap raised his arm to stop them. Rapidly, he descended the reviewing platform and, with his own holy hands, untied the quivering Jawala. Jawala collapsed at his feet and swore his undying loyalty.

"Release them!" Konstine's voice cut into Nagap's consciousness.

The procession of defendants continued throughout the better part of the day. The accusations ran the gamut from suggestive walking (two dunks) to lewd leering (also two dunks). No one was charged with lying, stealing or cheating, and no one was found innocent.

When the last defendant had been dunked, Nagap turned to Chuka.

"Are you pleased, Holy Mother?"

"I am pleased, my son. But have a care that your zeal for details in sexual matters does not lead the people to the wrong conclusions."

"Chuka, I ..."

"I am your mother. I formed your personality and your mind while you were still in my womb. I still know you better than you know yourself. My criticism was not intended harshly, only as an observation to help."

"I still do not know ..."

"I would not expect you to admit anything. If you are to be a supreme ruler, you must never acknowledge fault, even to me. But I do expect you to heed my counsel. Enough of this. I must bid you farewell for a while. I have matters to which I must attend. I cannot give you the full details now, but I will in the very near future."

"When will I see you again?"

"I am not sure. I can only say that it will be before another cycle of seasons has been completed. After all, you will be leaving here soon, yourself."

"How did you know that?" Nagap was genuinely incredulous.

"I told you, I am your mother. It has been seven cycles since you began acquiring power, and you still have brought less than one-third of the continent under your control. It is time that you expanded you territories. I know that you cannot trust anyone, save Rollof and Ondorf, with the details of your operation. Therefore, you will be leaving soon. I will see you while you are in the process of acquiring new villages."

"You are remarkable."

"A Holy Mother should be. How else could I have conceived you while estranged from my husband?"

The time came to inventory the confiscated goods. Nagap and Konstine went to the ORC, which stood for Official Repository of Confiscated goods. There was another line of people waiting for them at a table set up in front of the ORC.

Once Nagap and Konstine had situated themselves at the table, another set of quite different proceedings began.

"Name?" Konstine asked the first person in line. When the man answered, Konstine checked his name against a list.

"Oh yes. You were the one who told us about the Obusi couple. Let us see here, we confiscated several livestock animals, chickens, and twelve and three-quarter Nagapines. Sign here for your portion of the goods and follow this gentleman," he pointed to a brigade member, "to receive your reward."

The man signed the scroll quickly and followed the brigade member. Three months later he would return, but as a defendant, and have almost half his possessions confiscated.

At the end of the reward session, the totals were taken for the net profit of the church/republic. They had increased their holdings by twelve cows, sixteen horses, sixty-four chickens, two-hundred acres of land, one hundred and fifty- four Nagapines, and most important, eighteen quiphars. They would need speedy transportation to spread and maintain the new order.

When the others had left, Nagap and Konstine huddled together to make plans for the recruitment of new workers. They would need to have an ARI set up in every village they controlled.

22

The small, but burgeoning commune bustled with activity in preparing to celebrate the fifth birthday of its only child, Sombata, son of Jawala and Kalimba. There was Pianki, who, like so many of the others, had been away from his village when its water supply was polluted with the forbidden fruit. Finding himself an outcast in his own home, he left again and was drawn by the powerful, welcoming vibrations of the commune. He was accepted immediately. The commune grieved with him over the loss of his village and helped him adjust. Pianki, who loved tilling the soil, ignored his fields this day and painstakingly copied scrolls which Sombata would read when the time came.

Not all of the newer commune members had been away from their villages at the time of the water pollution. There were a precious few whose spiritual discipline had enabled them to fight through the tainted waters and escape to the commune. Of this latter group, none was more remarkable, especially to Sombata, than Shalina. Tall and big-boned, she exuded a strength that was not unlike Otumba's. Yet the most incredible thing about her was that she had only lived through twenty-three cycles of seasons, and had been able define her Megalight connection to the point where it could withstand the onslaught of the tainted waters. No matter what she was doing, she always had time to spend with Sombata except today. She rudely shooed him away while she prepared her special recipe for *galapos*, a syrup which would be spread upon their breads at Sombata's party.

Like any only child with a large, extended family, Sombata had grown accustomed to the kind of concentrated affection and attention that few children will ever know. Now today, which was supposed to be *his* day, everyone was too busy to even tolerate his presence. He longed for playmates his own age, other children to whom he would not always have to defer, as he did with the adults. At times like this, he could find only one place to be, and that was underfoot. After being told to move out of the way for what seemed to be the entire day, the tot stood defiantly in the midst of everyone, tiny fists perched on his even tinier hips, and loudly declared that all he wanted for his birthday was a way.

The activity stopped. The adults, visibly perplexed, peered at one another and at the child. "What do you mean, Dear, when you say that you want a way?" his mother asked him.

"Well, everywhere I turn, I am in somebody's way. I am in your way. I am in Daddy's way. I am in both grandaddys' way. If you give me a way of my own, then I will not be in anyone else's way, because I will be in my own way!"

The air remained still for the next several seconds as little Sombata's request began to settle in. Gradually, a single chuckle spread throughout the gathering, gaining momentum until everyone was laughing.

Kalimba set her son on her lap and kissed him. "My son, none of us really has a way of his own. There is but one way, and that is the way of the Megalight. When we bump into each other, it is because we are trying to get our own way, instead of following the way of the Megalight. The way of the Megalight is the way of harmony, like the way the high voices of the little birds blend with the deeper voices of the larger birds to make beautiful music. We have been so busy trying to make sure that everything would be nice, that we forgot that you were the reason we were doing all this in the first place. My beautiful son, you have taught us all something special today."

Once the small celebration feast had been prepared, they gathered and ate until no one could stand another morsel. There was singing, and the few young people danced, showing the different steps and variations reflective of their different origins. After the singing and dancing, they gathered around the fire to hear Menes tell a story.

Sombata loved to join the adults sitting around the fire, listening to Menes tell stories. It gave him a feeling of being grown up. While he would still get sleepy sometimes before the story was finished, he was becoming increasingly successful at fighting off the drowsiness. He was proud of his increasing ability to stay awake through an entire story, and his sense of belonging grew with each gathering.

This particular evening, Menes told a story about life before the Great Bang. In this story, the land had been taken over by a great evil. Incredible flying machines were used to kill people from the sky. The people that operated the flying machines also possessed magic lights that they used to turn all the other people into slaves.

There was one young man that the bad people could not catch. His name was Somtada. Somtada was very brave, even though he could barely use one of his hands, and he walked with a limp. When the evil people found that they could not capture Somtada, they kidnapped his girlfriend. Her name was Yavooda.

Somtada became enraged when he learned Yavooda had been taken. He polished huge slabs of metal until they shone like mirrors and whenever the bad people came around with their lights, he would use one of his mirrors to turn their lights back on them. He saved his girlfriend and restored all of the people back to their original states of mind, and everyone lived happily ever after.

"What did you think of the story?" Menes asked his grandson.

"I liked it, especially when the good guy turned the mirrors on the bad people."

"Why did you like that part?"

"'Cause it's how he won the fight."

"What energy did he use to defeat them?"

"The energy from their light rays."

"Where did that energy come from?"

"From them."

So, in other words, the hero turned the bad people's energy back on them. He did not have to use his own energy. Is that right?"

"Yep."

Menes arched an eyebrow at Sombata.

"I mean yes."

"Is there a lesson to be learned from that?"

"You should save your energy, if you can?"

"Close enough. The lesson is that whenever we face evil, we must give it every opportunity to destroy itself. As you get older, the things I am telling you tonight will become clearer."

"Yes, sir. But Grandpa, I have a question for you."

"Yes?"

"Well, in the story, there were good people and there were bad people. But you told me that all people are good. How can that be?"

Jawala and Kalimba pursed their lips and barricaded their

laughter. They stared at Menes as if to challenge him to reply.
Menes himself could not stifle a mild chuckle before he answered:
"You are quite correct, my son. There are no bad people. But there are bad decisions, and when good people make bad choices, they can act like they are bad people. Do you understand?"
"No sir. If the people are good, then why wouldn't they make good decisions?"
"Do you remember the time you were about to eat some berries and your father stopped you, because the berries were poisonous?"
"Yes."
"Well, that was an example of a good person- you- getting ready to make a bad decision: eating poisonous berries. Sometimes people make bad decisions because they do not know any better."
"But you always tell me that I will know better when I grow up. The people in the story were grown up. How come they did not know any better?"
"Life is a journey. Each of us has a path to follow, but we may choose not to follow that path. If we are going in the wrong direction, then it does not matter how long we travel, we still will not arrive at our proper destination."
"You still have not told me why good people act bad."
"That is enough for now. You are beginning to make your grandfather tired. It is time for you to go to bed," Jawala spoke.
"But I am not making grandpa tired, am I grandpa?"
"Well, if you are not making grandpa tired, you are starting to make *me* tired. I know you are stalling. I was your age once."
"Did you try to get out of going to bed when you were my age, father?"
"I am not Jawala," Menes interjected, imitating the Jawala of years gone by. "I am somebody else. Grown up."
Otumba nearly exploded with laughter.
"Was that how you used to try to get out of going to bed, Daddy? Tell me what you used to do."
"Well, I ..."
Laughter.
"Not another word. Go to bed!"
The adults remained around the fire and discussed their favorite subject: life with and without the Megalight connection.
"What will be required to return the people to a state of

harmony?" Shobogun asked.

"Nothing short of direct intervention by the Megalight, I suppose," Eloshima offered.

"But we know that the Megalight does not operate in that fashion," Jawala added.

"The problem is," Salikma joined in, "that once an individual has been disconnected, he will fight to maintain his state of disconnectedness. The blessings of the Megalight become abstract while his fear remains very real, very concrete. To borrow from Menes' earlier talk, he begins to make decisions based on protecting his illness, rather than attempting to gain any semblance of harmony."

"You are quite right," Menes added. "We have been so accustomed to growing and being growth oriented, that we have never really had to analyze that process the way we do now. No one can grow unless he has the courage to be wrong. When we are already correct there is no need or room for growth. As long as we are fed by the Megalight, we have the resources to allow ourselves to be wrong, so that we can be corrected. But if there is no Megalight connection, then the individual may not have the strength to seek out his faults and to accept them so that they might be improved upon. I am afraid that we have taken for granted the nurturing that has allowed us to accept ourselves to the extent that we have been able to change ourselves and grow."

"The entire community must understand that there is a divine imperative to grow that takes precedence over any personal fears," Salikma said.

"Which brings us right back to the original problem: How can change be affected when an entire community is comprised of individuals who are paralyzed by fear and pain?" asked Shobogun.

Godanza said, "Perhaps, the process of spiritual regeneration must be a gradual one. There have been rumors that the society which we left was at one time quite barbaric. And the Great Bang theory has never been disproved. It could be that even if the source of this great malady is eliminated in our lifetimes; the results may not be completely overcome for generations to come."

"What if the people are never reconnected?"

"Then someday there really will be a Great Bang."

Silence.

Everyone, except Jawala and Menes, collected themselves to return to their respective huts.

"You knew I was going to want to talk privately with you."

"I had surmised as much," Menes answered.

"That was no ordinary story you told earlier this evening."

"I can see that not all of my efforts in training you have been in vain. You are quite correct. How could you tell?"

"There was an edge. A sense of reality, of meaning coming through as you spoke."

"The story was a combination of fiction and a dream I had. I am sure that you know that the central figure in the story was your son. He is growing magnificently. Before he has reached his eighteenth birthday, he will be cured of the maladies that affect his hand and foot. Shortly thereafter, he will be called upon to fight the evil which afflicts our planet."

"Well, we know that Nagap is behind all of this. I cannot understand why my son would be called upon to deal with Nagap, when he and I are contemporaries. I know Nagap. To a certain extent, I believe I understand him. He is not really evil, just frightened. Our planet is being ravaged right now. What sense does it make that we should wait for a little child to do something about it when I am strong and healthy right now?"

"Did you ever stop to wonder why Shobogun taught your manhood group instead of me? Or why he made you do other chores when he had the other boys doing strenuous exercises?"

"Now that you mention it, I had wondered about those things."

"You are not nearly as healthy as you think you are. You must remember that your parents died of poisoning while you were still in your mother's womb. There was considerable damage done to many of your internal organs, including your heart. Shobogun lead your manhood group so that he could make allowances for your physical limitations; allowances which, had they been made by me, would have been construed as favoritism."

"I had no idea."

"Of course not. Your role in this cosmic opera has been to survive so that you might father the child who will deal with the adversary."

"But I still have a hard time trying to understand how my son could be the only person on this entire planet with the potential to deal with this evil."

"No one said that he was the only one with the potential. He is the one whom the Megalight has chosen. The Megalight is involved in our affairs, but in subtle ways. Perhaps some of those who died mysteriously so long ago could have been potential adversaries for this evil. Why was I not chosen? Could it have been that I was born at the wrong time to combat this evil directly, but at the right time to help train the one who would? There are so many things that we may never understand. But I will tell you this, I do not believe that Nagap is solely responsible for all of this mayhem.

"Why not?"

"I believe that much of what is happening now was set in motion before Nagap was ever born. His father was quite concerned- and with good reason, I might add- about his mother, prior to Nagap's birth. Her vibrations disappeared from his consciousness on the same day that your parents died mysteriously. I will never believe that your father could have mistaken a poisonous limpin for an edible one."

"Do you think someone killed my parents?" Jawala shrieked.

"Control yourself. I merely stated that the circumstances surrounding their deaths were peculiar. Lima's death was peculiar. He was one of the finest swimmers I have ever seen. When I traveled to Zambutu and interpreted Godanza's dream, I learned of still other strange deaths that ocurred in Zambutu at the same time. It may have been a coincidence, but there was something else that I learned about the people who made their transitions at the same time."

"What was that?"

"They were all known for having exceptional Megalight connections."

"That is truly fascinating. But what do you think is Nagap's actual role in all of this?"

"I wish I could say. It is quite obvious that his role is a significant one. But he is too obvious, too visible. Whenever one is faced with a mystery as spectacular as the demise of an entire civilization, one must first discount the most obvious answers, and work backward from the least imaginable. Finally, though Nagap is one of the brightest young men to come along in quite a while, he grew up without a context in which to plot all of these devious goings on. Owning land? Using currency? Utterly foreign concepts. I am afraid that he would need considerably more help than Rollof and Ondorf can afford him.

"But there is still another matter which we must discuss. Have you given any thought to Sombata's training? He will have no group with which to go through manhood training. What about traveling? He is approaching the age of his first overnight venture. What are you going to do?"

"I have given it a great deal of thought. I do not wish to expose him to any of the villages just yet. He is still too impressionable, and I am afraid I would not be of much help in explaining what I do not understand. With Nagap still possibly looking for me, it is too dangerous for him to travel to any village with any of us. I thought I would take him for a hike, spend the night in the wilderness, and then return the next day."

"When do you think he will be ready to be exposed to village life?"

"Sixteen?"

"Too old. He will need time to digest the experience, and grow in light of it."

"How about twelve?"

"I could not have thought of a better age, myself. Now it is time that we returned to our families- while we still have them."

The next seven years found the commune growing younger, as original members passed away and younger travelers replaced them. Alikum and Finola relinquished the ghost within months of one another. While their minds had relinquished responsibility for the actions of their adult daughter, Chuka, and their grandson to the Megalight, their hearts had stubbornly held fast. Their souls, stretched taut by the struggle, would at last find peace with the Megalight.

Then Godanza, Sombata's beloved grandfather, relinquished his physical form. Sombata had been brave throughout the memorial for Finola and Alikum, but he was unprepared to deal with the loss of his grandfather.

"It is not bad that you weep now," Jawala comforted his son. "But someday, you will realize that what has happened was best for Grandpa. He had lived almost ninety eight seasons. He was tired. He had done all that could have been asked of him, and now it was time that he be granted his rest."

"But I will never see him again," Sombata sobbed.

"Not in the form that you have known him. But in a higher, more beautiful form, someday you will see him. Someday you will see his true beauty, then you will love him even more than you do now."

"When will that day come?"

"When you too, have given up the flesh. Everyone must make a transition some day, but it is not something to fear. It is not the end of life, it is a part of life. In fact, it could be said that living and dying are the same thing."

"I do not understand."

"When you want to enjoy a piece of fruit, say an apple, you enjoy the fruit by eating it. But the more you eat, the less remains, until there is nothing left. You consume the apple but the apple has not been destroyed, it has become a part of you, supplying you with nourishment and energy. Had you not eaten the apple, it would have rotted anyway. Then it would have replenished the soil. When you consume the apple it is used for the best possible purpose, the same way you consume life by living.

"Each day that we live, we come closer to our transition. We die by living, and we live by dying. But nothing is destroyed, nothing can be destroyed. We can only change forms. Now, do you understand?"

"I thought I did, until you told me that nothing could be destroyed. Now, I am completely confused."

"Bring me that small piece of twig," he pointed toward a piece of wood on the periphery of the fire, "and be careful not to burn yourself."

Sombata handed his father the burning twig.

"Will the fire destroy the twig?"

"I thought it would, but now I do not know, Father."

"Very well. Let us observe."

They sat quietly for a few minutes, then Jawala spoke.

"Is the fire destroying the wood?"

"There is nothing left but ashes."

"But ashes do remain and smoke lifts into the air. So the wood is not destroyed. It is changed into ashes and smoke. Its form has been changed so that it is no longer wood; but it has not been destroyed, only changed."

"So?"

"So if a little thing like a twig cannot be destroyed, do you think that something as magnificent as Grandpa's spirit could be destroyed?"

"I guess not."

"Grandpa is fine. The older you get, and the more understanding you acquire, the more joy you will see when someone you love has made the transition. When you weep, you weep for yourself. When you get older, you will learn to love more unselfishly.

"Thank you, Father."

During Godanza's memorial, Sombata fought through the tears and, hobbling on his one good foot, danced, sang, and basked in the love that surrounded him.

23

"What is it?" Kalimba asked sharply, pretending she did not know what the matter was. She had heard many of Jawala's conversations with Menes, and many of his subsequent discussions with Sombata.
"Our son has entered his twelfth year."
"I can count."
"Let us TRY to remain civil. This is as difficult for me as it is for you. But it is necessary. You know why I have approached you. You know what I have come to say."
"Of course I know. I have been married to you for nearly fourteen seasons. I was no idiot when you met me, and I hate to think that I have regressed into one since then. Since you know that I know what you would ask me, then you should know what my answer is without having to ask."
"I did not come to ask you anything. I have come to inform you of when he must leave," Jawala regretted the words as soon as they escaped, but he had been truthful when he said that what he was about to do was difficult for him, and he resented Kalimba's making the matter even more difficult than it already was.
"Let me see if I understand you. You have come to tell me- not ask, but tell me- that you are going to send my twelve year old son out BY HIMSELF to visit a village where no one cares about anyone else, and no one is connected to anyone else? You have come to tell me this, and you expect me to cheerfully bow to your wisdom. If I understand you correctly, then I think it is time we checked the water around here, because whatever you have been drinking has been polluted!"
She turned her back to him as if to muffle her sobs. Later, she would share Jawala's pain in sending the boy away, but for now, she saw him endangering her only son. Her baby. How could he do such a thing?
"We have both known for some time, that the boy has been chosen by the Megalight Itself, for a special destiny. We have

basked in the honor of his selection without realizing the cost involved. We have brought shame to our training, for we both know that nothing is free; every gift, every honor which the Megalight bestows, exacts a price: the greater the honor, the greater the price."

"When will he leave?" she asked dryly, her mind clinging tenaciously to visions of the infant plucked from her loins.

"Tomorrow."

She turned to face her husband. His concern drew her to him. She embraced him, squeezing him as tightly as she could, trying to wring some sort of assurance from his body. She asked him if he would mind fixing the evening meal. She knew that this scene would be repeated: her son being sent off to some dangerous place for some dangerous reason. She would need the rest of the evening to herself. She would need to be alone to prepare for her only son's departure the next day.

The commune assembled early the next day to send young Sombata on his journey. Everyone, except Jawala and Kalimba, had a bit of advice to repeat. His parents could say no more than that they loved him, and that took considerable effort. Just before he left, Menes reached within the folds of his garment and handed the boy some small metal disks.

"What is that you are giving him," Kalimba found her voice.

"It is money. He may have need of it."

Kalimba bit her lip until it bled, but she said nothing. The idea that her child might need money dumped a frost in her chest that could only be removed by his safe return.

His heart pounding with excitement, Sombata hobbled across the desert sand toward Zambutu. He would make them all proud and prove to his mother that she had been wrong to worry so much about him. After all, he was almost a man! He tried to remember all the instructions he had been given: He was not to tell anyone where he was from. He was not to give his money away to anyone unless he was absolutely sure they needed it more than he. He was to be polite and courteous. He was not to ask anyone for anything unless he intended to exchange either his money or some form of labor in return. He was not to...

His bad foot made him stop more often than he wanted. He did not realize that few boys his age could have gone any further using two perfectly matched feet. Once he became angry for having to stop and complained about the foot. But he immediately begged the Megalight's forgiveness and offered as proof of his sincerity a litany of blessings for which he was grateful.

He had not yet learned enough to walk completely on top of the sand, but he knew enough to limit his sinking. The hot sun felt good, keeping his muscles limber, until it reached its zenith. He had not gone far enough in his manhood studies to allow the heat to pass completely through him, so he had to look for shade. When he found a shrub he rested and let his mind wander to what life in a big village must be like.

He had been told not to enter the village at night, so when it began to get dark, he built a fire and roasted some of the provisions Kalimba had packed for him. He would only be gone a few days, but she had packed enough nonperishables to last a month.

The sights, sounds and smells of Zambutu assaulted him the moment he entered the village. It seemed that everyone was busy doing something or going somewhere. Everyone seemed to be hurrying. He wondered if they hurried through their meditations. Was it possible to hurry through meditations? He stopped to watch a man putting the final ornaments on a strange wooden box.

"What you lookin' at, kid? Never seen a coffin before?"

"Coffin?"

"Yeah, a coffin. We're having a funeral today, and I'm getting ten Nagapines for this wooden box. You might be able to make some money too, if you want to scrounge up some flowers and see if you can sell them to the mourners."

"Funeral? Mourners?"

"Why do you keep repeating everything I say? Where are you from? Where are your parents?"

"I am from .. uh .. the North. My parents said that it is the custom for a young man to make a solo journey once he reaches his twelfth year, and I am now in my twelfth year."

"Well, you must be from pretty far up north. We stopped sending young men on solo journeys around here years ago. It has become too dangerous."

"My father and grandfather prepared me well for dealing with large predator animals."

"Who was talking about animals? I was talking about people. I am beginning to wonder if you are not from another time, as well as another place. Someone might try to take your money. You could get caught breaking one of the religious laws we have. There are so many of them that it is almost impossible not to break one, unless you want to just sit around all day and hold your breath. And who knows, you might get into trouble for doing that!"

"Well, I am not afraid," Sombata replied bravely. "The Megalight will watch over me."

"Son, don't ever let anyone around here hear you use that word again."

"What word?"

"The mmm...mmm...mmm.."

"The Megalight?"

"Yeah, that word. Don't ever say that word again. You could get into a lot of trouble."

"But why not? I do not understand. My parents always taught me that they were my Zarkonian parents, but that the Megalight was my real father and mother. They said I came from the Megalight, and that the Megalight just used them to bring me here. You are saying that I cannot utter the name of my real parent?"

"Boy, I don't know where you are from, but there hasn't been talk like that around here for many seasons. It is considered a sin to say that word. It is a sin for you to refer to yourself as a son of the Megalight. Around here, the Megalight has but one true son, and that is His Holiness, Nagap."

"Well, if people cannot say the name, mmm, then how do they pray?"

"There has been very little of that going on around here anyway, unless someone gets in some sort of trouble and needs something. But when they do pray, they do so in the name of Nagap, or the Blessed Mother."

"Is Nagap's name more powerful than yours?"

"That is another thing you must stop doing, asking so many questions. You could get us both branded as heretics or infidels or something if someone overheard us. Don't say another word about religion. As it is, I could have gotten a reward for turning you in for what you have already said. I'm getting soft, I guess, because I'm not going to do that. But don't push your luck."

Sombata was astounded. Never before had he heard anyone talk without making any sense whatsoever. Not only did the things the man said make no sense, but the *way* he said them made no sense either. He had expected life in the big village to be different, but not *this* different. He wanted to tell the man that his father had grown up with Nagap and that is grandfather had known both of Nagap's parents but decided against it. He wanted to ask the man if he had ever spelled Nagap backwards. Instead he just gawked at the strange man.

"Anyway, I can't afford to stand around here yapping with you all day. The funeral will be held in a couple of hours and I have to have this coffin ready."

"You never did tell me what a funeral was."

The man looked utterly exasperated. "It's a ceremony we hold when a person dies."

"Oh good! I have seen those before."

The next look the man gave Sombata could only be interpreted as an invitation to leave.

He stumbled away from the coffin maker and wandered into the area of an old woman who was sitting on a box, selling fruit. Although he already had more than enough provisions to last until he could get back home, he was curious about *buying* something.

When the old woman spotted him observing her, she motioned him closer.

"A growing lad like you must need a lot of fruit to stay big and strong. What's the matter with your hand and foot?"

"I was born this way."

"Somebody probably put a curse on you. But no matter, the money of the cursed spends just as well as the money of the blessed. Come, let me sell you some of this delicious fruit."

"Any two pieces for just one-quarter Nagapine. Give me your money, Dearie, and I'll select two juicy pieces for you. I'll give you my very best fruit."

Out of the corner of his eye, he could see three boys, about his age, watching him as he pulled the quarter-Nagapine from his pouch.

Once the toothless woman had the coin in her fist she picked two pieces of rotten fruit and tried to give them to Sombata.

Sombata looked at the woman as she extended her hands with the fruit. It was not a defiant look, so much as one of disbelief and pity.

"Go on, take 'em. A few bruises never hurt good fruit. Helps keep you regular."

Sombata continued to stare at the woman. His gaze began to penetrate, as if she were transparent.

"All right. All right. Take these instead." She reached below her booth and brought out two almost perfect apples. "I'll even throw in an extra piece just because I am so nice!"

Sombata just stared at the woman. He shook his head sadly and turned to leave.

"I'm sorry kid. I was just trying to make a living. I don't want your money. I don't need your money!" she cried as she flung the coin at his back.

As he bent over to retrieve the coin, the boys he had noticed earlier approached him.

"Hey, where are you from? You got any more money?" the largest of the boys asked him.

Sombata surveyed the boys who had surrounded him. They were about his age and size, except for the larger boy who spoke; but there was an immaturity, an arrogance, about them he found disturbing. They were smiling, but their smiles held more menace than warmth.

"I am called Sombata. I am from the North. And yes, I do have a few more coins," he answered stiffly.

"Do you want to play with us?"

"I am in my twelfth year. I have put the childlike things of my youth behind me. However, I do enjoy an occasional good game of Sklomb."

"Sklomb?"

"Yes, the game where someone thinks of a number and the others try to guess it. It is an excellent way to improve one's Meg... mmmm ... connection."

"Connection? What is this fellow talking about?"

"Excuse me, but shouldn't that be `About what is this fellow talking'?" the ubiquitous Menes influence loosed itself.

The boys peered quizzically at Sombata and each other.

They were so utterly undeveloped that they didn't even notice when Sombata probed them. His findings were repulsive: he could find no reflection of himself. Although they were all the same chronological age, he had nothing in common with them. They were almost completely lacking in discipline, compassion and seriousness; and their Megalight connections were so small that they were practically nonexistent.

"I have enjoyed talking with you. But I must leave you now. There are many things I must see before I depart."

"He sure talks funny," one of the boys observed.

"Wait a minute," the largest boy, whom Sombata had determined was their leader spoke. "Give us some money, and you can go anywhere you want." The boys tightened their circle around Sombata.

"What need have you of my money?"

"I need it to keep from breaking your face," the biggest boy exclaimed as he threw a punch at Sombata.

With his good right hand, Sombata caught the boy's fist in midair. The boy pushed and strained, as Sombata effortlessly held his fist motionless.

The other two boys gawked in disbelief at the sight of their leader- the toughest boy they knew- being bested so easily. Sombata was not even breathing hard.

"Don't just stand there. Jump him!"

The boys' reflexes to obey malfunctioned. They had done what he had told them to do because he appeared invincible. Here this kid grabs his best punch in midair-with one hand- and holds it there! The whole idea had been that the fight was supposed to be unfair. What they could not have known, of course, was that Sombata's rigorous spiritual and physical training had made the fight truly unfair- for their friend.

The bigger boy was about to yell a threat at his cohorts when Sombata squeezed his fist, forcing it open. Sombata then interwove his fingers with the boy's fingers and, clasping the back of his hand, pushed back on top of his hand, forcing it back on his wrist, and the boy onto his knees in pain.

Sombata perceived that the other two boys were weighing their fear of the bully on the ground with their fear of him. He looked deeply into their eyes.

"You do not have to join the evil this boy has tried to commit. You are free to walk away from this. I will not harm you, and he will not harm you, unless you give him the power to harm you. Walk away now, and try to learn something from what you have just witnessed.

Sombata's voice resounded with authority their fathers' had never mustered. They ran. When they had gone, he released his grip on the boy who, by now, writhed in the dirt.

"I am sorry if I used more force than was necessary. But it was important that you understand the pain which you intended for another. Perhaps, now we can be friends?" Sombata helped the boy to his feet.

"Friends! You are demon possessed! I'm turning you in. I'll get a lot of money for you. You, Demon!" The boy shouted his reply only after he was a safe distance from Sombata. He ran in search of a brigade member.

"Come here, quickly!" It was the coffin maker. "I saw what just happened. I knew it would not take you very long to get into trouble, that's why I have been watching you. Now, come quickly and hide."

"Hide? For what?"

"Why must you answer everything I say to you with a question? Didn't you just hear that boy say that he was going to get the authorities after you? Didn't you just hear him call you a demon? Don't you know what that means?"

"It means that he had a great deal of trouble accepting a lesson that he should have been taught long ago."

"Well, that may be true. But if the authorities catch you, you will be the one in serious trouble."

"For defending myself? I used my power in moderation. Why can't I just tell them what happened? Surely they can discern the truth."

"In the first place, you have exhibited more strength than a kid your age and size is supposed to have. In the second place, from the way you talk, you'll be sure to give the wrong answer to every question they ask you. And in the third place, you are not from around here. They will never take your word over that of a local boy, even if the local boy IS a rotten kid."

"Do you mean to tell me," Sombata asked incredulously, "that there is so little regard for truth here that the other boy will be believed and I will not, simply because he was reared in this area, and I was not?"

"It took you awhile, kid, but you are beginning to catch on. Now hide."

Sombata was scarcely out of view when the boy returned, followed by two members of the Zambutu brigade. They approached the old woman at the fruit stand. The coffin maker could see her pointing in his direction.

"Boy, if you know what is good for you, you will remain absolutely quiet. They're on their way here, and I have no intentions of spending the rest of my life in an automatic repentance inducer!" he whispered frantically.

"Blessings on you, good leaders," the coffin make gushed. "Is there something I can do for you on this fine day? I do hope that you have no need for my services. However, if they are required, they will be gladly rendered. And of course at special discounts, for the men who keep our village free from criminals, heretics, infidels and other vermin."

"Quiet!" the burly, bearded brigade member commanded. "We are looking for a youth- a strange looking youth with a withered hand and a deformed foot. We understand that he was around here just a few moments ago."

"Indeed he was. He was a strange one. A troublemaker if I ever saw one. A blasphemer, he was. I sent him away from my stand the instant he opened his mouth and started blaspheming."

"Which way did he go?"

The coffin maker pointed back toward the desert.

"Mind if we look around?" the guard asked rhetorically as he made his way around the stand. "What's in here?" he asked, pointing to the recently completed coffin.

"Nothing yet. It is to be used in the funeral today. Please feel free to look inside. But I must warn you that the coloring has not yet dried. You could get some on your pretty uniform, and it is almost impossible to remove from cloth."

"In that case, I'll take your word for it. But you do know the penalty for failing to come forward with information when we are looking for a suspect, don't you?"

"Oh, indeed I do. Indeed, I do."

The coffin maker banged meaninglessly on a piece of wood until the men had disappeared.

"Pssssst. You can come out now. Most boys your age would have been horrified of hiding inside a coffin. But you are nothing like most boys your age."

"And you are not like the other people here. I sense that, although it has been damaged and is in need of repair, you still retain a powerful connection. My name is Sombata and I am eternally grateful for your assistance."

The coffin maker simply stared at Sombata. He saw a twelve year old boy, but he heard a middle- aged man who displayed manners and a civility that had long been rendered obsolete in the current society.

"I am called Wabatani, and I am honored to make your acquaintance, I think. Stay here in my booth until I have delivered this coffin. It is not safe for you to wander around here. When I return, there is much that I would discuss with you." Before his words faded, Wabatani quizzed himself about the structure he had chosen for his last sentence.

When Wabatani returned, he brought with him a robe big enough to hide Sombata's telltale foot and hand. He wanted to know about the place where Sombata lived, and the people who reared him. There was something about this child that stirred vague, pleasant memories, feelings that had lacked expression for so long that they had receded to the twilight between existence and oblivion.

Wabatani had already proven his trustworthiness, so Sombata told him as much as he could about life in the commune.

"That explains it. You act as if you are from another time, because you are from another time."

"Yes, and you can return to that time with me. Would you not prefer the company of a small but loving community, where everyone cares for everyone else, to this?"

"Well, it is a thought, but ..."

"Have you a mate?"

"Are you sure you aren't twelve going on sixty?"

"It would be almost impossible to find a mate in this village who would not put her needs before yours- which is what I have been told a mate must do. I have a friend in our commune- she is big and strong, like you. But she is also very warm and loving, as you are. Her name is Shalina. If you did nothing but meet my friend, it would justify a visit to our community. Won't you come with me?"

"Well, even if I did decide to go with you- and I haven't said that I would, although I might- we would not be able to leave safely until after dark. Anyway, the funeral procession will be coming this way shortly. After that, I can get my money. By this evening, I will be able to let you know, one way or another."

"Why are you still concerned about money? If you decide to go with me, you will not need money."

"Even if I decide to go with you, and everything works out beautifully, there still may come a time when you or I will have to venture into a village. If that time comes, then it would be prudent to be prepared by having money."

"You are right. There is still much that I must learn."

"I was beginning to wonder. Here comes the funeral procession."

Sombata leaped into the air with a joyful yell. The mourners cut their eyes sharply at him with hatred. Some gasped. When he noticed the somber mood of the procession, he became so confused and embarrassed that he looked around for a place to hide. He crawled back behind Wabatani's stand. He did not have to be told to stay there. Nor did he have to be told to be quiet.

When he returned from collecting his money, Wabatani confronted Sombata.

"Do you want to tell me why you decided to act a fool when the funeral procession came by?"

"I was not acting a fool. Everyone else was acting like the person who gave up the flesh had been a fool."

"That was one of the most respected members of our community."

"I guess this is just more proof that what everyone was trying to tell me was correct."

"What are you talking about?"

"I know what I am talking about, but not well enough to explain all of these things to you. When you come to my dwelling place, there will be people there who will be able to explain things to you better than I can. My grandpa Menes, the mashari, can explain almost everything."

"You still have someone who goes by the title of mashari?"

"My grandpa."

"I have got to see this commune! My mind keeps telling me that you and the people of your commune are crazy, but something inside of me almost understands. I will be honest with you; I have been living here for many seasons now, and I still do not feel that I belong here either. I will go with you. I have to. If I leave you alone for more than the time it takes a quiphar to blink, I am afraid of what the consequences might be."

They left the village as soon as night fell, and Wabatani did not even bother to look back at the home he was leaving. As the temperature dropped, it became obvious that Wabatani knew less than Sombata about letting the cold pass through him. They built a fire and bedded down for a short night's sleep. As the next day turned to dusk, they were able to make out the faint outlines of the commune.

"By the time we get there, it will be dark. Will it be safe to enter then?"

"Why does that concern you?"

"Well, your people might mistake us for others they might not want around. Or they might think we are large animals and harm us before they recognize us."

"My people - *our* people do not act that way. They have no wish to harm anyone or anything. We only eat meat on special occasions, so they are not hunting, and they do not fear the animals, or any travelers. All are welcome."

"Somehow, I had a feeling you were going to say something like that."

By the light of the evening fire, they were soon able to make out individual people. Sombata and his mother eyed each other. Actually, they perceived each other's vibrations before they could see faces.

Seeing Kalimba lifted an enormous weight from young Sombata's shoulders. The strain of having been surrounded by so many negative vibrations, of dealing with a culture that made no sense, of feeling isolated save for Wabatani- these emotions which had forced him to dig within himself and produce a much older, wiser person than he naturally was- they all came crashing in on Sombata at the sight of his mother and he was gloriously transformed back into a twelve year old, with a twelve year old's needs. And right now the biggest need he felt was to hug and be hugged by his mother; so much so that he wasn't the slightest bit embarrassed or annoyed when she screamed, "My Baby, My Baby."

Kalimba's outburst alerted the others, and soon they were all gathered about the returning young hero. Their warm vibrations provided a salve for his battered psyche. Sombata motioned to Wabatani who had hesitated just outside the commune. "This is my friend, Wabatani. He saved me when there was danger."

Despite Jawala's struggle to ignore Kalimba's daggers when the word *danger* came out, she knew they had hit their mark. He turned to Wabatani.

"You are welcome here," and to the startled Wabatani's amazement, embraced him. Wabatani's amazement was compounded when the others followed Jawala's action.

The food was quickly prepared amidst the din of greetings, questions, and praises for the Megalight.

After hugging and kissing his grandson, and before offering his questions and observations, Menes watched with amusement as the boy tried to comply with the onslaught of conflicting messages.

"Eat your food, you must be famished," gushed Kalimba.

"Tell us more," Shalina added.

"Were you frightened?" Shobogun questoned.

Yet even Menes was captured by the compelling story which

Sombata wove of the strange place Zambutu had become.

The flurry of interruptions and questions did not bother Sombata. He basked in the attention he received. As Sombata interacted with the others, Wabatani tried to piece together what it was that made these people so completely different from those he had left in Zambutu. Their manner of speaking, the questions they raised, and the horrified sadness which they expressed over events which Wabatani had long accepted as parts of normal, everyday life, all insisted that these people were really quite weird. Yet beneath the weirdness, the peculiarities-it was obvious that they really did not understand ownership-there was a comforting, yet unsettling familiarity, like returning to the home where one lived as a toddler.

"Sombata, you have made us all very proud of you. Not only have you survived a solo visit to a strange and hostile environment, but you have also returned with a fine new friend.

"I sense the flow of the Megalight in you, and I also sense that it is yearning for expression," Menes continued, turning to Wabatani. "You possess great love and great power. Unfortunately, your virtues have suffered due to the unyielding demands for conformity in the environment which you left. There is much that we would share with you, learn from you. You would honor us if you would consider staying here."

"I agree," Shalina added, a bit too enthusiastically.

Wabatani was dumfounded. This elderly man whom he had just met had seen right through him, and spoken with a candor that Wabatani had thought reserved for a father and son. Had anyone in Zambutu spoken so candidly to him, particularly without the benefit of a long relationship; he would have been angry, embarrassed, or both. Yet the tone of the man, the warmth with which he spoke, removed any threat from his words and left Wabatani with a feeling of warmth and belonging which he had not felt in a long, long time. Also, Shalina's interjection did not hurt matters either. If indeed, this was the woman whom Sombata had been thinking of as a possible mate, then the boy was even more insightful than he had any right to be.

"Tell me, did you grow up in Zambutu?" Menes continued.

"No. I was one of the wilderness people from up north. We lived mostly in isolation in the mountains and forests. We visited different villages to establish and maintain ties and to keep abreast of whatever the latest developments might be, but we pretty much stayed to ourselves."

"That explains your size. The few wilderness people I have met have been rather large people. I was about to ask you a few more questions when I realized that I have allowed my curiosity to outweigh my manners. If my inquiries make you the least bit uncomfortable, please say so. I would not be surprised if life in Zambutu would enhance one's need for privacy, and we certainly do not wish to invade yours."

These people are sure polite! Wabatani thought to himself, trying to recall a distant time when such manners were the norm. "No, by all means, please ask what you will. It has been many season since anyone has taken such an interest in me," he answered truthfully.

"How is it that you came to live in Zambutu? It is obvious that you do not resemble the people there."

"I left my people in search of adventure, knowledge, and, if possible, a mate; although not necessarily in that order. I wandered to the village of Zambutu. At first, I was repulsed by the way the people acted there, so I traveled on to the other villages of the cluster: Milanhi, Saroppo, all of them. Yet, everywhere I turned, I found the same thing: no one cared about anyone else. Before I knew it, I was back at Zambutu. I basically stayed there for lack of a better place to go. I had no desire to return to my people as a bachelor. Eventually, I began to blend in with the others."

"Since you have lived in Zambutu, have you eaten the same food, and drank the same water as the others?"

"Pretty much so. Although I have carried one habit with me from my days in the mountains that everyone used to say was kind of silly.

"Well, as I am sure you know, in the mountains you share the streams with a number of different large animals that use it for more than just drinking. If enough animals fertilize your drinking water, you can become fatally ill. Since we could never be sure of the water, we always boiled it before we drank any. Everyone in Zambutu told me that it wa no longer necessary to boil my drinking water, but when you have grown up doing things a certain way, it becomes difficult to change. I still boil my water."

"That's it!" Menes led a chorus in exclamation.

"That's what?"

"That explains why you are here, why you resonate with us

the way that you do. There is much that we must explain to you, and even more that we must reteach you. But here, you will have a chance to finally end the war that has been raging within you."

"What war?" Wabatani asked timidly, almost afraid of the answer.

"The war between who you have been conditioned to become, and who you were intended to be. You see, there are two major components which comprise an individual: he is the sum total of his experiences, and he is the result of his interpretation of his experiences- the unique decisions he makes based upon those experiences."

"Huh?"

"You must forgive my father," Jawala added; "he has the ability to confuse everyone."

"I will explain myself in greater detail later, without the assistance of our critic here," Menes nodded toward Jawala. "For now, let me say that if you give us a chance, I know that you will find peace here. I know that you are a bit nervous about us, despite the attraction that you feel for us. But the issue is not whether you can trust us, it is whether you can trust the spirit that has already told you that you can trust us. When you have learned to trust that spirit- that quiet voice which speaks from the very core of your being- then you will never be nervous about making decisions again."

"I must admit that I am nervous, although at the same time you have made me feel remarkably comfortable. You have spoken more truth than I am accustomed to hearing, and I am afraid that that is something that will require a certain amount of adjustment. I feel the same good feelings toward all of you that I felt toward the child when I first saw him, even though I thought he was the strangest boy I had ever seen. If you could have seen the way he handled that old fruit swindler and the other boys, especially the one who was so much bigger than him. I have never seen that much strength in a child that size, but then I cannot recall seeing so much perception in people as I have seen in you tonight, either. Although I am utterly confused, each passing minute makes me feel more and more like I belong here."

"You feel that way because you do belong here. As for the strength of the child, he has been blessed with an extraordinary Megalight connection...."

"Excuse me, but don't you feel awkward, using that word, mmmm."

"Megalight? Not at all. The word only means something because we agree on what it means. There is no name that is great enough to truly convey the power, creativity, intelligence, and love to which we refer when we say Megalight'."

"I have a lot to learn. Please, forgive my interruption, I would hear more about the boy."

"I was saying that because of Sombata's Megalight connection, the other boy did not have a chance against him. The other boy was entirely limited to whatever strength was contained in his body. Sombata is a vessel. He does not depend upon his own, limited, energy; that is, when he is following his teachings properly. But enough talking for now, you must be exhausted." He did not mention Sombata because he was already asleep, his head cradled in his mother's lap.

"We will have many seasons to continue our dialogue."

24

*F*eathers. Ninety-Seven. FEATHERS. Ninety-Eight. FEATHERS. Ninety-Nine. FEATHERS! One Hundred. Sombata released the imaginary feathers on his arms and head, and, in so doing, made room for the very real rocks in their stead. He lowered his arms allowing the heavy rocks he had placed upon them to fall to the desert floor. Carefully, he removed the remaining rock from his head. He opened his eyes and turned around to survey the sands he had just crossed. No footprints. Not one. Jawala had taught him to walk on top of the sand; the added weight of the rocks had been his idea.

What to do next. He had performed every task that Jawala, Shobogun and Menes had been able to conceive for him. He had even added variations- like the rocks- to those tasks, to make them more difficult. Though his body ached for rest, his mind craved new challenges.

He recalled Jawala's recollections of his manhood training: how all the boys got into trouble when one of them made a mistake, and how they had to learn to depend upon one another and help each other through many of the obstacles. His father had been lucky. He had had a peer group with whom to share the anxieties he felt when his body began to change in the grasp of puberty. Jawala and Menes had continued to be supportive of Sombata as he struggled with his emerging manhood, but they were not going through it *with* him. He was sure, despite his father's assurances, that puberty did not bludgeon other young men with the same anxiety that had been reserved for him.

Things would be different, once he had performed the manhood ritual. Not only would he would completely belong to the adult world, but he would also have the chance to finally exorcise the demons that had intruded upon his soul ever since his trip to Zambutu more than five seasons ago. While everyone around him had oozed with pride over the way he had conducted himself, the experience had left him feeling unsure of himself.

Yes, the others had been proud, but could they could not have really understood how relieved he had been to embrace his mother when it was over. No one could take from him the notion that he was not overly relieved when he returned home, or that his relief did not prove the weakness within him. He wondered how he would have fared had Wabatani not been there to intervene on his behalf.

Perhaps it was the lack of peers that forced him into a relationship with himself that was uniquely intimate and demanding. Or maybe he held an intuitive sense of destiny that drove him toward perfection. Whatever the cause, Sombata hinged his hopes for redemption on the successful completion of manhood training.

Despite his almost unyielding expectations of himself, there was one success of which Sombata was enormously proud: Wabatani and Shalina. They had been attracted to each other immediately. Each having been denied the comfort of a complementing other for so long, they bypassed much of the courting ritual and were married within three months. Sombata's greatest honor came when they asked him to be the arachmo, or godfather of their first child.

He was trying desperately to capture the attention of the child, by then a toddler, when, as the last rays of the sun faded from the sky, a boisterous young man penetrated the camp's psychic defenses and interrupted its serenity. The young man galloped his quiphar directly into the middle of the commune.

The young man loudly proclaimed that he was a member of BORE, which he explained, with obvious condescension, stood for Brigade Of Religious Enforcement. He told them that since their commune was not charted they were already in serious trouble for not being in compliance with the laws of tribute, as well as any other violations he might happen across. Furthermore, it was his duty, he informed them, to ensure that no gaps existed in the spread and practice of NETAP; which, he further explained, stood for the Nagapine Economics, Theology And Philosophy.

Initially, many of the commune members found the young rooster with the wren's feathers rather amusing- distasteful to be sure- but a comical diversion from the mundane realities of everyday life, nonetheless. He attached such grave importance to the most trivial and in many instances downright nonsensical issues. And he was smart. He knew he was smart. He answered all of their questions with the greatest of ease. He defined faith as the ability to adhere to the Nagapine Doctrine without question or notice of any inconsistencies, hope as what should occur when one is in the pursuit of a young woman -- after all, without hope, why bother? -- and charity as being forthcoming in turning in one's neighbor so the Republic might reap greater rewards.

Although they were well aware of the young man's contempt for them, the commune members brought him food and drink as they would any stranger, all the while chuckling to themselves at his pompous and ridiculous ways.

For his part, the young brigade member became increasingly agitated by the strange ways of the commune. They were civil, but not subservient. They appeared to be too stupid or uncivilized to understand the gravity of their situation. Nor was he able to impress upon them his importance, how the report he would submit would impact upon their primitive and pathetic ways. In a moment of largess, he had offered to submit a good report on their behalf, yet they accepted the offer with the same nonchalance they had shown his threat of a bad report. He wondered if they mated with the apes, then chuckled to himself at the gross mental images the thought produced. No matter, he would bring a sense of civility to these heathens.

"Move your behind! Bring me more food and wine, and bring it NOW!" he commanded, at Otumba of all people.

The young man ceased to amuse.

Otumba whirled around and barely stopped herself from delivering a blow that surely would have caused the brigade member's spirit to give up the flesh.

"Young man," she said evenly, striving not to throttle the ignorant young fellow, "I think you had better leave, before you further endanger your safety."

"You *DARE* to threaten me?" the young brigade member was almost hysterical in his indignation. He drew back his official club in order to teach the wretched hag some respect.

Otumba neither flinched nor twitched. Promptly the entire village surrounded the young man. Their faces melted away, and only their eyes remained; penetrating, searing eyes. Their powerful minds invaded his like tiny suns invading the cold or like lights -- *mega*lights -- invading darkness.

He fell to the ground, writhing under the onslaught. They withdrew their forces. Someone brought him a cup of tea that would help revive him. When he could stand, they pointed him toward the guest tent.

In the morning a different, quieter young man rode out of the village, but not before they had made sure that he would not convey anything about his experience with them to anyone else. Upon returning to his brigade, he would begin a decline in efficiency that eventually would lead to his dismissal. He would wonder aimlessly for three seasons before returning to the commune, this time asking to stay and learn. Although his experience with them did not reconnect him, it put him along the path for reconnection: it gave him humility.

The episode with the young brigade member produced more mental cud for the thoughtful young Sombata to chew. It increased his already deepening hatred of disconnection. He loved those who were connected, pitied those who were not, and loathed the difference. It seemed so unnecessary, so nonsensical that anyone should become alienated from themselves; and hence, everyone and everything else; not just other people, but the land, the streams, the animals, everything, especially the Megalight. It seemed to him that people who did not grow were actually wasting their lives. The waste of a life was a thought almost too horrible to bear.

Something had to be done, but what? He wondered about the entire commune traveling from village to village, turning their minds on the disconnected and at least imparting some sort of humility or healing. Then he remembered from discussions with Jawala and Menes that the Megalight would never allow them to force healing on the people. They would have to want it. There had to be something, but what? He decided to approach his father and grandfather.

"What would you do?" Jawala asked.

"I do not know. I just know that something has to be done to end all of this suffering. People are suffering without even knowing it."

"They know they are suffering," Menes added; "it is just that they have become accustomed to suffering and prefer it to the challenge of reconnection."

Jawala raised his eyebrows inquisitively at Menes who nodded approval.

"Some day, my son, you will be called upon to do something about the terrible problems that plague our planet. I cannot tell you when. All I can say is that you will have a considerable role to play. All you can do for now is to continue in your studies and when the time comes, you will be ready."

Since that talk, Sombata's efforts took on a new zeal that astounded everyone, even Menes. He dedicated and rededicated himself toward his lessons so that Menes, Jawala, and Shobogun were forced to push themselves just to keep new material coming to the growing lad.

He barely blinked when Jawala told him it was time to be circumcised. He was back walking around in two days less than any of the boys with whom Jawala had been circumcised. The more difficult the task he was given, the more enthusiastically he tackled it.

Then the time came.

"It is time that you were cured, my son. This will be the final step in your becoming a man," Jawala announced proudly one fine morning.

"Father, I can find no words to express what I am feeling now. Tell me what you would have me do. There is no mountain too big for me to climb, no river too wide for me to cross, just tell me and I will do anything!"

"Your task will not be so difficult. You have nothing to prove. You have been proving yourself all along. Tomorrow morning, you will accompany me and several others to the Mudan river. There, you will dip yourself seven times in the river, each time giving thanks to the Megalight for having been made whole. When you emerge from the river on the seventh time, you will have been made whole. And you will emerge as a *man*."

Sombata could not believe his ears. All the work he had done just to pass the manhood training, and his father was telling him that all he had to do was to dip himself in a stinking river seven times? How could his own father deny him the chance to prove himself?

"Father, how could you do this to me? All this time that you have been telling me that I could do anything that any other person could do, I have believed you! Now that the chance has finally come for me to prove that I am as much man as any other, you want to take that away from me. Dip myself in the Mudan river? I could have done that when I was a baby! If it weren't for this bad foot of mine, and this bad hand, you would probably have me climbing some tall mountain or capturing some great beast."

"It is not the way you think," Jawala tried to soothe his

headstrong son."

"Oh, isn't it?" Sombata was practically out of control. "Was it not you who taught me that manhood was not something that just came automatically with the passing of time, that it had to be earned? Was it not you who taught me that manhood came before everything else, that one must never prove unworthy of the title of `man'? Was it not you who taught me that if a man cannot prove himself worthy to become a man, he will never prove himself worthy to become a true vessel of the Megalight? Who was it that taught me all of those things? It was you, Father, and now you want to take everything away from me, because you think I am an invalid! How could you do this to me? How?" Sombata was near tears.

"Very well then," Jawala heard someone else speaking through him, "if you insist, bring me back the egg of a torrocos bird. Then you will be cured. Then you will be a man."

"I'll leave right away," Sombata brightened. "And when I return, I will bring you the biggest torrocos bird egg you have ever seen. I will make you proud of me!"

Jawala's tears clouded his vision of his son running away. He wished he could take back the challenge he had given Sombata. He turned toward the heavens, but even the sky seemed to disapprove of him. Even though he had done what he had been forced to do, he still could not justify his actions. He felt small. And alone.

"Have you seen Sombata?" Kalimba asked later that evening. "I have not seen him for hours. I wonder where he could be?"

Jawala sighed deeply, then told her what had happened.

Her eyes flashed brilliantly. Her entire body jerked involuntarily.

"Fool! You did WHAT? You sent my baby where? Are you out of your mind? Do you know what kind of teeth a torrocos bird has? Do you know what kind of claws a torrocos bird has? Do you know how quickly a torrocos bird's venom can paralyze a cow? Kill a full-grown quiphar? And you did what? You sent MY baby, MY baby, to get a torrocos bird's EGG. Are you CRAZY?" She shrieked as she began to pound her husband's chest with her fists.

She pummelled until her arms grew weary and her screams turned to sobs.

"My baby," she moaned, "I've lost my baby."

Jawala felt as if he had swallowed an entire field of kimomo beans. For a time, he could say nothing, do nothing. Finally, he was able to embrace his woman.

"He'll be back," he whispered softly to her. Then to himself, "I know he'll be back."

25

"We'll stop and rest for a moment," Nagap called to Rollof and Ondorf as he dismounted his quiphar. They traveled almost exclusively by quiphar since Nagap had become prominent.

So many things had happened and so many things had changed in the nearly twenty cycles of seasons since that fateful debate with Jawala. He had become the planet's most important man, and its busiest. He found that governing his existing territories required so much of his time that it was becoming increasingly difficult to get away to cultivate new villages and territories. So much of his time was now taken up with overseeing his overseers and checking on the people who checked on people that he developed a genuine fondness for the times when he could get away and explore a new forbidden cave with Rollof and Ondorf.

Getting away put him in a reflective mood; so much so that he almost felt a twinge of gratitude when Rollof brought him dried meat, and Ondorf brought wine without having been asked. Rollof and Ondorf, who would have thought that some day they would become his most trusted and valued assistants.

He pulled out his pouch of trusty happy powder. It would make his food and wine taste better. It would make his thoughts fly faster and the trip inside the cave more intense. Ah, the cave; how many seasons had it been since he had last ventured into one? three? four? The caves were where it had all begun, where his master plan had found flesh.

In those early days, he, Rollof and Ondorf would have to do everything: all the bruising and soothing of egos, the planting and nurturing of the seeds of discontent, all of it. Now, they would simply pollute the waters, then send someone else to do all those things. After an appropriate amount of time had elapsed and the people's dissatisfaction had been built sufficiently, Nagap had only to arrive in the villages and be greeted by his anxious new subjects.

Without the talking drums- he had banned them because he found them irritating and reminded him too much of things he would rather forget- he relied on a network of quiphar riding messengers who formed the hub of his communication network. Because quiphars were the fastest animals big enough for a man to ride, private ownership of them was banned. They were to be used only for the official business of the church/republic.

As the happy powder took effect, he wondered again about Jawala. After all those seasons, he had never been able to forget about him. How could Jawala have escaped his rule? Perhaps he had not. Maybe he was a loyal subject whom Nagap had overlooked in one of the larger villages. No. If Jawala was in one of the villages he controlled, he would know it. Somehow he would know it.

His mind continued racing. He wondered which of her mammoth being spaces Chuka was occupying at this time. While she played the role of Holy Mother almost to perfection, she could also be quite annoying at times, criticizing and advising as if he were still a child. Her criticisms irked him, even thought he knew he could trust her. It was strange, he thought to himself, how he had built an entire empire entirely upon distrust, and yet trust had become the one thing he longed for most. That was why Rollof and Ondorf had become so special to him over the years. They had no ambitions whatsoever, independent of his destiny. He liked that. They were as loyal as Chuka, without the nagging.

There was a good chance that he could trust Biloxin, the metal worker who now supervised the production of the coins. Of course there was also a slight chance that he could not be trusted, so Nagap had someone watching Biloxin, while someone else watched Biloxin's watcher. The same with Konstine. All the watching and counter-watching was necessary, but also quite tiresome. Only Rollof and Ondorf, whom he had come to regard almost as his children, required no supervision other than his.

"We've had enough rest," he announced. When he noticed how sluggishly they responded, he guessed correctly that they had not stopped for nearly as long as the happy powder had him thinking they had. "Anyway, the two of you can rest when we get to the cave, unless of course, you have decided that you want to go inside this time."

"No, No, No, we'll be happy to rest outside the cave, as always,"

Ondorf answered.

That was another thing Nagap loved about Rollof and Ondorf; they never changed, never grew.

A few hours later they arrived at the mouth of the cave. Sarcastically, Nagap beckoned Rollof and Ondorf to join him in the cave. Then he entered alone.

The warm exhilarating feeling, enhanced by the happy powder, bathed him as he descended deeper into the cave. Each trip inside a new cave produced a sweet mixture of feelings as the familiarity of caves in general combined with the excitement of the new, distinct cave.

Something about this particular cave made it feel more unique than most. He had already regarded this trip as being somewhat special because he knew that this would be the last cave he would encounter for a great distance, perhaps twelve days of intense quiphar riding. There was something unusual about this cave, that he could not quite identify. He decided that if the cave were truly unique he would find out soon enough. He made his way through the darkness- he had long since abandoned any form of carrying light in favor of allowing the cave to draw him along naturally- when he realized that he had long since passed the point at which he normally would already have gathered the fruit before he sniffed the slightest trace of its aroma. He was sure that there was fruit inside the cave. He had never been in one that had no fruit. Yet there was also something else that was quite interesting about this peculiar cave.

There was something nebulous in this cave, something he had never encountered in another cave. He was being drawn deeper and deeper inside by something more than mere fruit. As his anticipation heightened, he was almost tempted to light his carrying lamp, but the happy powder reminded him that as the Chosen One, he required no light.

The tunnel meandered, veering down to the left, then up to the right. The ever widening and narrowing trail seemed to wander forever, with so many sharp turns that he not only lost his sense of direction, but he also began to wonder if he was even still inside the cave, or if he had ventured into some sort of brave new world. How big could a cave be? He had already traveled the length of at least four normal- sized caves when, in a clearing, he spotted light skimming the top of an overhead ridge. Upon climbing the ridge, only his heart and lungs continued to function. The rest of his body became as stone in protest against the obvious and outrageous deceit which his eyes perpetrated against him.

There, in the middle of a forbidden cave, rose, as if to challenge the very sky, the most incredible being space. Bright lights assaulted his eyes. Glowing spheres, mostly white, some orange, blue, yellow and red, produced an unbelievable brightness. There were statues and furniture carved out of the rock itself, and a network of tunnels leading from just about every direction in and out of the space. The roof of the being space must have been at least fifty-feet high. Even Nagap, had he been able to imagine it, would have had difficulty claiming such a being space for himself.

Yet the opulent being space as not nearly as astonishing as the man who occupied its center. If the being space was bigger than life, then its occupant was bigger than life, death, and dreams combined. Seated upon a humongous, ornate throne, carved entirely out of the back of the cave, was a man who was almost twice as big as anyone Nagap had ever seen.

The man was enormous, and he wore funny clothes. In place of a robe, he wore what appeared to be two separate pieces of tight fitting clothing that clung to his arms and legs. Different pieces of the same material covered his torso and his arms. The bottom half of his apparel separated along his legs and disappeared into another strange, shiny material which covered his calves all the way down to his feet. His feet were completely covered by the hard looking, shiny material. His clothing was like a loose fitting layer of skin almost.

"Welcome, Nagap," the man's voice boomed louder and deeper than any Nagap had ever heard, "I have been expecting you."

Nagap could not speak.

"It is indeed ironic that the man of a thousand speeches should be rendered speechless at the sight of his mentor."

Nagap's voice remained on hiatus.

"I can appreciate your shock at meeting me. Unfortunately, you do not have the luxury of indulging that shock. While I like the look of you, you must still pull yourself together to make the best possible impression on your mentor."

"Mentor?" the voice returned and decided to act on its own.

"Actually, more than mentor. I could truthfully say that I am your creator."

The giant's last statement challenged Nagap back to a semblance of himself.

"My creator? No one created Me! I am His Holiness Nagap, the Grand Exalted Ruler of ..."

"... the Brigade of Religious Enforcement," the giant interrupted. "You are also The Only Begotten Son of the Megalight. You are The Imperial blah blah blah. Look around you. Do you no think it just a tad inappropriate to try to impress me with your pathetic titles?"

The hated feeling that Nagap had escaped for so many seasons returned. His chest began to fall into his stomach and his shoulders hunched forward. It was a sensation he thought he would never have to experience again. Without thinking, he took two steps toward the strange man.

"I wouldn't do that if I were you," the man said as he began to rise from his seat. The man rose and rose and rose until it seemed that he would not stop until Nagap's grandchildren reached maturity. The man did not stop rising until he had reached a height in excess of nine and one-half feet.

Nagap's nerves abandoned him.

"That is better," the giant said, having made his point, and returning to his throne.

"Who are you? What have you to do with me? How did you know my name? Why do you call yourself my mentor? Where..."

"One question at a time, my good fellow. But before you indulge your questions, there is someone here that I think you might want to see." He clapped his enormous hands twice, and a familiar form materialized within one of the tunnels.

"CHUKA! What are you doing here?" Nagap raced to embrace his mother. "Has this man harmed you? Has he threatened you in any way? I can summon my brigade and ..."

"Be patient, my son, and the proper conclusions will come to you. There is no need to jump to them," she spoke gently as she embraced him.

"What do you mean?"

"I am here because I want to be here. This man has already been deeply involved in our lives for many seasons. You must listen to him. There are many strange and wonderful things which you must learn from him. He has promised me that he will not hurt you."

"Excellent counsel, my dear. I was just about to introduce myself, but that might appear rude, since Nagap's trusty servants are not present."

"It would take hours to retrieve them. I left them back at the mouth of the cave."

"I am afraid you took the most indirect route to get here," the giant replied as he pulled one of several levers affixed to the cavern wall. A huge stone slab slid to one side, revealing the trembling Rollof and Ondorf huddled outside.

Nagap, trying hard to retrieve his chest from his gut, commanded.

"Don't just sit there, you fools, get in here!"

Unfortunately, Nagap's authority was no match for the incomprehensible sights within the cave. The two men remained motionless, paralyzed by fear and amazement.

"Rollof, Ondorf, my good fellows, you are welcome here. Please come in and join us so that I may close out the damp night air." The giant's voice acted as a hypnotic command, lifting, directing, and ushering the two men into the cave without disturbing their comatose states of being. Like sleepwalkers, they entered.

Nagap's left eyebrow began to twitch, as if sweating palms, burning eyes, a throbbing head, and falling shoulders and chest were not enough.

"Now that everyone is here, let me properly introduce myself. My name is Darinus. You have all heard rumors that life on Zarkon was once quite different than the period into which you were born, and that the previous civilization was destroyed by a tremendous catastrophe known as the Great Bang. Well, I can assure you that all of those rumors are correct. I can assure you of this and much more, because I am from that era."

"But no one could live that long," Nagap gasped as his curiosity overtook his indignation.

"If you will kindly desist from interrupting me, I will explain everything to you, momentarily. Now then, as I was saying, Prior to the Great Bang, our civilization was dominated by the most ingenious devices ever constructed. Being spaces, as you call them, were constructed on top of each other until they scraped the very sky. We built great flying machines that held hundreds of people and could transport them from one end of the planet to the other in a matter of hours. We had even greater flying devices that left the planet and flew to the land of the stars. We could transmit images and information almost anywhere, almost instantly.

"The more we learned of transmitting information and images, the better we became at manipulating them. We were the true masters of thought management, but not the way that you have been taught to think of it. Thought management in our time did not mean that each individual controlled his own thoughts. Rather, the men of power, the cognoscenti, controlled and manipulated the thinking of everyone else. They were true magicians, capable of creating desires, then changing those desires into needs. They could make the poorest of the poor throw their money away on a fragrance or on wearing apparel by convincing them that the product was essential to their well being. They manufactured reality. As the ability to create reality increased, our need for what you now call the Megalight, diminished to the point where we were in direct competition with It. We did not have to take things; we could make people want to give us what we wanted."

"What you see about you represents only the last vestiges of the technology that once was. Is it too bright in here for you?" he asked rhetorically as he dimmed the lights with a dial.

"Perhaps, you care for some music," he offered broadly as he placed his finger on the strange table setting next to his seat. A small, but intense beam of light appeared from one of the objects and struck another round object. Peculiar music filled the chamber.

"Would you like it louder?" he demonstrated the volume control," or perhaps softer," he almost whispered as he brought the volume slowly down to inaudible before turning the machine off.

Chuka smiled reassuringly at her befuddled son. Rollof and Ondorf simply took up space, as they were not yet able to function.

"I am sure you are all wondering," Darinus continued, relishing his guests' inability to digest that which he had already placed before them, "how such a magnificent society could have destroyed itself. The answer is quite simple. The very elements that made our society great, almost guaranteed that it would be destroyed.

"Since we decided that we had no need for the Megalight, we searched for something else- something more compatible with our way of life- with which to justify our existence. We found the answer in competition. We called it our competitive edge. It was our competitive edge that made us great. Whenever someone built a tall structure, someone else had to build one taller. If one person- actually it wasn't a person, it was a collection of persons called a company- but I'm getting ahead of myself, I'm sure you are beginning to have difficulty following me as it is," the giant began to ramble as the fond remembrances- remembrances that had been locked away for too long- began to unfold and the glory of his society replayed itself in his mind. "Whenever one group built something fast, the next group had to build it faster, and so on. Our competitiveness enabled us to conceive and create things which no other civilization ever has, or will.

"Unfortunately, it was our competitiveness, coupled with our advanced technology- technology just means inventions- that ultimately destroyed us. Competition for control of the resources led to skirmishes, and skirmishes to wars, which eventually led to full blown global conflicts. The third such conflict decimated our civilization. Your culture grew from the ashes of ours."

"I was the premier military scientist of my day. I had created the perfect formula to destroy all who opposed my government. It was just the right strength to bring the rest of the planet to its knees. But the fools would not listen to me! They insisted on tinkering with my device- nothing was ever strong enough for them, nothing was ever big enough for them- until it would, and did, not only destroy our enemies but us as well.

"When it became clear that no one would listen to me, I vowed that I would never again allow my genius to be controlled by others. I realized I had been a pawn, and swore that someday I would do the governing. But in the meantime, I hid myself in this cave. I studied all of the ancient mystical arts and combined that knowledge with my own scientific method to provide a serum that prolongs life. Little did I realize that a side effect of the serum would be the re-activation of my growth glands. You see, four hundred and thirty years ago, I was five feet and four inches tall. I have been growing at a rate of ..."

"Almost an inch a decade," Nagap offered almost involuntarily.

"It is good to see that your excellent mind is still functioning. I had begun to wonder if anything I have been telling you had sunk in, given the glazed expression you have been displaying."

Darius' last taunt reached the one thing in Nagap that could bring him out of his state of semi-shock: his vanity.

"After all these seasons of wondering whether there really was a Great Bang, I would be lying if I said your story was not fascinating. But I think I could enjoy it more, if I understood what it has to do with me," Nagap struggled to project some sense of control.

"Come, come, my dear protege, given your well documented intellectual capacity, surely you have deduced by now that I have been the guiding force behind all of the developments for which you claim credit. Who do you think wrote the pamphlet that has provided such inspiration for your campaigns?

"Many seasons before there was a Nagap, I took a solemn oath to someday return this planet to its former greatness, the only difference being that this time I would be the ruler. Since it is difficult for a man my size to get around without drawing an inordinate amount of attention to himself, I recruited a band of assistants, not unlike yours.

"While I am not completely familiar with this Megalight connection business, I do know that it makes people virtually ungovernable. I also know that those with extraordinary connections cause adverse reactions in those who do not have the connections. I equipped my assistants with highly sophisticated instruments which would monitor heart and perspiration rates. Then I sent them out among the people. I tabulated the results and- taking a number of factors such as age, title, and the personal observations of my workers into account- was able to identify and eliminate those persons who had the greatest Megalight connections and hence, posed the greatest threats to my campaign. In your village, that meant the parents of your arch- rival, Jawala. You see, just as you have had your people watching each other, I too, have been watching you.

"Your own mother would have fallen into that category as well, except that there was something about her that I could not bear to eliminate. Instead, through a series of actions- landscaping and mirrors- I arranged to have her visit a forbidden cave while she bore you. In effect, I recruited her and you.

"My plan has worked quite well. Thanks to that meddlesome Menes- I would have had him eliminated as well, except that I thought him too old to pose a threat- there are still a few people out there somewhere who might create problems for us down the road. But for the most part, things have gone better than even I could have anticipated.

"My plans have taken shape because you have played your role so well. I have been controlling events while you have been parading around, thinking you were in charge of everything. But that is as it should be. If you had had any humility, you would have been absolutely worthless to me. So far, you have provided ample proof of my wisdom, because you have been a brilliant lieutenant."

Nagap plummeted into absolute turmoil. A few hours before, he had been the uncontested ruler of much of the continent, and now this freak was trying to tell him that he was nothing more than a mere errand boy. He felt confused, betrayed. The man had made him feel small- something he had sworn he would never allow anyone to ever do again since the debate with Jawala- and he had done it in front of Rollof, Ondorf, and Chuka. Through his confusion and despair, there was but one emotion that rang true and clear: he wanted to kill Darinus.

26

Like a heartless taskmaster, Sombata ignored the pain and fatigue in his muscles as he continued his assault on the mountain. "Just a little bit further," he kept saying to himself. This was the third day of his climb. There had been times when the mountain had seemed so unyielding that Sombata had almost thought it be to alive. The mountain could fight him all it liked, he would not be denied.

He had foraged just enough nuts, berries, roots and leaves during his sojourn to maintain his strength. His aching muscles and empty stomach helped distract him from the deeper pain he felt whenever he thought that his father had not had enough confidence in him to allow him to undergo the rigors of manhood training. He had thought about it until he had made himself dizzy, and he still could not understand why his father had shown so little confidence in him. No matter, soon he would return with a genuine torrocos egg and there would be no lingering doubts. He would be a man.

Then he spotted it. Just above him and a little to his right was a ledge, maybe four or five yards wide. On that ledge set a torrocos nest, complete with egg, practically beckoning him. There was no bird in sight. Once he reached the nest, he realized he had not given much thought to his next dilemma: how to get the egg down the mountain. While he had two strong arms, he could barely grasp anything in his left hand. The torrocos egg was the size of a small watermelon.

He sat for a moment to think of a solution, when an idea hit him that he liked so much that he was forced to congratulate himself. He would dismantle the nest and reweave it into a backpack!

He had scarcely begun dismantling the nest when he heard a horrible screeching sound directly above him. He turned just in time to stare into the bulging red eyes of the mother torrocos bird as she swooped upon him. The torrocos resembled a sixty-pound bat. Her membrane span was a minimum of twelve feet.

Her wide mouth revealed large, sharp teeth.

Instinctively, he threw both arms across his face. The bird's sharp talons narrowly missed Sombata's eyes and locked onto this forearms. Struggling against him, the bird brought its ugly head so close to Sombata's that its whiskers brushed his cheek. The torrocos' neck veins bulged as it stretched its head to bite Sombata's face. While the torrocos' talons were dangerous, its bite was fatal. Her hot, putrid breath fell heavily upon Sombata's face. He almost gagged. Her venomous saliva dripped on to his cheeks, searing his skin.

The burning saliva, the bared teeth, and the talons piercing his arms all combined to produce a terror in Sombata that grew until it exploded in an incredible outburst of strength. Using his right arm, he ripped the torrocos' claws away from his left arm. He screamed as he felt the torrocos' talons ripping away his flesh. Supporting himself on his left arm while grasping the bird with his right, he jerked himself upward to gain just enough leverage to hurl the bird away.

Frantically, he charged the bird, driving it to the side of the mountain. The torrocos wrapped its membrane around him. He felt the bird bobbing its head, trying to get a bead on him. He stopped struggling for an instant. Death charged at his head. He ducked. The torrocos bit through the membrane . Her teeth sank deeply into one of her own major arteries. Her blood spewed across the membrane, dripping onto Sombata. He untangled himself as the bird slid to the ground. He found a large rock and hoisted it with both hands over his head. He was about to heave the rock onto the bird when he made eye contact with the wounded animal for the first time. When his eyes met the bird's, it became a fellow living creature, a creature filled with pain a sorrow. The torrocos stared at the egg as its eyes began to fill.

"This is not how I was reared," Sombata thought to himself. He dropped the boulder harmlessly down the side of the mountain. He reached for the bird's wound, but the frightened animal snapped at him. *There is no living thing with which you cannot empathize,* Jawala had taught him. He would have to hurry. There wasn't much time. He tried to penetrate the bird's mind, but it was too small. Frantically, he rummaged through the teachings stored in his brain trying to find one that fit. The harder he tried, the more frantic he became. Every second counted. He knew he had received a lesson that would tell him what to do, if he could just focus on the right one. The seconds continued to elapse. Then he realized that he was working against himself.

He breathed deeply and allowed himself to vanish from his consciousness. Nothingness. Of course! In nothing, there is no large and small, there is nothing. He began to lose himself, to stretch himself psychically so that he could shrink himself mentally, to accommodate the bird's small brain. There was no room for the guilt he felt for having injured the bird. He could neither rush, nor dally, he simply had to allow his inner resources to carry him through at the proper rate. He reduced his thoughts to feelings, then simplified those feelings. He made contact.

"My baby and I wanted only to live in peace," he received from the bird. "I am dying, and my baby will not be able to survive without me."

"I did not mean to be so cruel, " Sombata responded. "Please, if you will let me help you, you can live. I did not mean to harm you. When you are well, I will leave. I will not bother your egg again. I never meant to harm either of you. Please forgive me."

He thought he had gotten through to the bird, but there was only one way to be sure. Gingerly he placed his hand at her face. The torrocos' venom was optional; she could either bite him venomously, or she could harmlessly lick his hand. She licked his hand.

He spied a kukasia plant growing out of the side of the mountain. Using soft twigs from the nest, he tied the leaves into place over the bird's wounds. Only after he had made the torrocos as comfortable as possible, did he realize how much his arm and face hurt.

Carefully, he lifted the wounded animal and placed her on top of her egg. He spent the night forcing himself to awaken every few hours to attend to the torrocos' wounds. By morning, the wounds had almost completely healed.

He had just hoisted himself over the lip of the ledge when he heard the torrocos' loud "kaaa ... kaaa." He returned to make sure the bird was all right. She licked his hand again and made a few whimpering sounds. She was telling him that she and her egg would go with him.

27

"I will get something to eat a little later. Right now I want to get an early start on the harvest," Jawala told Kalimba as he prepared to leave their being space.

"What's the matter, don't you want some nice EGGS?"

Jawala glared at Kalimba.

"I am sorry. I have given a lot of thought to the things you have been trying to tell me. I know that you did not enjoy sending Sombata away. It is just that it has been nine days since he left. It seems that my discipline deserts me when my only child is involved."

"I understand. But while we are on the subject, you should know that when he does return, he will soon have to leave us again, and the next time he leaves, will be for an extended period of time."

"I had feared as much. How much time will we have with him before he has to leave us again?"

"Does it matter? If he stays with us one day or a hundred days, we will miss him the same when he leaves."

"You are right."

Jawala stepped out of the being space, then quickly ducked back in. "There is someone out here, I think you might want to see."

Kalimba caught his meaning, sprung from her seat, and was outside in an instant. Her son approached, followed by an egg-carrying torrocos bird, She raced toward him, then stopped abruptly. She realized how right she had been when she had screamed that she would never see her baby again. This was not her baby walking toward her. He was different. He was a man.

Soon the entire commune had gathered for a second time to welcome Sombata home from a perilous journey. He told them what had happened, although he rushed those parts of the story that he knew would upset his mother.

"Son, you have given us more pride than any village would ever have any reason to hope," Jawala spoke. "You have returned with the egg, and you did not kill the bird. Do you now know why I had to send you on this mission?"

"Yes, sir. I was arrogant without even realizing it. I insisted on paying for something that had been offered as a gift. It was almost as if I wanted to determine how my blessings would come, instead of accepting them however they were presented. My light was shining, and everyone knew it but me. The mission was only necessary because I made it necessary. Before I could make contact with the torrocos, I had to make contact with myself. I saw myself in ways I had never experienced before. I saw my own immaturity, my own selfishness. I am sorry that I forced you to send me on this journey. I now realize how difficult it must have been for you. But I have grown. I will accept any task you assign to me, and I will accept it gladly."

"Sombata," Kalimba joined in, "you have learned the single greatest lesson that anyone can learn in life. You have learned humility. Humility is not easy. Those who proclaim it the loudest, always possess the least of it. I am so very proud of you, and I will always thank the Megalight for this day."

"As usual, your mother speaks with wisdom. But let us not destroy the boy's, uh, excuse me, the *man's* new-found humility will all these compliments. We have serious business that must be discussed.

"Sombata, tomorrow we will go with you to the Mudan River. There you will dip yourself seven times. Upon the seventh time, you will be made whole."

28

"Chuka, I cannot believe that you have agreed to become Darinus' bride. Am I not the one who made you the Blessed Mother? What do we need with him?"

"Nagap, this man offers something that no one else can offer. He offers immortality! What good will all of the power you have acquired be when we are both dead and gone? Besides, nothing can happen between us until I have grown to a size that is compatible with his. Even with the accelerated formula that he is preparing for me, that would require a minimum of fifty seasons."

"But still, Chuka. The thought of him calling you his bride is in itself disgusting. He is an Airopin!"

"Nagap, you have just committed the worst sin any ruler can commit: you have begun to believe your own propaganda. We have ruled successfully because we have been able to keep the people focused on their differences instead of their commonalities. Race is important only as a controlling mechanism. When you start to believe the lies you tell the people, then you become unfit to lead because you become one of them."

"You are right, as usual," Nagap placed just enough emphasis on usual to give it a sarcastic twist. "But I still have worked too hard over the years to get the kind of power I have now, and I am not about to turn it over to some overgrown freak. He has been using us, manipulating us without our knowledge."

"That is quite true. But while he has been using us, we have been using him. You used his knowledge to put the empire together in the first place."

"That is true, and I am going to keep it together, without him. I am going to get the formula for both of us, then we won't need him."

"Be careful, my son."

"I will, Mother."

Nagap made his way from his mother's quarters and through the labyrinth of tunnels inside Darinus' mammoth headquarters. He was looking for Darinus' working space. In the week that had passed since his initial encounter with Darinus, he had learned his way around the first two levels of the cave. The lower levels had been declared off-limits. Imagine, someone trying to tell his holiness, Nagap, where he could and could not go! He was about to enter the passageway that he was sure led to Darinus' working space when:

"May I help you?" Darinus startled him.

"Am I glad to see you! I was on my way to my quarters and I must have taken a wrong turn somewhere."

"My dear fellow, there is about as much likelihood of your getting lost as there is of your outsmarting me." Darinus clapped his huge hands and the second largest man Nagap had ever seen- he must have stood almost six and three-quarter feet tall- materialized. The one-eyed, hooded, man seemed vaguely familiar. Nagap screwed his face trying to place the man. Darinus, seeing Nagap struggle for recognition, explained:

"This is Olphemus. I could not help noticing your attempts at recognizing him. There is good reason that he should seem familiar to you. He brought provisions to your being space when you were but a mere child.

"You see, Olphemus is my oldest and was at one time, my most trusted assistant. He has been with me more than one hundred seasons. But he disobeyed me once, and had to be punished. Olphemus, tell our young guest what happened."

"Many seasons ago," the man spoke slowly, unsteadily, his voice a testimony to living without life, "Our leader embarked upon a campaign to eliminate those persons who were most closely associated with the Megalight. There was a particular family that radiated the Megalight superstition so powerfully that Darinus ordered that the entire family be destroyed.

"Our leader," Olphemus insisted on using the ugly phrase that syphoned Nagap's curiosity and replaced it with irritation, "produced a deadly strain of zhubu flies. While the family slept, I dropped small dollops of a special jelly that attracts the zhubu fly on their bodies. By morning, the parents were dead, but the infant remained alive. I could not bring myself to kill it- it was just a harmless baby boy- so I took it far away from the village and left it at another hut. I hoped that the new home would not be as deeply involved in the Megalight connection nonsense."

"And?" Darinus prodded the unhappy fellow.

"I was wrong. The new home was even more involved in the

Megalight connection that the original home."

"Nagap," Darinus asked, "Can you guess where Olphemus took the child ?"

Nagap studied the question for a few moments. How could he possibly know the answer? Wait. There was a hazy recollection of a story about Jawala's father, Basalt, having been delivered to Menes' being space one night.

"Menes?"

"Excellent.

"Then the stories I heard of how no one could believe Basalt could have been mistaken about a poisoned limpin ... you?"

"A little makeup can fool any limpin expert."

"Now, Olphemus, explain my reaction when I discovered that my orders had been disobeyed."

"You explained that because of my many seasons of loyalty and obedience, my life would be spared," Olphemus' drawling voice began to stretch itself, as if straining under the weight of a powerfully painful memory. "But you also said that my disobedience could not go unpunished," Olphemus' voice began to quiver.

"Perhaps, it would be best if I resumed the story from here. Suffice it to say that before he disobeyed me, Olphemus had two very good eyes."

Nagap felt like someone had dropped a lump of burning coal in his stomach. Over the seasons he had ordered hundreds of people punished for all sorts of bogus charges, and all kinds of goods confiscated, but to put out someone's *eye* because he had not murdered an *infant*? This man had killed Jawala's parents! He wondered how many other people Darinus has killed, how many Darinus *would* kill. Nagap had always deluded himself into believing that any and all of his actions were justified, but not for one second had he ever stopped to consider himself evil. Until he met Darinus, he had not been sure of what evil really was. Now he knew. Evil was Darinus.

Since he had entered the cave, Nagap had strived to maintain his composure, to assure Rollof, Ondorf, and especially himself, that he was still firmly in control, even if the circumstances indicated otherwise. But this pathetic man's story visibly shook him.

Until now, his quest for power had been a game. He had managed to obliterate the seriousness of his actions with a little happy powder. He had set out to get respect and admiration.

Somewhere along the line, everything got changed. Now things had gotten really complicated. He thought back to the many opportunities he had discarded for developing his Megalight connection. He wondered where he would be, what he would be doing, had he taken those opportunities. It was too late now. He would have to live with his decisions.

With the gift of time, his ability to plan and scheme would return, but for now, he reeled under the weight of an overdose of reality.

"Olphemus," Darinus' voice came from a faraway fog, "escort our guest back to his quarters."

Like a lost child, Nagap numbly followed Olphemus.

Darinus called after him.

"I realize that it must be unsettling for you to suddenly find someone else in charge. It must be terribly difficult to accept the current situation; and if I were you, I would probably be experiencing the same feelings of wishing to revolt that I know you are feeling. However, I have made an extremely generous offer to you and your mother. While I can sympathize with you, my patience is not unlimited."

"Why DID you make such a generous offer to us?"! Nagap managed to ask.

"Because even *I*," Darinus' voice dropped to the point of being almost inaudible, "get lonely sometimes. But I must warn you that I have powers that you could never imagine. If you force me to clap my hands again, it will not be to summon a servant."

29

"It has worked! He has been made whole!" the faraway voices proclaimed. Sombata could barely hear the voices over the thunderous boom of his heartbeat, as he pulled himself from the muddy waters of the Mudan River. Summoning courage from the innermost recesses of his heart, he peered through the translucent curtains formed by the water droplets on his lashes. Attached to his wrists and ankles were the greatest, most perfectly matched sets of hands and feet.

Sombata collapsed into the arms of Jawala, Kalimba and Menes, as the others surrounded him with hugs and kisses. Sombata, Jawala, Kalimba, Otumba, Wabatani, Shalina and yes, even Menes, they all cried as one in an outpouring of love, relief and gratitude.

Sombata held his left hand high above his head; and, for the first time in his life, made a fist. He flexed his fingers and made yet another fist, and another.

When the tears had finally subsided, they walked slowly back to the commune. The next night there would be feasting and singing and celebrating. This evening was reserved for quiet reflection. This night would be filled with quiet prayers of thanksgiving.

Seven evenings later, Sombata huddled with Jawala and Menes.

"I feel the time has come for me to leave," Sombata spoke with as little emotion as possible. "I have been in meditation, and it has come to me that the time has come for me to begin my involvement in the battle to restore sanity to our planet. There is always the chance that when someone wants something badly enough, he can allow his desires to interfere with the true message his spirit might have intended. What do you think of what I have said?"

Jawala deferred to Menes who, although he moved a bit more slowly, was as mentally keen as ever. Menes said:

"Your father and I have both known that you would be

leaving us shortly after you received your blessing. We have also known that you would have to be the one to know when the time had come. We have been waiting for this moment. We know that what you speak comes from truth and not desire."

"When will you leave us?" Jawala asked, sensing that his son had already made his decision.

"Probably tomorrow. My feeling was that I should head toward the Northwest, although I have no idea why I feel that way."

"Your connection is functioning beautifully; that is why you feel that way," Menes answered him. "If you were to draw a map of the home villages of the last five or six converts we have received, you would find a pattern indicating a northwesterly path of the negative forces."

"Mashari, how do you always know these things?"

"Son, don't even bother. I have been knowing him a lot longer than you have, and I have not been able to figure it out either."

As Sombata prepared to say his farewells, Jawala placed a small hand-carved figurine around his neck.

"This was made for me when I was a baby. I never met the man who carved it. He was Nagap's father. Keep this with you. It will serve to remind you that the people who oppose you are just people the same as you; they just have made some bad decisions."

"Thank you, Father."

There would be no long farewells this time. There would no hand wringing, or crying. A man was leaving on an important mission.

"Limba!" Sombata called to the torrocos he had named after his mother and who had since become his almost constant companion. The torrocos, her five-day old baby clinging to her neck, accompanied him as he disappeared from view.

Limba's company proved invaluable during the grueling journey across the desert sand. Sometimes she flew directly between Sombata and the sun, providing shade, and cooling from the flapping of her membrane. At one point he projected his thought toward the overhead bird, warning her that she had better not do "you know what" while she was directly over him. Limba's shriek sounded a great deal like laughter.

The bond between man and bird flourished as the journey continued. He loved to watch the torrocos care for her baby during the evening. Sometimes he would help feed the apparently insatiable baby bird.

Each evening, after the birds had fallen asleep, Sombata spent long hours in meditation, cleansing himself of any negative feelings or doubts he may have picked up and praying for guidance. As a result of the previous evening's meditation, his path might change slightly on any given day. Sometimes he could not know why the path had been altered. Other times, the new path led to water or food.

Shortly after leaving the desert area, they approached a large lake. Sombata wanted to walk around the lake- it was so huge that the other side was barely visible- but his inner voice insisted that he swim it. He chuckled to himself as he remembered the time when he would have ignored the voice and followed what appeared to be the most logical course. He tied his clothes and the figurine into a bundle which he hung around Limba's neck.

As the shock of the cold water following the hot sun began to wear off, Sombata found himself almost completely relaxed as he stretched his muscles in the water. Ten hours later, however, he began to have serious misgivings as his arms became increasingly weary.

So much of his energy was absorbed in staying afloat that he did not see the large dorsal fin as it approached him. Fortunately, the ever watchful Limba noticed. She shrieked and charged the fin, causing its owner to alter its course significantly. Sombata felt a powerful tug at his ankle and felt himself being pulled down beneath the surface. He looked down to see his entire foot- the one that had just been healed- engulfed in the mouth of a full grown zeman. Zemans were shark-like mammals which also had the ability to leap as high as thirty feet into the air.

His lungs half filled with water, Sombata curled his body downward to grasp the beast's jaws. Thanks to Limba, the zeman caught Sombata's foot with the side of its mouth where its teeth were smaller and dull. The zeman's front teeth would have ripped his foot away instantly. Images of his family and friends flooded Sombata's brain, supplying an intense rush of adrenaline, as the water flooded his mouth and nose. *Not my good foot! I just got that foot well!* he shrieked angrily to himself as he forced the beast's jaws apart.

He rushed toward the surface as the zeman pursued. He dodged its attack and grabbed its fin. The zeman carried him to the surface. They broke the surface. The air tasted sweet as

Sombata coughed, trying to clear his lungs. Limba charged the zeman, but the beast leaped at her causing her to swerve sharply. The baby torrocos yipped loudly as it lost its grip on its mother's neck. Limba angled herself in such a way that the baby was able to regain its grip. Fearing for the baby torrocos, Sombata waved Limba away. He would have to deal with the zeman alone.

With one hand holding the dorsal fin, Sombata ran the other along the back of the zeman until he found the small hole through which zemans breathe. He looped one leg over the zeman's back and began projecting to the zeman: *I have blocked your air supply. Continue to fight me and we both will die!*

Sombata had never heard of anyone ever being able to communicate with a zeman. Their small brains and aggressive nature made them unlikely candidates for telepathic projection. Sombata breathed deeply, filling his lungs as much as he could, in anticipation of the zeman's next manuever. The zeman dived abruptly beneath the surface. Sombata released his grip on the breathing hole and held fast to the dorsal fin with both hands. When the zeman resurfaced, Sombata found the breathing hole and blocked it again. He left a slight crack between his fingers as a peace symbol which he hoped might help in the telepathic projections.

A pattern of diving and resurfacing developed with enough regularity to enable Sombata to time his projections. With timing, his projections became more and more effective. Eventually his thoughts began to seep into the zeman's dull brain. Gradually, the zeman's manuevers became less sharp. Their time on the surface increased. Sombata widened his fingers the tiniest bit, to allow the zeman more air each time they returned to the surface.

Fortunately, the zeman carried Sombata closer to his destination. By the time the zeman had calmed down enough for Sombata to completely remove his hand from the breathing hole, they were less than two miles from the shore. There were men fishing alone the shore. When he came within two hundred yards of the men Sombata stood on the back of the zeman and began waving and shouting to them. When he came within fifty yards, he released the zeman and swam to shore.

The men gathered around Sombata as he emerged from the water. They stared at him as if he were a flying quiphar. Sombata surveyed himself, thinking he must have grown a third arm or something.

"I am called Sombata," he addressed the gathering. He sensed that although they acted strangely, the fishermen were still connected. "I have journeyed a long way and would appreciate your allowing me to partake of your hospitality."

"It is he!" one of the men cried.

"He has come to us!" shouted another.

"His Holiness has come. The True One. The Chosen One. The only one who could walk upon the water!"

"Walk upon the water?" Sombata mumbled to himself as he tried to ascertain if it was he or the fishermen who was mad. Like a jolt of lightning it struck him: they had seen him stand upon the zeman's back and mistaken that for walking on the water!

He knew his laughter could be taken as rudeness, but in his state of near total exhaustion, he lacked the energy to keep it in. When he had regained his composure and wiped the tears from his eyes he promised to explain everything to the men once he had rested and eaten. Limba landed on a rock next to Sombata. "This is Limba and her baby. They are my friends."

30

As the months passed since Nagap had been caught trying to sneak into Darinus' working space, he found himself increasingly struggling with internal conflicts, frustrations and doubts. Grudgingly, he had been forced to admit that Darinus possessed knowledge and techniques that were far more effective than anything he could have imagined.

Darinus' methods had eliminated the need for powdering the forbidden fruit and making repeat visits to the various streams and rivers. He provided them with containers- larger than wine jugs but smaller than barrels- in which the fruit juice was poured. The containers were constructed from a wondrous material that was light, strong, hard, and yet malleable. Darinus called it 'plastic.' They punched small holes into the containers just before placing them in the different water supplies. Darinus had explained that the containers would then release a small but steady stream of the fruit juice that, after a period of three to four weeks, would gradually take effect. Using Darinus' method, villages could be conquered in less than half the time that Nagap's procedure required.

Though the powdered fruit was no longer needed for contaminating the streams, Nagap continued to produce it to replenish his personal supply of happy powder. Yet it seemed the more he mixed, the more quickly his supply of happy powder vanished; which was odd, considering that he was the only one who used it. But after nearly twenty seasons of almost complete control, being forced to relinquish his authority to Darinus left Nagap in need of the solace which only his happy powder could provide. His world had been shattered and he knew no other place to turn.

There were times when Darinus' charm could make Nagap *almost* relax his guard. Yet just about every time Nagap allowed himself to get the least bit comfortable, Darinus would do something to reassert his position of superiority.

There was the time that Nagap had wanted to go out and get

reports from Konstine and Biloxin, but Darinus overruled him, saying that his people were completely aware of Konstine and Biloxin's activities, just as they had been of Nagap's. Had Darinus explained his decision privately to Nagap, he might have been able to accept it. But he had squashed his authority in front of Rollof and Ondorf.

Darinus' evil both repulsed and seduced him. His decisions were uncomplicated by considerations of the pain or anxiety they might inflict on others. He was the epitome of what it meant to be disconnected. Nagap had always been jealous of Jawala's connection, now this giant appeared to be so much stronger than he precisely because he had no connection whatsoever. The man was ugly to the point of being fascinating.

Aside from indulging in his happy powder, there was little Nagap could do other than to feign complete acquiescence as he bided his time. He had been born to command and, even though he still lacked a specific plan, he was convinced that he could overthrow Darinus. Sooner or later, Darinus was going to make the one mistake that would be his last. Nagap would see to that. In the meantime, Nagap developed an almost cheerful attitude toward Darinus' commands and demands. He offered suggestions, and almost apologized when they were not accepted, which was quite often. He studied Darinus- his moods, likes and dislikes- as he grew in his role of faithful servant. He became so effective in the role that he could almost see Darinus congratulating himself for choosing, not just Chuka as a future bride, but also Nagap as his prospective stepson.

He remained quiet during the regular meetings Darinus conducted unless called upon or Darinus' mood dictated more input.

"Is there anything unusual to report today?" Darinus asked to open one such meeting.

"There is," the assistant answered meekly, his head bowed.

"Then speak up! I am not an ogre, am I, Nagap?" Darinus was obviously in a good mood.

"He is not an ogre," Nagap stated dutifully; any pain which might have been involved in the exchange having been banished by the happy powder.

"We have brought the majority of the eastern continent under our control. Yet there is a small fishing village, not more than a half day's ride by quiphar from here, where very strange things seem be happening."

"Be specific," Darinus' good mood appeared to be waning rapidly.

"Four brigade members have visited the village on four different occasions, and each time they have returned suffering from some sort of brain damage."

"Brain damage?" Darinus sat up, his good mood having been completely erased.

"What kind of brain damage?"

"They seem to have lost their sense of purpose. They do not seem to remember why they visited the village, or even why they are members of the brigade. They were incoherent. Each of them mumbled something about being unworthy. Do you wish to interrogate them personally?"

"No. I cannot allow my existence to become too widely known until after we have determined the source of this problem. Are you sure their water supply has been treated?"

"Absolutely. I would stake my life on it."

"You already have. You are all dismissed, except for Nagap, Rollof, Ondorf and Olphemus."

When the others had left, Darinus turned to Nagap:

"What do you make of this report?"

The question penetrated the fog of euphoria which the happy powder had provided Nagap.

"I would say that either we have defective brigade members, or we are not the only ones who know about slipping things into water or food."

"Does anyone else have any thoughts on the matter?"

"Whatever the reasons, the fishermen are obviously in rebellion and must be brought into compliance," Olphemus offered.

"I know that, dolt!" Darinus was clearly becoming agitated.

"How would you suggest that we bring them into compliance?" Darinus directed his question at Nagap.

"I don't know. Give them a week, and if they have not changed, then maybe you should kill them. It would set an example," Nagap replied flippantly as he struggled to maintain the euphoria which Darinus seemed intent upon destroying.

"Not only do I detest that answer, but I detest the attitude with which you gave it! I suggest that you remove whatever else it is that you have on your mind, or I will see to it that you will have no mind on which to rest anything!"

Darinus' outburst shattered Nagap's haze and brought him tumbling back down to the present. He had worked too long trying to appease Darinus and win his confidence to let an overdose of happy powder betray him.

"I am sorry. It is just that I have so much confidence in you that I really did not give the matter the attention which it justly deserves." Nagap's words may have been syrupy, but underneath, the strain of dealing with Darinus was becoming unbearable.

"I do not have the ability to formulate a plan," he continued to massage Darinus' ego, "but I will be honored to carry out whatever instructions you might give me," Nagap's voice blended the proper quantities of sincerity and humility.

"That is much better," Darinus answered as he began to settle a bit. "I think someone knows what we are doing, and has figured out a way to counteract our measures. Nagap, you are the only one I can trust on this mission," he paused long enough to glare harshly at Olphemus. "I want you to take Ondorf and Rollof with you and investigate this village. Do not let them know who you are or why you are there. Just observe. Find out what you can about them. Do they have a leader? If so, learn all you can about him. Make sure you carry plenty of money with you. You may have to buy your way out of some situation. Any questions?"

"None, my leader. We will leave this evening," he forced himself to answer. Without the effects of his happy powder, Nagap found each encounter with Darinus more nauseating than the previous one.

Under cover of nightfall, Nagap, Rollof and Ondorf departed the cave. Nagap surprised his helpers by changing directions after they had gone not more than five yards.

"The village is the other way," said Ondorf.

"Fool. Don't you think I know where I am going? Of course I know where the village is. But that does not mean that we are going there. You two have been with me long enough to know that Nagap accepts orders from no man, no matter how big he is!"

"We thought you liked Darinus. Isn't he our new leader?"

"I am your leader, as I have always been! As far as liking Darinus, well, that is what I wanted you to think; or more importantly, that is what I wanted Darinus to think. Did you hear that idiot say that I am the only one he could trust? Hah! Those are the exact words I have been waiting to hear before I made my move. Come, before the night is over you will know once again that only I am your master. I found another entrance to the cave: one that will lead us to a spot directly above Darinus' sleeping chambers."

When they arrived at the designated location, Nagap rolled a large stone to the side revealing a narrow tunnel. Nagap crawled down the tunnel, biding Ondorf and Rollof to follow.

Nagap pulled a small carrying lamp from beneath the folds of his robe, illuminating Darinus' horizontal outline on his sleeping plank. He stole upon the form. He drew a huge dagger and, estimating the location of Darinus' heart, plunged the dagger into that spot.

White light flooded the room.

"I was afraid that you might return like this," Darinus spoke from the corner of the chambers. I had wanted you to be the son I never had, yet I feared that you were already too much like me to be trusted. I warned you not to force me to clap my hands again."

"Darinus, wait ...let me explain!"

BOOOOM

A thunderous noise rang out as Darinus' huge hands came together violently. The noise was too loud to have been made by clapping, even with Darinus' humongous hands. A strange odor followed the noise. Neither Ondorf nor Rollof noticed the metal device Darinus had concealed in his hands as he returned it to a secret compartment in his clothing.

Nagap crumpled to the floor. He lay dead, a bullet hole in his forehead.

Soon the other servants began to descend upon Darinus' chambers. Then Chuka arrived.

Immediately, she knew that her blood soaked son was dead. She stepped woodenly, haltingly, toward her son. Mechanically, she rocked his head in her arms.

"He left me no choice. It was either him or me," Darinus pleaded.

He might as well have been talking to a wall.

She picked up the knife that had fallen from Nagap's hand. Her mind having deserted her, her body plodded unevenly toward Darinus.

"Please, do not make me hurt you too," Darinus sounded almost frightened as he backed against the cavern wall. There being nothing in her to retain them; Darinus' words passed effortlessly through Chuka as she continued stalking, the knife in her upraised hand.

She did not notice when he pulled the lever against the wall. Nor did she see the floor slab move just as she was about to step on it. Her screams droned on for what seemed an eternity as she plummeted down the apparently bottomless open pit.

"Are there any questions?" Darinus asked with the air of a conquering hero.

Rollof and Ondorf were too petrified to blink. The rest of the servants bowed their heads.

Effortlessly, Darinus carried Nagap's limp body to the open pit and deposited it. Then he returned the slab to its original position.

"Ondorf, you and Rollof are to follow the instructions that I had given your dear, departed leader. Leave in the morning. Find out if the fishermen have a leader, and if they do, learn all you can about him. But be *discreet*. There is no need for any further demonstration of the consequences of betrayal, is there?"

Rollof and Ondorf shook their heads vigorously as they turned to depart.

Darinus smiled sadly to himself as he retrieved the pamphlet that had fallen from Nagap's robe, its title: *Governing The Accelerated Advancement of Civilization.*

31

*R*ollof and Ondorf marched stiffly into the main chamber of the cavern.

"Your most exalted lordship ..."

"All of those titles are not necessary with me. I know who I am. Now, get on with the report."

"Yes, your lordship."

Darinus rolled his eyes upward, as if some relief might be found on the cavern ceiling.

"The fishermen are led by a mere boy of less than twenty seasons. His name is Sorata."

"Sombata, you moron,"

"Who are you calling moron? Moron."

"My patience grows thin!"

"Forgive us, Excellency. The fishing village is quite small, but it is different from the others."

"In what ways?"

"Well," Ondorf gulped the air trying to give himself courage. "We tried very hard to do everything exactly as you told us. We did our very best not to let them know who we were or why we were there. We said we were just passing through and just happened to see their campfires, but ..."

"Go on, continue," Darinus tried to sound sympathetic. He did not want them to be too afraid to speak.

"It felt like they were able to look right through us."

"They let us know that they did not believe us," Rollof continued for the faltering Ondorf, "But that it did not matter. They said they would tell us anything we wanted to know. It was like they were telling us that they really did not care what we did, or what we knew; because they didn't think we could pose any kind of threat to them. It was almost like they could see us, but we couldn't see them."

"What about their leader?"

"He was the most strange of all. He did not act or look like a leader. He was very kind and gentle. He never raised his voice, yet everyone listened to him. Next to your exalted self, we have never seen anyone command that kind of respect before.

"He took one look at us and said that he knew why we were there. He said he knew we were spies, but that we were his brothers before we became spies. It was the strangest bit of reasoning I have ever heard. Anyway, he told us his parents were Jawala and Kalimba. Neither of us knew anything about Kalimba, but we are from the same village as Jawala ..."

"I know who he is. That strain still survives!"

"We denied having a leader, but he insisted that he wanted to meet you anyway. He said he wanted to help you open your Megalight connection so you could see your own goodness."

"He said WHAT?"

"He said ..."

"I heard you the first time. It was a rhetorical question. Do you think he would fight me?"

"That is doubtful. He said that it is not possible to hurt another without hurting oneself. He sounded like he meant what he said. We even tried to get him angry, but he kept saying that he understood."

"Hmmm. This young man is either a genius or a complete fool. But if he were a fool, I doubt seriously that he would be able to organize an entire village around him. I want you to return to this village. Tell this Sombata that your leader would meet with him. I will give you the specific time and location."

He strode to a corner table and retrieved a helmet. The helmet had been made with the negative energy radiating minerals found in the cave, combined with an alloy of various metals. It had been polished with a wax that contained the forbidden fruit juice. Caressing the helmet, Darinus turned to the assembled servants.

"We shall soon see if the so-called Megalight connection can withstand the raw power and cunning intellect of Darinus!"

32

The early morning grass was cool against Sombata's feet as he made his way to the appointed location. He wrestled with knowing that essentially all people are the same, and yet feeling that Darinus would somehow be completely different from anyone he had ever met. He rehearsed several opening statements and found them all unsatisfactory. Having prayed, meditated and prepared himself as best he could, he knew he should have been feeling more confident than he was.

He could not help wondering why Darinus had insisted that he bring some of the fishermen along. He hoped it was not to provide an audience of witnesses, for that would mean that Darinus was truly determined to fight him.

Against the blue horizon, he saw them approaching. For a time he was puzzled because it appeared that the approaching band consisted of one adult accompanied by small children. As they neared, he realized that the small children were grown men, and that the adult figure was actually a giant.

Once they had come within twenty yards of one another, the giant waived his hand, motioning his entourage to stay back.

In the spirit of reciprocal etiquette, Sombata did the same.

Sombata surveyed the walking mountain. He was enormous! He was also quite strange. His dress-the strange sphere that adorned his head- his gait- all very different, as if transported from another world. He knew the man represented the thing he hated most-disconnection, and yet he could not help being fascinated by the man's *difference*. He wondered if he would ever be able to find himself within the man's spirit.

Tentatively, Sombata sent small blasts of psychic energy at the strange hulking figure. First he tried a gentle probe. Nothing. Then the thoughts he tried to send died before reaching their destination. After having contacted a torrocos and a zeman, Sombata was bewildered that he could not begin to approach a fellow human being. Had the man blocked his energy, Sombata would have understood. But the difference in having his energy blocked and what Sombata encountered was the same as a fighter having a punch blocked and swinging through an apparition. *"How is this man stopping me?"* he wondered to himself.

"So, you are the one they call Sombata. You are the leader of the fishermen," Darinus spoke first in an effort to establish his authority.

"I am Sombata, but I do not claim to lead anyone. I have shared what little knowledge I have with these fine people and they have been very receptive."

"You realize, of course, that I have come here to destroy you?"

"It would be no surprise if that were your original intent. I came to talk, to meet you. A portrait has been painted of you that indicates a man with no connection to anything, or anyone, whatsoever. During my twelfth season, I became acquainted with many strange and horrible things, but never have I encountered anyone who is completely irredeemable. As long as the Megalight exists, such a person cannot exist. Therefore, I cannot believe this of you. I would know you better. Where there is discord with the Megalight, there can only be pain, fear and emptiness. I have learned that much. That which I cannot offer you, my father and grandfather can."

"You're a long-winded little bastard, aren't you?"

"I understand that it is quite natural for the disconnected to respond with insults whenever faced with a truth they find distasteful. But if I provide a target for whatever pent-up frustrations or hostilities you may have, and the venting of those negative feelings makes room for the Megalight in your consciousness, I will gladly suffer any invectives you might hurl at me." As he spoke, Sombata continued struggling with why his messages had been intercepted before they could land inside Darinus' mind. Then it ocurred to him: *It must be that strange looking sphere he has adorning his head that is blocking my thoughts!*

Sombata's compassion rubbed salt in the wound that was Darinus' soul. His nostrils flared as his eyes narrowed.

"You DARE to speak to me like this? FOOL! You *still* do not realize who and what I am. The only reason you are not dead now, is because I want to know the person I am about to kill. There could be little pleasure in destroying you without first knowing whom it is I have destroyed, now could there? But your babbling is wearing thin, and if you want to prolong your life for a few more minutes, I strongly advice that you change your tone.

"Do not think that I do not know what your are trying to do. Your puny little thoughts will have no effect on me. I am Darinus. I have the greatest scientific mind in the history of this planet!"

"I can see that you have an excellent mind, but can you imagine what you could accomplish if that mind were used as an instrument of the Megalight?"

Darinus could stand no more. He raised his staff and, aiming for Sombata's head, brought it down with all his might. Sombata avoided the stick but continued to press his point.

"Know this. I am Sombata. The first three letters of my name stand for `Son Of Man'. You cannot kill me. I am your evolution."

Darinus swung his huge stick again, but missed the more nimble Sombata. He was so infuriated that only death by clubbing or choking- no impersonal bullet- would satisfy him.

"I am what you must become. I am your brother, I am your son. I am..."

"And I am the one who killed both your grandparents!"

Sombata was so stunned that Darinus' next swing caught him glancingly. Darinus' blow, although grazing, would have been excruciating, had there been room for the pain. Sombata continued to hop about, absent mindedly avoiding Darinus' clumsy attacks as his mind tried to digest what his heart could not.

The dancing around to avoid Darinus' ongoing attack sped the process. Sombata's shock quickly gave way to remorse- for Darinus. There was something pitiful beyond description about this man who would rule, and yet was cruel enough to kill two people, and then tell their progeny about it. Sombata shivered at the ugliness he might have found, had he been successful in probing him.

But as Darinus continued flailing about with his staff, Sombata's sadness relinquished its hold for the onslaught of pure, raw anger. The next time Darinus brought his staff down, Sombata grabbed it and flung himself feet forward into Darinus' chest, knocking him off-balance. Darinus tried to lunge for Sombata, but Sombata dived through his legs, and with both feet, kicked him hard in the buttocks, sending him sprawling.

Fueled by strength that came, not from the Megalight, but

from his fury, Sombata lifted a small boulder, and was about to crush the giant when something in Darinus' eyes- just as something in Limba's eyes had done before- stopped him. Then he thought of a way of hurting Darinus more than killing him would: He would remove his helmet and present him with a true mirror of himself. Nothing could be crueler.

He fell upon Darinus and yanked at his helmet, dislodging it without completely removing it. Then Darinus gained enough leverage to hurl Sombata away.

Out of nowhere, Limba swooped down upon Darinus and removed his helmet. Darinus reached into one of his secret compartments and brought out his gun. There was a loud bang, and Limba fell hard to the ground.

Sombata's rage exploded. He dived at Darinus' ankles and yanked them from under him. He pounced onto Darinus' chest. His mind blanked as it melded with his biceps, triceps, wrists and his fingers as they tightened around Darinus' huge neck. Had he been able to hear the gurgling sounds issuing from Darinus' throat, they would only have encouraged him. He could see nothing, hear nothing. Every fiber, every cell, every molecule of his being focused on one mission as never before: to kill Darinus.

Then some small object insisted on swinging into his view with each rocking motion of the choking. Somehow the object forced itself into recognition. The object was attached to some chord which in turn was attached to all his years of training, training so intense that it began to bring him from his trance.

The object was the small figurine that Nagap's father had carved for Jawala when he was a baby. It told Sombata what he himself had told Darinus: that they were one. Horrified, he came to himself, and released his grip on Darinus' neck. He turned his back and kneeling, tried to fathom all that had happened in this fateful encounter. For a time- Sombata did not know how long- he had completely lost his identity.

As Sombata recovered psychologically, so too did Darinus recover physically, only faster. He hoisted the same boulder Sombata had almost used to kill him. Holding the rock high above his head, he stepped toward Sombata.

Sombata whirled and stared into Darinus' eyes. He sent to him that he could commit no evil that would alter the fact that they were brothers.

With no helmet to protect him, Darinus was bombarded by

Sombata's messages. They clung to his brain and allowed no room for escape. The truth robbed him of his purpose and identity.

He dropped the boulder on top of himself.

Sombata turned to the fishermen and assured them that the evil campaign which had plagued their planet had finally ended. He told them that the time had come for healing.

As he spoke, in a distant corner of the western hemisphere, a toddler gnawed on a piece of forbidden fruit.

ORDER FORM

To order **The Megalight Connection,** please fill out this order form and mail, along with your remittance, to:

E & L PRESS
P.O. BOX 1967
CHICAGO, IL 60690

NAME: _____

ADDRESS: _____

CITY: _____ STATE: _____ ZIP: _____

QUANTITY ORDERED _____ x $9.95 = _____

ADD $1.50 POSTAGE   TOTAL: _____

Please contact E & L Press for discount order information.

Illinois residents please add eighty cents sales tax.

ISBN 0-9622869-5-8